FINDING HOME

A SWEET CONTEMPORARY GAY ROMANCE

BLAKE ALLWOOD

BLAKE ALLWOOD PUBLISHING

Content Warnings

Homophobia
Controlling Parents
Attempted Kidnapping

Join Blake's email list to get advance notice of new books and receive his occasional newsletter:

www.blakeallwood.com

MM Romance
By Blake Allwood

Transitions Series
Aiden Inspired
Suzie Empowered (MF Romance)
Bobby Transformed

Chance Series
Love By Chance
Another Chance With Love
Taking A Chance For Love

Romantic Series
Romantic Renovations (1)
Romantic Rescue (2)
Romantic Recon (3)

Melody Series
Melody of the Heart
Melody of the Snow

Road to Rocktoberfest Anthology
Changing His Tune - 2022

Coming Home Series (2023)
A Long Way Home
Family Home
Discovering Home
Finding Home
Bound For Home
…and many more

Novellas
Tenacious
Moon's Place

Romantic Fantasy
By Adam J. Ridley

Big Bend Series
Love's Legacy (1)
Love's Heirloom (2)
Love's Bequest (3)

The Witch Brothers Series
Emerald Earth (1)
Diamond Air (2)
Ruby Fire (3)
Sapphire Water (4)

Science Fiction
By Adam J. Ridley

Superhero Series
Emergence

ACKNOWLEDGMENTS

Special thanks to the following amazing people who helped me get this book finished and into your hands.

Jo Bird: Editor
Renee Mizar: Editor
J.P. Jackson: Beta Reader

And of course, a big thank you to my husband who puts up with my endless stories and handles the formatting and final publishing of all my books.

ONE

LANCE MCCARTNEY

*C*RAP, I SAID TO myself as I stood at the front door of the beautiful late nineteenth century Queen Anne. The house that belonged to my brother. Correction, my *estranged* brother.

I took a deep, steadying breath as I willed my finger to press the doorbell, pleased it was warm enough today that my breath didn't make misty white clouds. When I'd left Long Island a couple days earlier, it had been well below freezing.

"Shit, I can't do this," I said out loud and turned to leave the grand porch, almost bumping into three girls who had appeared out of nowhere on the steps behind me.

"You shouldn't say shit, especially in public," the tallest, and I assumed the oldest, girl said. From what I could tell, she was somewhere around ten or eleven.

"Sorry. I was just leaving."

One of the younger girls, maybe a twin to the other, stepped onto the porch and directly in front of me, preventing me from leaving.

"Why were you standing at our front door? Are you trying to rob us?" she asked as she put her hands on her hips.

I almost chuckled. The girl couldn't have weighed over fifty pounds, but it was clear she wasn't one to be ignored. And that she wouldn't budge until I answered her.

"Um, no...I'm here to see my brother."

All three girls gawked at me. "Why would your brother be at our house?" the older one asked.

"He owns this house."

"Nuh-uh," the little powerhouse said. "This house is owned by my Uncle Gib and his husband, Uncle Allen. And if you've got a problem with that, we can call the sheriff."

I smiled then, unable to stop myself. "I'm your Uncle Allen's brother."

"And how do we know you aren't lying?" the third girl, who'd been silent up until now, asked.

I sighed. They had me there. "If you get Allen, I'm sure he'll confirm it."

All three girls gave me a lingering stare before they apparently needed to converse. Scooting far enough away that I couldn't quite make out what they were saying, they huddled together at the bottom of the porch steps.

I assumed they were discussing whether or not I should be trusted.

Luckily, they were entertaining enough to cause the ball of anxiety in my stomach to ease a bit.

Finally, the girls pulled apart. "You can sit on the swing and wait to speak with our grandmother. Otherwise, we'll think you're a thief and call the sheriff."

I chuckled before agreeing to their terms. These girls were a force to be reckoned with. Somewhere deep down, I was proud of them for being cautious and not blindly trusting some stranger claiming to be long-lost family.

They escorted me to the porch swing, and each girl sat across from me. They were clearly in no mood for more conversation, so we sat quietly until it became awkward and a little bit too cold. I opened my mouth to ask them some random question just to break the silence.

"Shh," the oldest one said, putting her hand up in front of her. "We aren't supposed to talk to strangers, but we're not letting you out of our sight, either. So, you can just sit and wait. Grandma will be here any moment."

I nodded, again having to work hard not to smile. I should thank the trio for effectively keeping me there since I'd been ready to bolt earlier. My brother and I weren't close and, despite some regrets I may have about it now, we never had been. The three pairs of eyes looking upon me with suspicion were evidence enough of that. It'd also made it incredibly difficult to even come here.

With little more to do than take in the scenery, I gazed out over the gardens. Even in the dead of winter, I was impressed by their beauty. I hadn't noticed them earlier because my nerves had been too frayed.

I was just about to stand up and tell the girls I'd return later when an adult was home when a new Lexus turned the corner and began its slow progress toward the house. When it pulled into the driveway, I immediately recognized the person inside as Allen's mother, Catherine.

I cringed. This was their grandmother? My father had been married to Catherine when he'd had an affair with my mom. I didn't know her well, but I'd always felt that I was a reminder of that transgression, especially since my mother's pregnancy was the excuse Dad had supposedly given for the divorce. Well, *that* divorce, since he later married and divorced my mom, too.

I waited in silence as the knots in my stomach began to re-tighten.

Catherine started up the porch and took one look at me and sighed. "Nice to see you, Lance," she said but her body language made it abundantly clear she felt the opposite.

"Girls, I see you met your uncle Allen's brother, Lance. Lance, what brings you to this part of the world?"

I smiled at my three little guards, whose eyes had grown the size of saucers at the confirmation of my identity. They didn't seem too pleased to learn I wasn't a burglar they could have hauled off to the slammer.

When I returned my gaze to Catherine, I simply shrugged. "I've come to see Allen."

Catherine looked at me for several long moments before her attention shifted to her granddaughters. "Girls, aren't you supposed to be raking and bagging leaves? If we get more rain, you know it's going to be too soggy to do it. Your uncles both said it was your number one priority this week."

The girls nodded and stood to go. The quietest one waited until her sisters had left the porch before she came over and whispered, "I'm glad you didn't have to get arrested."

I winked at her, then lowered my head so as not to laugh at the seriousness of her expression.

She quickly scurried off the porch and followed her sisters around the side of the house.

As soon as the girls were out of earshot, Catherine came over and sat in the glider facing the swing.

"Why are you really here?" she asked, sounding wary.

I cleared my throat, hoping to wet my mouth after it had gone dry in anticipation of the conflict I fully expected to happen.

"I'd, um...I'd rather discuss that with Allen."

"Allen isn't home and won't be back until the weekend. He and Gib are attending a medical conference in Atlanta."

All the courage I'd mustered up whooshed out of me like a deflating balloon. I hadn't just swallowed my pride; I'd choked on it. What the hell would I do now? Dad had kicked me out of the house, suspended my credit cards, and even blocked the savings account I'd been shoveling money into from odd jobs over the years. I had no cash left after spending my last few dollars to get here.

"Is there a hostel or somewhere cheap I can stay until he gets back?" I asked.

Catherine looked at me funny. "Why somewhere cheap?" she asked.

"I've got fifty dollars, and I'd still like to be able to eat," I burst out. "Fuck, forget it." Maybe I could find a shelter or something. Did those even exist in the backwoods of nowhere, Tennessee?

I stood and was about to walk past the woman when her hand shot out and grabbed mine.

"Lance, did your father kick you out?" she asked. The sudden softness in her voice, either out of genuine concern or just feeling sorry for me, nearly did me in.

I'd held it together since I'd left. Of all the people in the world to break down in front of, I'd have preferred it not to be the very person who likely hated me the most. Not that I had any control over the reason—my very existence.

"I'm um...I'm just going to go," I said as I wiped away tears with my sleeve.

"You're not going to go if you've got nowhere *to* go. Allen would want you to stay here, Lance. Besides, he'll want to know what happened."

I shook my head. "This was a bad idea. I shouldn't have come."

Dashing off the front porch, I was once again stopped by the three particularly intense-looking little girls.

"Grandma said you need to stay, so that's what you're going to do," the eldest girl said.

I hadn't been able to hold back the tears, so I collapsed onto the front step and buried my face in my hands. I'd put myself in a horrible situation and now I was stuck in a mortifying one.

As I wept like the useless lump I felt like, the girls all came closer and sat near me. Before long, the twins had burrowed up to my sides and the oldest girl was kneeling on the step in front of me.

A few moments later, Catherine came down the stairs and put her hand on my shoulder. "Lance, I'm not sure what's going on, but Allen would want you here. You're his brother, which makes us all family."

"Except that's not really true, is it?" I asked, not daring to open my eyes. I was just beginning to get a grip on the tears, and I didn't dare look into the four pairs of eyes I could feel staring at me. I knew if I did, I'd melt back into an emotional puddle.

"Come on in. I'll show you to the guest room and then, after you take some time, you can come tell me...tell *us* what's going on."

I really didn't have a choice. Fifty dollars wasn't enough to get by, even for one night, let alone the rest of the week until Allen returned.

I got up and followed Catherine into the house. The twins stayed attached to my sides and I could hear the other girl following behind us.

I was still swiping at tears, so I didn't fully take in my surroundings. Still, I could tell the interior of the house was just as amazing as the outside, and perhaps I could explore some later. As it was, though, I just wanted to get into the guest room and pull myself together without an audience.

We walked up a magnificent stairway, and my artistic wannabe architect's heart took over. The mahogany railing was decadent. Even in my current state, I couldn't resist running my hand over the wood. I welcomed the momentary distraction.

Catherine and the girls showed me to a second-story room at the front of the house. "This will be your room while you're here, Lance. There's a bathroom attached, so you won't have to share with the girls."

I walked in and placed my backpack on the floor next to a beautiful, oversized chair. The bed was a four-poster made of rich ebony wood. I wanted to ask if it was original to the home but tamped down my curiosity. Now wasn't the time for small talk. I just needed to be alone for a while.

"Come downstairs after you've had a rest," Catherine said, and I watched as the three girls' concerned faces disappeared as she closed the door.

Two

Jake Hudson

"**T**ODD, MAN, WE'VE GOT to get this ironed out. What's taking so long?"

Todd, one of my best friends and the contractor leading a massive building restoration project in downtown Crawford City, shook his head.

"One, you keep sending me more clients than I have time for. Two, the project keeps growing; and three, I haven't gotten the final plans back from the architect."

I sighed. I knew I was impatient, but my excitement for the project had only ramped up since a fire destroyed the original building.

"What can I do to speed things up?" I asked.

"You can be freakin' patient for a change," Todd said, sounding frustrated.

"That's not my strong suit," I said under my breath.

When Todd didn't reply, I glanced around at the other tables. We'd arrived at the Crawford City Cafe early, but the place was filling up now, which wasn't surprising since it was one of the most popular places in town.

An older woman came out of the kitchen and asked if I'd like more coffee. I watched her pour and looked up just in time to see her wink at Todd. When she left, I shook my head. "Everyone in this town thinks I'm a crazy person."

Todd chuckled. "You're a little nutty, but they like you. Don't always understand your big city ways, is all."

"Hmph," I muttered and took a deep breath, letting it out slowly. "Todd, I know the project has continued to grow, and that's mostly my fault since I bought the two empty buildings next door. But can we at least *start* talking about phases?"

"Yes, and no. The project is costly, Jake, and all the other co-owners besides just you and I need to be involved in any decisions. Dad, Doc, Allen, and his mom all have to see the plans and agree with them. Then we need to convince the town council as well. You can't push this stuff."

When I frowned, Todd put his hand on my shoulder and squeezed. "Listen, I know I was upset with you springing the other two buildings on us. I still say you should've consulted us before you purchased them, but I also know plunging headlong into things is more your style. In any case, we all think this will ultimately be an amazing project for downtown, and put Crawford City on the map. It'll also give our town a lot more commercial potential, which is very much needed. Still, you just need to be patient, ride the ride, and let it unfold at its natural pace."

I didn't say anything, just reluctantly nodded in understanding. I received this same lecture from Todd and all the partners every time I tried to push things forward. My best friend had me pegged, though. I do tend to dive headfirst into things at breakneck speed and expect everyone else to do the same. That served my career well, but not so much the other areas of my life, relationships included.

I'm not sure why I felt so impatient with this project. It's not like I didn't have a hundred and one other things to worry about. My PR firm had just signed on two new country music stars and I had a shit ton of work to do for them, but there was something special about Crawford City.

The place kept drawing me back and not just because Todd, his husband Ash, and their three screaming but adorable children were here, although that meant a lot. I felt more at home in the small town than I'd ever felt anywhere else, including my current home in Nashville. More than once, Todd and Ash had tried to convince me to move down and buy a home, but that didn't feel right. I had no interest in mowing yards or messing around in flower beds as a homeowner.

As I'd been lost in my thoughts, Todd had begun chatting with the café owner about her new husband, Mr. Cole, Jennifer Cole's dad. Jennifer was one of my first clients, and her rise to the top as a supermodel had helped lift my career as well.

Jennifer was also one of my best friends. When she and Todd were roommates years ago, they took me under their wings. As an awkward street kid, they helped me feel, for the first time, like I was someone worth knowing.

As Todd and Mrs. Cole finished chatting, she turned her attention to me. "You doin' okay, Jake?" she asked.

I smiled. "Yes, ma'am. I'm afraid if I drink any more of that coffee, I'm gonna wash away."

She winked at me and turned to go in the back. In the past few years, that had become more common as well. I'd been coming to town more to visit Todd and Ash, and the locals had begun to know me on a first-name basis.

That felt good... and right. I had spent most of my childhood in a small town closer to Memphis than Nashville, and the people there were hateful even before they'd learned I was gay. They knew my name, but few used it. "Hey, boy. Hey, you..." That was the standard way I was referred to, even in school.

Tennessee isn't known for being welcoming to those of us flying the rainbow flag. I was pretty sure my hometown was more the norm, so the open and accepting town of Crawford City was special. I always felt so at ease coming to visit.

"Well, time to get to work. I have to help with the triplets tonight. You gonna come over to help, too?" Todd asked.

"That's a hell no," I said, earning myself some looks from those around us. "The agreement is you've got to get them out of diapers first, then Uncle Jake's duties will begin."

Todd punched me playfully on the arm. "You know you want in on the full dad experience, diaper changing and all. You're just playing hard to get."

I pretended to gag. "Not likely! I'm not a baby person. I swore after I was kicked out of my parents' home, I'd never change another diaper as long as I live."

A flash of sadness crossed Todd's face, as it always did when I referred to my backwoods family and how they'd thrown me out at fourteen for being gay.

"Besides," I continued, "when your young'uns start entering all those talent competitions, that I'm gonna put them in, you're gonna need help to transport them. Then it'll be Uncle Jake to the rescue. Trust me, you'll thank me later!"

"We'll see," is all he said, and I was thankful to have put him off the sympathy conversation I'd grown to hate.

I tossed down enough money to cover our meal and give Mrs. Cole a big tip. Having struggled financially for so many years, I'd made it my mission to be as generous with money as possible, and all the more so in places where I knew the people. I felt like I owed Jennifer for helping me get my start. Knowing that the café owner and Mr. Cole were now together, I felt tipping extremely well translated in some small way to showing my gratitude toward them.

Todd and I parted ways as soon as we stepped outside. He took off toward his truck and I decided to walk through downtown and spend some time checking out the project site.

I'd just come around the corner when I bumped shoulders with a guy who'd been looking the other way. His backpack fell to the ground, and I reached down to pick it up as he apologized.

"No prob..." My words stuck in my throat as I laid eyes on the beautiful man. His eyes remained downcast as he grabbed his backpack from my hand, then apologized again before rushing down the street and disappearing behind the old town hall.

I thought about following him, but that would be a bit too stalkerish, so I shrugged it off. I'd certainly never seen the man around here before, but damn, I would love to see him again. The prospect caused my heart to do a little leap in my chest. Crawford City didn't get many tourists on weekdays this time of year, so maybe he was visiting someone in town? He had seemed rather skittish, though...maybe he needed a place to stay? That thought caused an altogether different sort of pang in my chest.

I leaned against the building across from where our building project still just looked like an empty lot and thought about my life. I'm not sure why, but I was feeling particularly nostalgic at the moment. Maybe it was Mrs. Cole's cooking.

I'd lost everything–my family, my so-called friends, my home, my security–when I'd been forced out of the closet as a teenager. I had roamed the streets of Nashville for several months before getting tangled up with the wrong crowd, staying in an abandoned house with several other kids who were selling drugs, shoplifting, and even prostituting themselves out just to survive. The police raided the house one night, and I was caught up in the arrests.

Since the police didn't have evidence that I'd done anything illegal, they turned me over to children's services, who instantly moved me to a group home. I never had the same desire as some of the other kids to run away from there. It was a hundred percent better than anywhere I'd lived before. I grew up in squalor, the oldest of seven kids, and God only knew how many more my parents had after they threw me out.

At the group home, I had two roommates, who were both annoying as hell and whose feet stank so badly we slept with the window open. Still, I had a warm bed, plenty of food to eat, and clothes that hadn't come from a thrift store or worse, the dumpster. I also liked my counselor, Anita, a stereotypical lesbian who rode a Harley to work and had tattoos up and down her arms.

Within a year of moving into the group home, Anita and her wife, Claire, received their foster care license and began doing respite care for me. In other words, I got to hang out with them on the occasional weekend and on holidays. We'd remained close over the years, and I still considered both women more a mother than the woman who'd given birth to me.

I resumed walking toward the project site when my phone dinged with a text message. I laughed when I saw the name. Think of the devil...

Claire: *Can you come to dinner this weekend? Anita's cooking.*

Me: *Think of the devil and she'll text you every time.*

She quickly texted back a smiley face. As the dots popped up, indicating she was typing another message, I thought of how my life with her and Anita had unfolded. The two women were tough as nails, but I'd liked them from the moment we met. For my sixteenth birthday, they asked if I would be willing to live with them permanently. What kind of fool would I have been to say no to that?

Claire: *I'm not responding to the devil comment. You know I have enough mean in me to qualify. So, you coming to Sunday dinner or not?*

Me: *No. You made the mistake of telling me Anita was cooking. I'd rather avoid that disaster if at all possible.*

Her response was a laughing emoji.

Claire: *You're coming, or Anita will come get you. I promise to stand guard over the food.*

I chuckled. Anita was tough on the outside but buttercream on the inside. Her bark was one hundred percent worse than her bite, but I knew not coming home wasn't an option.

Me: *Okay, but if the food tastes like crap, I'm forcing you both to take me to McDonald's.*

Claire: *Forcing, huh? We'll see. Come early. Anita wants to show you something.*

I laughed. That usually meant she wanted me to help with one of their never-ending projects around the house.

Me: *See ya around four.*

When she sent a thumbs up emoji, I put my phone back in my pocket and looked over to where I'd lost sight of the skittish man. After regaining my footing living with Claire and Anita, I'd promised myself to never hesitate going after what I wanted. Men were no exception. Our brief conversation had reminded me of that.

Life was too short and uncertain to have regrets, so if I were interested in a man, I went for it. Regardless of knowing if he were gay, bisexual, pansexual, or not, if he caught my eye, I'd ask him out. Sure, that tactic had resulted in a fat lip or black eye more than once, but my batting average ranked pretty high compared to the strikeouts. Did the mystery man play for my team? I figured since my attraction to him was so strong, it'd be worth finding out. But first, I had to find him.

THREE

LANCE

I WOKE UP AFTER unintentionally falling asleep on the big, plush bed. It'd been a rough week. First, my decision not to go back to medical school. Then, facing my renowned surgeon father and explaining to him that I didn't want to follow in his footsteps by becoming a doctor.

I'd expected the blow-up, but not being kicked out of the house without a penny.

If my stepmother had still been around, I'm sure Kassidy would've helped calm things down. However, Dad was in the throes of divorce number three, and since he'd cut her phone off, I had no way to get in touch with her.

I had five hundred dollars in cash that I'd pulled out of my account to cover expenses for a trip I'd planned to make with a couple of guys I knew from college. If it hadn't been for that, I'd have really been screwed.

Those supposed friends were not sympathetic to my plight and went on the trip without me. So, the only choice I'd had was finding Allen.

I stretched and tried working the kink out of my neck. I could hear noise coming from the first floor and, after splashing water on my face, I went downstairs.

"Lance, you're just in time," Catherine said the moment she spotted me.

"For what?" I asked stupidly.

"To help with supper, silly," one of the twins said.

The look on Catherine's face told me I was about to be put through my paces.

I was pulled into the obviously newly renovated kitchen and placed at the island. I ran my hands over the granite countertop, admiring how beautifully it accented the dark wood cabinetry. I tended to like more modern finishes in a kitchen, but this seemed to fit the grand old Victorian perfectly.

One of the girls plopped several large wet potatoes in front of me, then handed me a bowl and a weird-looking tool.

"What am I supposed to do with this?" I asked.

All four females stopped what they were doing and looked at me quizzically, as if I'd spoken a riddle. "You peel the potatoes," the oldest girl said.

I could feel my cheeks reddening with embarrassment. "Um, I don't know how."

They continued to stare at me until Catherine shook her head and took the weird device from my hand. She picked up one of the potatoes and began scraping it, removing the outside.

"Here, now you try it," she said, trying not to sound condescending but failing.

I tried and dropped the potato several times before I finally got the hang of it. By hang of it, I mean I didn't drop it.

When I ended up scraping my thumb with the peeler, they rushed me to the sink to stop the bleeding.

"I don't have any experience cooking," I said, half apologizing. "Dad's cook always prepared our meals."

Catherine made some sort of exasperated noise in the back of her throat as she finished cleaning my thumb and applied a Band-Aid with images of Disney princesses to the wound. I couldn't help but giggle as I looked at it.

After the mishap, they put me to work, wiping the counters and keeping things clean as the others pulled the meal together. One of the girls rewashed the potatoes, even though I hadn't gotten any blood on them, then peeled them at lightning speed.

The girls chattered about everything from kids in the neighborhood to creatures they saw in the garden. I'd somehow been allowed into this strange circle, even though I was clearly there just as an observer. The inclusion made me feel oddly at home, despite my nerves.

When their chatter died down, one of the twins looked pointedly at me. "What's your last name, Mr. Lance?"

I smiled at her and said, "Same as your uncle Allen. I'm Lance McCartney."

"So, that makes you our uncle too?"

The question, which sounded more like a statement, took me by surprise. I hadn't thought of these girls as my nieces. I mean, I knew there had been a tragedy in Allen's husband's family, but I only heard bits and pieces. Then, as now, I'd only been on the periphery of Allen's life, never directly involved.

Guilt swept over me. Here I was asking for my brother's help, but I'd done everything in my power to keep him at arm's length my whole life. I had to swallow hard around the lump that formed in my throat as I thought about how I'd never been there for him like a brother should be. I'd be surprised if he didn't kick me out the moment he heard I was here.

"Yeah, I guess I am your uncle...sort of anyway," I managed to say.

"Cool, you're Uncle Lance then," the other twin said.

I smiled. "What are your names? We haven't been properly introduced."

"I'm Ruby," the twin I'd come to think of as the shy one said.

"I'm Margie," the other twin responded.

The oldest girl was busy at the sink, and I figured she was avoiding answering me.

"She's Chrissy," Ruby said. "She's older than us. Margie and I are twins."

I had to stifle my chuckle. As if their looking identical wasn't clue enough of that.

"It's nice to finally meet each of you," I said.

Chrissy came over then and, with a slight frown, asked, "Why haven't we met you before now?"

Her question felt like a gut-punch. Luckily, before I had to bumble through some bullshit answer, Catherine came to my rescue and told the girls to go do their other chores while she finished preparing the meal.

I watched the girls go and knew Chrissy had my number. I would eventually have to explain my absence from their lives if I hoped to have a chance at a relationship with these girls–my nieces–and with Allen.

After the three left the kitchen, Catherine finished putting the potatoes on the stove and then sat across from me. "Did you tell Allen you were coming?"

I shook my head. "No, I don't have his number."

"You couldn't ask your dad for it?"

I shook my head again. "Dad and I aren't speaking."

"I see," Catherine said while looking down at her hands. "I'm trying not to pry, Lance, but I'm in charge of the girls while Allen is away. Having you show up out of the blue, and being cagey as to why, is very disconcerting. You might not think so, but you have always been a member of this family and we care about you."

I looked at her for a long moment. I'd spent most of my life hating her and Allen, more for what they represented than anything else: a relationship full of unconditional love and support that I'd never experienced myself.

Allen seldom spent time at Dad's during my childhood. When he did come to visit, Dad drilled him like he did me. Still, every time he left to go home to Catherine,

Dad would refocus his energy–and criticism–on me. It didn't take long for me to resent both my brother and his mother for making my life miserable. Allen always had a safe haven to escape to, away from our father, but I never did...until now, hopefully.

"I dropped out of medical school, and Dad kicked me out of the house," I blurted.

Catherine shook her head, and an expression of disgust crossed her face. *Great*, I thought, *here comes the lecture.*

"Lance, your father is a grade-A asshole. I'm sorry to drop a truth bomb like that, but that's God's honest truth. I'm guessing he cut you off financially, too, since you said you've only got fifty dollars to your name."

A feeling of shock or relief for her believing me, I couldn't tell which, hit me hard. All my father's friends, and girlfriends for that matter, with the exception of my soon-to-be ex-stepmother Kassidy, always took his side. "You're being insolent," the woman he'd cheated on Kassidy with, and whose name I couldn't remember, had told me right before Dad washed his hands of me.

When I didn't respond, Catherine sighed. "Honey, I've watched your father come after Allen time and again when he didn't do exactly what he wanted him to do. I've often wondered how you fared all alone with his ridiculous expectations."

She got up, grabbed a sponge out of the sink, and ran it over the countertop to clean up what the girls and I had missed earlier. Judging by the pensive look on her face, though, our conversation wasn't over.

"I try very hard not to disparage your father to Allen, and I'll offer the same courtesy to you. It's no secret he and I don't get along, but you should know that both Allen and I always worried about you. I've wanted to pull you under my wings more than once. Anyway, you're under my care now, while you're here," she said. "Don't worry about a thing. We'll get you settled, and Allen and I will do what we can to help get you back on your feet."

I stared at the woman, speechless. I was having the hardest time reconciling her with the person I'd demonized throughout my childhood. The woman who I thought hated me for being the reason her husband left her. The woman who hated me for keeping Dad from Allen. Guilt clawed at me over my apparent misperceptions of who she really was all these years.

"I-I'm not sure what to say."

Catherine chuckled. "Say *Thank you, Catherine*."

Her candor made me smile, even as my eyes stung with the threat of more tears. "Thank you, Catherine."

"Now, why don't you go back upstairs and get a shower? No offense, honey, but I can smell you from here. Supper should be done by the time you get back down, and you can meet your nieces in a more official way."

I nodded and stood to go.

"Oh, and Lance, you better have an answer for Chrissy. She is the guardian of this little tribe, and she'll want to understand why you've avoided them all this time. These girls have experienced real and terrible loss and won't be patronized."

I nodded again, though I didn't fully understand the loss they'd suffered, remembering only bits and pieces of their story. Regardless, I could tell Chrissy was going to be a tough character, and damned if I didn't like her more because of it.

Four

Jake

"So, when are you gonna settle down?" Claire asked, then smiled, knowing she'd just stirred a pot that wasn't part of our dinner.

I rolled my eyes. "Oh my god, are you two going to start this again? What's the rush? I mean, seriously, I'm only thirty-one."

"Claire and I had been married five years by the time I was thirty-one," Anita said as she stirred the actual pot on the stove.

I glanced at the red-colored liquid in the pot and all but shuddered. I hadn't had the nerve to ask what exactly she was cooking.

"I haven't met anyone I want to settle down with. Besides, I'm happy being single. Not everyone has to be, or even wants to be, coupled up. Heck, I might need two or three husbands, like in a reverse harem, to keep me satisfied."

Anita chuckled as Claire shook her head. The two had been on me like white on rice for the past few years now, trying to get me to commit to one person and settle down.

The truth was, I really did want that. I envied what Anita and Claire shared, going through life side by side with another person. I wanted to wake up every day knowing that person—my person—would love me for a lifetime and always have my back. And, if we were truly fortunate, maybe one day we could pay forward Anita and Claire's generosity by giving a home to a young LGBTQ person who'd been kicked out of their own family.

The biggest obstacle to finding my Mr. Right was that the men I attracted tended to be...sluts. Not that there was anything wrong with finding pleasure in... pleasure. A quick, no-strings roll in the hay could be amazing and blissfully free of the relationship troubles that could come with having a boyfriend. But meaningless hookups were also just—empty.

Watching Todd and Ash get together had seemed like a foreign concept to me at the time. Not that I could ever compare my love story to theirs, assuming I ever got my own. Those two had been in love since childhood, although their road to 'happily ever after' hadn't been without some bumps and outright potholes along the way. If I wasn't so damned happy for their happiness, I'd probably be jealous.

"What'cha all contemplative about?" Anita asked when I fell silent.

I chuckled. "Nothing, just thinking about Todd and Ash and how strange it must feel to be in love with someone your whole life like that."

"Stranger things have happened, but I think most people meet and fall in love gradually. Take Claire and me, for example. We met in college. I'd never laid eyes on her before then, and now look at us."

"An old married couple?" I snidely asked, knowing I'd get a rise out of her with the age comment and hopefully tone down the scrutiny on my nonexistent love life.

"Hmph, come taste this and tell me what you think."

I cringed. "I'd rather not," I said and earned a disapproving glare from my foster mom.

"I didn't ask if you wanted to. I *told* you to come taste it."

"Oh my god, I'm going to end up in the hospital tonight with food poisoning. Why didn't you just let me take us all out to eat?"

"'Cause I'm learning some new recipes and you're my guinea pig."

"Ugh," I said but dutifully picked up the spoon Anita had set out for me.

I dipped it into the boiling concoction, then blew on the piping hot spoonful to cool it down some. I didn't need a scorched tongue on top of potential food poisoning.

I closed my eyes, tried not to breathe, and stuck the spoon in my mouth.

My eyes shot open seconds later. "Wow, that's...wait, did Claire make this?"

Anita swiped me with the back of her hand and told me to put my spoon in the sink and get out of her way.

I complied but stared in wonder at my foster mom. "Seriously, nothing you make ever tastes... um, edible, but I can actually stomach this. What's changed?"

"She's begun taking classes with the kids at the shelter," Claire said as she came in behind me.

"Really? Why didn't you take those classes years ago instead of spending over a decade trying to poison me?" I asked, not at all kidding.

Anita gave me a withering look. Then, ignoring me, she switched the stove off and announced it was time to eat.

She served the beef stew in real bowls rather than the usual plastic crockery, and we sat at the dining table that only got used for our all-out-war card or board games. I guessed having a decent meal to eat was special occasion enough.

I crumbled soda crackers into my steaming bowl like I'd learned to do as a little boy living with my birth family and dug into it.

"Oh my god, this is really good, Anita. I can't believe you cooked this."

She shook her head and frowned. "Was I really that bad before?" she asked.

Both Claire and I nodded at the same time.

"Oh, remember the time she made deviled eggs and tomato soup?" I asked and Claire chuckled.

"God, it was awful," she said. "As if those two things should ever be served together as a meal anyway. Good grief."

"I swear, that's when we were raising all those chickens for your school project and they'd all started laying at once," Anita recalled. "I had to do something with them. We had eggs coming out of our ears."

I laughed. "That wasn't the only place they were coming out of! Your deviled eggs about did me in. It's a wonder I didn't have to stay home from school the next day."

"Whatever," she said, but chuckled. "I've told you how my mother was all about women serving their men. I refused to learn to cook 'cause the whole *that's what women do* thing pissed me off."

Claire sighed. "Even so, you didn't need to try to kill us, did you, dear?"

Anita gave Claire a look, but it didn't last long. She'd never been able to stop from smiling when Claire gave her the business.

We continued our typical benign bickering until we finished our meals. We sent Anita on her way and, as was family tradition, Claire and I cleaned up the kitchen.

Claire spooned the rest of the stew into containers and stuck most of them in the freezer. She left a couple in the refrigerator, and I recognized those were meant for me to take home.

"Hey," I whispered, "is all her food that good now?"

Claire shook her head and whispered back, "No, but she's improving. To be honest, she worked on that really hard to impress you." Then, as was her way, she chuckled thinking about her wife's antics. "Thanks for carrying on about it. She'll be on cloud nine for the rest of the week."

I smiled. I had a deep and intense love for my foster mothers and knowing I'd brought some joy into their lives always made me a little giddy.

When we finished cleaning, Claire hugged me. "Sweetheart, Anita wants to ask you something about your birth family, but she's afraid it'll upset you. I wasn't going to say anything, but this might be important."

The seriousness in Claire's voice gave me pause. We rarely spoke about my birth family. Not that it was a taboo subject for me, there just wasn't all that much to say. The truth was, I didn't think Claire or Anita knew much about them.

"No, it's fine. What's going on?"

Claire sighed deeply. "Come on, let's have a sit-down in the living room and I'll let Anita ask you."

I sat on the sofa. Claire went into Anita's office to get her and came out a few minutes later and sat next to me. Anita emerged in short order, carrying her laptop, and plopped down on my other side.

"I was debating whether or not to show this to you, but I guess Claire let the cat out of the bag."

That put my nerves on edge. It wasn't like my foster moms to beat around the bush like this. Usually, they were straightforward, even demanding. Especially Anita, who dealt with some of the most rugged, hard-ass street kids at the group home where she worked.

Anita opened the laptop and clicked through a couple screens before pulling up the image of a boy.

"Does this young man look familiar?" she asked.

Besides being chubbier than I was at his age, the teenager certainly looked a lot like me. I read the description next to his picture.

Derek is a polite, well-mannered, and respectful young man. He is generally happy and outgoing and easily able to build positive relationships with peers and adults. Derek likes fishing, swimming, playing tennis, and other outdoor activities. Despite his difficult past, he has a positive outlook on life and has a way of encouraging his peers to do what's right. Derek loves playing Pokémon, video games, drawing pictures, and anything mechanical.

I looked at Anita, then Claire, and saw concern etched on their faces. "Who is this?" I asked, confused.

Both women sighed sadly. "We aren't sure, but we think this could be your brother or maybe a nephew," Anita said. I continued looking at them, utterly speechless. "I get a list of the children who are becoming eligible for adoption. The state sends out their photos and descriptions every month. It's sort of a way for them to encourage adoption. I noticed how much this young man looked like you and so I called the social worker. Although she couldn't go into detail, she did tell me he grew up in the same small town you did."

"When did he come into foster care?" I asked, my mind reeling.

"Just under a year ago. What they can disclose to me is limited, but if you are his blood relative, I think you could get more information."

"I-I mean, it's possible we're related, but the only reason I was in care was because I'm gay. My parents weren't abusive or even neglectful before they found out about me."

Both women shook their heads. "We don't know any more than that, but honey, if he's your family, we thought you'd want to know."

I stared in silence at the laptop and the longer I did so, looking at the young man I'd never met before, the more I thought it possible, maybe even probable, that we were related. Same color hair, same weird cowlick on the left side of his head. He even had the same small, pointy nose I sported.

"Is his last name Hudson?" I asked.

"Yes, same as yours," Anita said. "Derek Hudson. He's fifteen."

That sealed the deal in my mind. Whether the kid turned out to be my long-lost brother, cousin, or kin of some other kind, I owed it to the both of us to find out. "I'd like to know, yeah."

"Are you sure this isn't going to be...too much?" Claire asked. I knew she was remembering the long days and nights I'd spent as a teenager trying to process losing my family. My childhood trauma had reared its ugly head, and it took all of Anita's training as a counselor plus Claire's natural maternal instincts to keep me from completely falling apart.

They'd been my rock back then and still were in many ways. I felt down to my core that Derek needed someone solid in his corner right now, too, and I could be that for him.

"I'm sure it's going to be a lot, but I think I'm up for it. I need to try, at least."

"Okay, I'll let the social worker know you're a potential family member. They should be able to determine if you are right away, since you aged out of the system."

"Yeah, okay. Cool," I said and managed a small smile despite my already frayed nerves. At some point during our conversation, I'd begun pacing the room and only now realized it as I looked at the two women still sitting on the sofa.

"You okay?"

I went over to my usually stoic foster mom, bent down, and kissed her cheek. "I'm good, Anita. Overwhelmed a bit, especially since he'd be sixteen years younger than me, but my birth parents weren't fans of birth control. I have no doubt Mom would continue having kids until she couldn't, so it shouldn't be surprising if more siblings came along in the years since they kicked me out."

"Well, we're both here if you need to talk about it, okay? We just couldn't imagine you not wanting to know if one of your siblings ended up in the system."

"You're right. Yeah, it's a lot to digest and I'm sure it'll hit me even more later. If he is my brother, it's gonna hit me even harder, but I do wanna know him and why he's in the system."

Both my foster moms stood and enveloped me in a group hug like they had back when things got really bad. I just smiled and let them love me. I learned a long time ago, when the heart was raw, it was best to let the people who cared nurture you. In the end, it's what I really wanted anyway.

FIVE

LANCE

BY THE TIME ALLEN and Gib returned home from their work conference, the girls and I, and to some extent Catherine, had developed a distinct fondness for each other. At least, that's how it felt to me.

The girls were a lot to handle. Running around creating havoc, but also causing both Catherine and I to laugh at their antics. Their energy and playfulness even rubbed off on me some, which brought on a general feeling of positivity I'd never felt before. It helped temper the feeling of dread at the prospect of Allen being less than receptive to my being here.

Ruby had become my ally, and although Chrissy had yet to decide whether or not she trusted me, Ruby seemed to keep things between us civil. I definitely owed the eight-year-old a lot for helping me feel so welcome.

However, the welcome mat was quickly rolled up, at least in my mind, when Allen walked through his front door.

The girls were all over him and Gib, asking what they'd brought them in between hugs. Even though I could tell both my brother and his husband were leery of me, they smiled at the girls and handed out presents. Mostly freebie-type stuff they got at the conference, like stress balls in the shape of hearts, writing pads, and dozens of pens and highlighters, but the girls seemed as happy as it if were Christmas.

After everyone got settled, Allen gestured toward the door and asked if I'd be willing to go for a walk with him. I knew this was his way of getting me in private so we could talk about why I'd come.

I cringed inwardly, but agreed. I'd spent years treating Allen like warmed up shit, especially after I got old enough to refuse his company and could blatantly avoid him. Now, I could only hope it wasn't time for him to return the favor.

Today was a lot colder than the day I'd arrived, so we bundled up and walked toward town. Neither of us spoke until we had nearly reached the town hall and the row of interesting little shops I didn't have money enough to patronize.

"So, what brings you to Crawford City?" Allen asked. I knew Catherine had probably filled him in somewhat, but I figured I still owed him an explanation.

"Dad threw me out," I said with a sigh.

Allen just nodded, and we continued walking. We came to an ancient-looking donut shop, and he led the way inside. A man not much older than me stood behind the counter and smiled when he saw Allen.

"Hey, Jamie," Allen said. "I want a double scoop of Rocky Road. Lance, what would you like?" When I hesitated, he added, "My treat."

"Um, thanks," I said, not making eye contact with my brother. Obviously, I couldn't afford to pay for anything, but knowing Allen also knew that left me feeling as embarrassed as I was appreciative.

The thought of eating ice cream on such a brisk winter day made my whole body shiver. "Do you have hot cocoa?" I asked, hoping to combat the chill I'd caught on our walk. I couldn't quite wrap my head around why a donut shop even sold ice cream.

The guy nodded and asked if I wanted whipped cream on it. "Yes, that'd be fine."

After the guy rang Allen out and handed us our treats, we walked to the corner and sat at an antique-looking table and chairs that had definitely seen better days. Allen asked, "So, what do you plan to do?"

I took a sip of the piping hot cocoa, knowing I'd delayed this conversation as long as possible. "I don't really know, Allen. You have to know if I'd had any other option, I wouldn't have come here." I knew my words sounded harsh, but that's honestly how I felt.

Allen looked down at his two scoops and sighed. "That makes me sad, Lance. I've never understood why you and I are estranged, but this probably isn't the time to discuss that."

He took a bite of the ice cream, then swallowed. I glanced out the window at the town I had yet to explore, trying to keep my anxiety at bay as I waited for Allen to gather his thoughts. I wondered if he knew that, like it or not, he basically held my future in his hands.

"You're more than welcome to stay with us. Mom said the girls have taken a liking to you. Of course, Chrissy is convinced you're an imposter come to spy on us. But that's mostly my fault for introducing her to young adult mysteries."

I chuckled, partly in relief that Allen wasn't throwing me out, and partly because the girl was definitely suspicious of me.

"Listen, I won't stay long, just long enough to get a job and find my own place." I took a couple more sips of hot cocoa, mostly to give myself time to find the courage for what I needed to ask him. "Do you know anyone who's looking to hire a medical school dropout?"

Allen took a deep breath and let it out slowly, obviously digesting my words. Apparently, Catherine hadn't spilled the beans on that crucial tidbit. "Probably not until I understand more about *why* you dropped out."

I shook my head. I figured I was gonna get it now. Allen had followed in Dad's footsteps, after all. He was now second-in-command of pediatrics at a prestigious Nashville hospital. Of course he'd be disappointed in me, same as Dad.

"I'm not made for medicine. I wanted to be an architect and still do, even if it's only a pipe dream at this point. I told Dad, and he went berserk. You'd think I'd told him I wanted to become a tennis coach or something."

Allen laughed. "Funny enough, I used to fantasize about becoming a tennis coach when I was in med school."

"Really?" I asked, surprised. Dad spent years conveying, with all kinds of cutting remarks, how superior Allen was to me in every way except one. "I always kicked your ass at tennis whenever Dad made us play each other. There's no way anyone would've hired you as a coach."

"Yeah, well, there's a reason it was a fantasy. Seriously, though, med school's hard enough on those of us who *want* to become doctors. If you don't, you made the right choice by dropping out."

"Really?" I asked again. "I mean, I figured you'd take Dad's side."

"Rarely," he said, looking amused. "I try not to, as often as possible."

I frowned at that, totally confused. "According to Dad, you were more like him than me. Ambitious, hard-working...I can recite the list. You didn't let fanciful thinking get in the way of making mature decisions, unlike me."

Allen threw his head back and laughed out loud. "Oh my god, he really *was* shooting you the bull."

Now I was really confused. Shooting me the bull? I'd never heard that expression. "Is that a Southern thing?" I asked, and Allen laughed out loud again.

"Probably. Hey, you need to talk to Mom. Dad and I were at war until I moved out here. Hell, I moved out here to get away from him!"

My eyebrows shot up to my hairline at that. I couldn't believe what I was hearing. When Allen caught my shocked expression, he sighed. "Listen, Dad and I have come a long way. I mean, we have something resembling a relationship now, but for the most part, he's made my life difficult."

He reached over and put his hand on top of mine, which caught me off guard. Needless to say, Allen and I had never been even remotely affectionate toward one another, and seeing the concern in his eyes now made mine misty.

"Lance, I always felt bad that you were stuck there alone with him. I had Mom, who had a good, solid head on her shoulders and didn't expect me to become a mini version of her. If you don't want to be in medical school, good for you for having the good sense to get out now, before you ended up hating your life. If you want to be an architect, be a damned architect. Dad isn't living your life, you are."

He finished off his ice cream and tossed the paper cup into a trash can sitting next to our table. My cocoa had pretty much gone cold, so I tossed it too.

"I don't really know what to say, Allen. Dad always compared me to you, even though you were hardly ever there. I felt like a worthless little brother who could never measure up. That's why I avoided you all those years. You didn't want to be around me as a kid, so why should I want to be around you as an adult? It's why I didn't come to your wedding. Not that you really wanted me there, anyway."

Allen sighed and I could literally feel the sadness coming off him. "Actually, that broke my heart. I mean, I'm beginning to understand why you weren't there, but we can deal with that later. God, I'm so glad you're here now."

Allen stood up, and the next thing I knew, I was being pulled into his arms. "I'm sorry I wasn't a better big brother to you growing up. I promise to be the best brother I can be from here on out, and I'm proud of you for taking charge of your life. Knowing you pissed Dad off in the process has made my entire year!"

I couldn't help but laugh. I'd really misunderstood my brother and his mom. *What the hell, Dad?* I thought to myself. Why had he worked so hard to make me think they hated me? Probably because he knew if he didn't, I'd have begged to move in with them...and maybe they would've even let me.

The thought made me smile, and when Allen pulled back, he was grinning, too.

"Hey, I have an idea. Our friend Todd is in the construction business and I'm sure he'd give you a job. You could learn all about the business while working toward an architecture degree. Is that something you'd be interested in?"

I had to admit, the idea intrigued me, if not for one crucial detail. "You know I don't really even know how to swing a hammer, right?"

"That's what you'd be learning. I'll ask Todd to take you on as a free intern, and I know for a fact if you work hard, he'll do what he can to train you."

"I don't know, Allen. I need to make money. I don't want to become a burden on you, not any more than I already am."

"You're not a burden, Lance, you're family. I tell you what, I still have some of the money our grandparents set aside for our education. Since Dad still controls yours, I'm guessing you're never going to see it. But I got lucky with undergraduate scholarships and Dad actually paying for medical school for me, so I didn't have to tap into mine for that. If you work for Todd and need the money to help get you through college to become an architect, I'll sign it over to you."

I couldn't believe what I was hearing and looked at Allen like he'd grown horns. "You're giving me your inheritance from Grandma and Grandpa McCartney?"

"Sure. I was going to turn it into a trust for the girls, but their mom and dad had good life insurance, and Gib and I are doing well financially, so they'll be fine. If it helps you get through school, I'm happy to."

The tears came unbidden, and I had to blink hard to try to keep them from falling.

Allen put his arm around me. "Ah, little brother, don't get worked up. It's not that much money."

I spat out a watery chuckle. "It's more than the fifty dollars in my wallet. That's all I've got to my name."

"Yeah, it's more than fifty dollars. It's enough to pay all of your tuition and for the basics while you're earning your degree. Want me to introduce you to Todd?"

"Hell, yeah!" I said and threw both arms around my older brother in a bear hug. I had no words to express my relief that I wasn't going to end up on the street. The fact that our grandparents' money—Allen's money, really—might help me achieve my dream of becoming an architect was more than my brain could even process.

Six

Jake

THE WEEK WAS HELL. My client, Titan Franks, was a beast to deal with. *Entitled, over the top hillbilly thrust into stardom* was the most generous way I thought about him. The last time we'd met, he'd literally rubbed my head and called me Jakie Poo, like I was his damned dog.

Titan's career had taken off after he sang at the Iowa State Fair as part of the free entertainment lineup. A concertgoer posted a video of his performance and it went viral. Not long after, he contacted my PR firm seeking representation, and I signed him that day. I couldn't deny the man's immense talent, but damn, he sure could rub me the wrong way.

My only saving grace was I'd hired a major player in the music industry public relations world to directly managed Titan's arrogant ass. This let me keep him at arm's length most of the time. When I assigned her to the asshat, she quickly agreed, thinking I was giving her a promotion. God help me, if it wasn't for her, I'd have fired him as my client the minute the words 'Jakie Poo' came out of his fucking mouth.

Lexie Richards, on the other hand, was God's gift to everyone who worked behind the scenes of country music. She was cute, funny, down to earth, and knew exactly what she wanted before anyone even asked. She wasn't a newcomer to Music Row, and it showed in her professionalism on every level. Working with her was one of the highlights of my week.

Unlike some of my other clients, Lexie had no qualms about singing in bars, honkytonks, or anywhere else that had a stage and audience willing to listen. Hell, I think the woman had sung in every venue Nashville and most of Branson had to offer. She was hungry for success and willing to grind out every miniscule ounce of it anywhere she could to achieve her dreams. Those were the types of clients I loved to represent.

She'd been cast to sing on a TV series where her character had been killed off before she hit it big. Even though the show wasn't the biggest blockbuster to hit that year, Lexie's performance had thrust her into the public consciousness. It was my PR firm's job to keep her there and, if we were lucky, push her even further into the spotlight.

I'd been preparing to meet with Lexie when Anita called.

"Hey, I know you're busy, but I just got off the phone with Derek's social worker. I thought you'd like to know what we learned."

I sat speechless for a moment, caught completely off guard. I hadn't expected to hear about Derek so quickly, let alone while at work and about to meet with a client. "Yeah, of course. Is he my brother?"

"Yes, he's the baby in your family."

I took a long, deep breath and let it out on a sigh. "Wow, Anita, that's a lot to process."

"Why don't you come on over and spend the rest of the day with us? You probably need some family right now."

"Thanks, I really appreciate it, but I'm too busy. In fact, I've got a client coming in at any moment."

"Well, call if you need us, okay?"

"Yes, ma'am," I said and hung up, just in time for Lexie to walk in.

I quickly tried to push that very loaded information out of my head and, like any good PR professional, I pasted a smile on my face like my life hadn't just been flipped upside down.

Of course, Lexie saw right through me. "Jake, honey?" she asked in her sweet, twangy way. "You look like someone just kicked your favorite dog. Drop that fake smile and tell me what's happened."

I chuckled, for real. "My God, you don't miss a damned thing, do you?"

"Oh no, honey, not in this line of work. You gotta know how to plow through the bullshit if you hope to survive."

I sighed. "I'm not trying to bullshit you, Lexie. I just got some difficult news. But maybe good, too? Hell, I don't even know what to make of it."

"Well, spit it out," she said matter-of-factly, and I almost did before shaking my head.

"I'll tell you what. Let's get through our meeting and if you agree to the plan I'm proposing, then I'll push it off onto my team and you and I can go get a drink...or fifty."

She chuckled. "Baby, you know I don't drink any longer, but I'm happy to go with you. I can be your designated driver."

I'd forgotten Lexie was a recovering alcoholic, and I cringed. "I'm sorry, Lexie, I wasn't thinking..."

She put her hand up. "No, that's my cross to bear and I don't expect others to change their lives to accommodate me. Hey, I have a better idea," she said. "I'm gonna hang out with my best friends tonight and we're gonna watch *Steel Magnolias*. They're gonna drink and I'm gonna laugh and cry 'cause that movie always messes me up. Wanna tag along?"

I thought about it for a moment and was about to say no, but the look on Lexie's face told me that wasn't really an option.

"Okay, but not until we're finished here. You're my last meeting of the week and my assistant will fire *me* if I don't get this plan to her so she can have her weekend off."

Lexie smiled. "Well, let's get to it then."

We had more than an hour's worth of planning to go through. Lexie had brought up that she wanted to record a special benefit album for the children's hospital in Memphis. I begged and pleaded with her to let us use it as a public relations spotlight for her, but she'd flat out refused until I showed her how using it as PR could increase the sales by over fifty percent, thereby benefiting the hospital even more.

"So, what you're telling me is, this is a win-win?"

"It is, and I'll explain to the good people at the children's hospital why it's so important."

I'd done just that the week before and had to navigate all their legal teams to ensure the hospital's trademarks were handled appropriately. It had been quite a lot of work to ensure everyone was onboard with what we had planned.

Lexie looked over my suggestions and only shot down one idea. I knew it was a long shot, but it had her sitting with the kids and singing one of the songs on the album to them.

"I'm not going to exploit ill children so we can raise money," she said.

"It's not really exploitation if they agree to it. Plus, the money raised will go toward ensuring they continue receiving medical services for free."

Lexie absolutely refused. Since I'd expected as much, we set it up so she would sing to an audience that included the children. A special performance just for them. The cameras wouldn't focus on any child in particular, but as they panned the crowd, it'd be clear the children were there.

She grudgingly agreed, but only because I managed to convince her doing so had the potential to bring significantly more money into the hospital.

By the time we finished, both of us were tired. I phoned my assistant Charlie and asked her to come in. She'd spent most of the last week in Memphis with me, so I knew she understood all the work that needed doing on this particular endeavor. She only needed to be updated on how we were changing the plan from Lexie singing to just the kids, to her giving a mini-concert for the kids, their families, and the hospital staff.

When Charlie left, I leaned back in my chair and said, "I'm ready for that diversion now."

Lexie went to the little loveseat at the back of my office and picked up the guitar I kept there. I worked with so many singers, I'd learned you never knew when an acoustic guitar might be necessary.

"The dawn is always darkest before the sun starts to shine..." Lexie sang, her voice as clear and beautiful as any star out there.

As I listened, chills sprinted up my spine. This would be a hit, I could feel it, and I was willing to bet it was one of her originals since I'd never heard the song before.

Lexie sang of hard times, of losing one's way when staying hidden in the darkness.

After belting out the last note, she put the guitar down. "So, you ready to spill yet?"

I couldn't stop grinning, and I wasn't about to let her change the subject so fast. "First, I'm gonna say that song is amazing, and I wanna know when you plan to release it."

She shook her head. "That song is my song. I wrote it when my husband and I split and after I'd accepted the fact that I was a raging alcoholic. I'm not sure I'll ever be ready to put that one out for the public to hear."

"I understand," I said, willing to drop it for now. "Lexie, what do you know about my history?"

"Well, I read in a magazine you were a foster child, and that you pulled yourself up by the bootstraps. That's actually one of the reasons I signed with you. You're no stranger to struggle and you're willing to put in the work, same as me."

I smiled at that because, as usual, she'd made a solid assessment. "Yeah, and did the article tell you why I was a foster child?" I asked, knowing full well that it hadn't.

"No," she said, shaking her head.

I sighed. Talking about my birth family always made for a difficult conversation, no matter how many years had passed. "It's no secret, I'm gay. Although the article you're speaking about didn't bring that up, plenty of others have. I grew up in a tiny town about fifty miles east of Memphis. My parents were, and probably still are, deeply religious, so when a kid I went to high school with caught me looking at half-naked men online, he told everyone in town. My parents wasted no time kicking me out. I've not seen them or any of my siblings since."

Lexie nodded in understanding. "Jake, honey, tonight you're gonna meet my ex's brother. He was kicked out of his home for being gay, too. You've got to know that doesn't change how I feel about you."

I smiled over at the woman I was becoming fonder of by the day before shaking my head. "I appreciate that, Lexie, but that's not why I'm upset. My foster moms discovered that I have another sibling in the system, a brother I didn't even know about. They weren't sure he and I were even related when I met with them last weekend, but they confirmed it to me right before you walked in."

"Oh, honey, why didn't you put this off? We could meet any old time. You should be with them now."

I put my hand up, chuckling. "'Cause this planning meeting was, and is, a priority. You're doing a huge thing for those kids, but it's also really important for your career too. I don't know my brother's story, don't know why he's in foster care. I'm guessing I'll learn more come the weekend, but for now, I'm just trying to wrap my mind around it all."

"Well, thank you for telling me," Lexie said and came over to pull me up out of my chair. "Come on, we'll head over to that little dive you have right around the corner from here, and you can have a drink while I have a Shirley Temple."

I smiled and let her lead me out the door.

We laughed as several people in the bar tried singing karaoke, all of them horrible. Right before we were about to leave to meet her friends for the *Steel Magnolias* movie night, Lexie got up, put on Patsy Cline's "Sweet Dreams," and belted out the song so perfectly that people had to look around to see if Patsy had somehow come back to haunt the place.

We left to a round of applause and, of course, a lot of yelling for an encore. "You love getting an unsuspecting crowd riled up, don't you?"

"There's no feeling like it in the world," she said as she winked at me.

Enjoy it while you can, I thought to myself. I had a strong feeling that once this hospital album got traction, our girl wouldn't be able to stand up in a karaoke bar and anonymously belt out Patsy Cline any longer. I just hoped she knew what life changes that kind of success was about to bring her.

SEVEN

LANCE

"HEY, TODD, DO YOU have a moment?" my brother asked into his phone while I sat across from him.

"Cool. Yeah, thanks. They're good. How are the little ones?"

He laughed heartily at whatever his friend had said. I felt a little awkward eavesdropping, albeit on only one side of their conversation, but then again, I was the reason Allen had called.

"So, I won't keep you long, but my brother just came into town, and he's wanting some experience working in construction. He's hoping to become an architect and needs some hands-on learning."

There was a long pause before Allen shook his head, his eyes flicking to mine. "Well, no, I don't think he has much experience at all."

Allen's calm demeanor gave nothing away as far as how his friend had reacted to that last crucial detail. Not to be overly dramatic, but I felt like my future hung in the balance of an otherwise casual conversation between friends, and I fought the urge not to pace. The suspense left me with nervous energy that I had no choice but to pack down.

"Cool, yeah, it'd be more of an internship at this point, letting him shadow you and your workers." He laughed. "Well, that's something you can take up with him." Allen nodded and smiled, which eased my nerves a fraction. I couldn't imagine him sounding so jovial if his friend had balked at the idea of basically mentoring me.

"Why don't you meet us at the café? My treat, and you can meet him personally. Great, see you in about an hour," Allen said, then paused before chuckling. "I'm a pediatrician, I know how to avoid changing diapers, so I'm a no on that one. But sure, we do. In fact, I'll ask Gib and we can make plans while we're having lunch."

He said a goodbye, then hung up, and his grin widened as he looked at me. "Well, we better buy you a set of gloves 'cause Todd said he doesn't do interns, just free labor."

I cringed. "I know you told him I have no experience, but does he know I'm clueless? Like, I barely know the difference between a Phillips and a flathead screwdriver."

Allen shrugged. "I'm guessing since he knows me and how I grew up, he'll suspect you are."

Allen's face grew serious then. "Lance, Todd is one of the best people I know. He'll definitely be tough on you, but if you're willing to try, he'll teach you."

I struggled with mixed emotions in the hour leading up to our lunch with Allen's friend. On the one hand, I was excited to be trying something I'd only ever dreamed of. On the other, I was terrified I'd be bad at it. Growing up, I'd never had a chance to do anything with my hands, let alone manual labor. Dad was adamantly opposed to it. "You've got surgeon's hands," he'd say. "Don't mess them up before you've grown into them."

I was literally shaking when we got to the café and sat down. The server took our order just as a tall and ruggedly handsome man walked in to join us.

Allen got up and hugged him, then introduced us. "Todd, this is Lance. Lance, this is Todd."

I smiled at the man. "Nice to meet you."

"You might want to reserve judgment on that. Your brother here tells me you're looking for some hands-on experience in the construction industry."

I nodded and smiled nervously, trying not to give away how freaked out I was about all this.

He seemed to catch on, though, and offered me a friendly smile. "Well, let's sit down and you can tell me about your experience in construction."

That's when my smile fell and I couldn't hold back a cringe. "Well, I don't really have any," I admitted. "That's why I'd like to work for you. I mean, intern for you. Knowing how things are built will help make me a better architect...someday."

I still wasn't totally convinced my someday would come, but I had to put all of my cards on the table. I owed it to Allen for believing in me more than I did myself. Todd pondered for a moment without responding, sipping at his newly filled coffee cup while my nerves continued running amok.

"Well, my business is completely inundated at the moment, so I don't have a lot of time to train you," he said, and I felt all hope seeping out of me like a deflating balloon. "But if you're really interested in learning, I can put you with my second-in-command. I'm going to be completely honest with you though, your first few weeks will be nothing other than fetching things for me and the other workers. Until you're experienced enough around a job site, you'd be a huge liability to me being in the middle of the action."

My game plan for this interview had been to act nonchalant, but I'd never been good at hiding my emotions. The smile slipped out before I could stop it. "I honestly can't wait."

Todd chuckled. "You say that now."

Todd quickly texted someone and a moment later, received one back. "Can you start tomorrow?" he asked, looking up from his phone.

"I can start now," I said before I could stop myself.

Todd laughed. "Okay, Linc said he'll pick you up tomorrow morning at Allen and Gib's place."

I looked confused. "He knows where I'm staying?"

Todd smirked. "Well, it is a small town, so people you've never even met likely already know things about you. You'll get used to it. But yeah, I mentioned you were staying with Allen, and we did the work on their house, so Linc knows where to go."

"Oh," I said as my thoughts shifted to Allen's beautiful Queen Anne home. "It's really well done. Did you put the kitchen in?"

Todd nodded. "We did that, Chrissy's room, and all the bathrooms. The rest just needed sprucing up. The Cross sisters had kept it pretty well-preserved. We just had to do the basics."

I was confused again, not knowing who the Cross sisters were, but I shrugged and smiled. "I can't wait to be involved," I said and was about to ask more questions when I looked up, straight into the face of one of the most handsome men I'd ever laid eyes on.

My mouth went dry, and I completely lost all ability to talk as I stared at the man who was staring back at me with equal intensity.

Todd cleared his throat. "Hi, Jake. What brings you out today?"

That broke the momentary spell, and only then did the man–Jake–look away from me. "I came to find you, but I didn't know you were in a meeting. Sorry to interrupt."

"Not really in a meeting. Pull up a chair and join us for lunch. If you guys don't mind?" Todd asked us.

When Allen shook his head, Todd glanced my way, and I could see a barely repressed smile. He probably saw my cheeks had turned pink and I couldn't exactly blame it on the cold outside. My audible gulp must've been confirmation enough because Todd nodded toward the empty chair at our table and Jake sat down. Right next to me.

"Jake, you know Allen, and this is his brother, Lance. Lance is going to come work with us for a while. He's needing some experience in the field before going to architecture school."

I felt Jake's eyes on me again, and my damned blush deepened in response. Good God, I needed to get myself under control before I really made a fool of myself in front of my brother, my new boss, and this gorgeous man.

"Cool, so you're going to be in town for a while then?" he asked.

I nodded and met his eyes, hoping my voice didn't crack. "I hope so. My brother has agreed to put up with me while I finish my schooling. Do you live here too?" I asked, crossing my fingers in hope under the table like some lovestruck schoolboy. I felt ridiculous but couldn't help myself.

Jake shook his head. "No, not yet. I live in Nashville, but I'm here a lot."

"A lot more than he needs to be," Todd said, and he got a nasty look from who I suspected was a friend.

"It wouldn't feel that way if you'd get started on our project."

"I already said..." Jake put his hand up to stop Todd from talking. They both sounded at least mildly annoyed, but from what I could gather, it seemed mostly like good-natured teasing.

"You already said... I know, but that doesn't mean I can't keep asking."

"Or turning up like a bad penny," Todd said, smirking, and Jake rolled his eyes.

"So," Jake said, turning his attention back to me. "You're going to school to be an architect?"

"Well, that's yet to be official, but I'm hoping."

"You'll get in, and you'll do terrific work. Your passion for it will show in everything you design," Allen said with a huge grin. I had no idea where my brother's confidence in me came from, but I was grateful for the boost. He must be a truly amazing father.

"Good, we've got a project that needs an architect, one that doesn't drag his damned feet," Jake said and looked over at Todd.

Todd chuckled. "Tom isn't dragging his feet, my friend. You are being impatient. So, tell me why you're here? I know it's not just so I can buy you lunch."

"I have a couple of new friends I met the other night and thought it'd be fun to have them come to Crawford City to check it out. I thought I'd drop by to see if I could talk you into hosting a get-together."

Todd cocked an eyebrow at Jake. "Dude, I have three little hellions that take every ounce of effort to keep under control. You think your friends would want to come babysit? 'Cause at this point, that's what a party at our house would be."

Jake's face fell, and I wanted to reach out and take his hand to comfort him. *Where the hell did that come from?*

I didn't know this man from Adam, and I already wanted to make the world right for him.

I looked over at Allen, silently pleading for him to offer his home for the get-together.

Allen caught my expression and cocked his eyebrow, very much like the way Todd had a moment ago. We silently communicated and Allen didn't even try to hide his smile. "Hold on, Jake. Let me text Gib and see if we have time to host your friends. When were you wanting them to come out?"

Jake smiled so brightly I'm surprised it didn't blind everyone at the table. "They work during the week, so it'd work best if it was on a weekend."

The smile never left Allen's face as he texted Gib. Within moments, his phone dinged with a reply. "How about the weekend after next? I've got both days off."

"Perfect. Thank you," Jake said and quickly texted his friends. A reply came almost immediately. "Lexie said she needs to hear back from the rest of them, but she thinks it's a go."

"Hmm. So, since both Gib and I work insane hours, why don't you take Lance's number, and he can be our point person for all this."

I looked at Allen with mouth agape. Blushing, I turned back to Jake and rattled off my number.

"L a n c e M c C a r t n e y," he said, enunciating each letter as he typed them into his phone. Like spelling my name correctly was somehow important...like *I* was important.

I knew I was blushing so much that I could've lit up a lighthouse in the middle of thick fog.

Jake finished typing and looked up at me, smiling. "What're your plans right now, Lance?" he asked.

"Um..." I looked over at Allen, then Todd. Both were grinning at each other like Cheshire cats and giving no indication that their afternoon plans included me. "I-I don't know if I have any."

"Good," Jake said, almost too quickly. The man's face really did glow when he smiled. "I'm going over to the new project site downtown. If you're going into architecture, maybe you'd like to come along and take a look."

I really did want to go along and take a look. A whole lot of looks actually, and not just at some future job site either.

"Yeah, that'd be good. Allen, do you need me for anything?"

My brother had the most embarrassing grin on his face—embarrassing to me because we all knew the reason behind it—and he shook his head. "No, you two go on and check out the project site. I'm gonna finish my lunch, then walk back up to the house. I'll get your food to go."

Jake and I stood up, and before I forgot, I shook Todd's hand and thanked him for the opportunity to work for him.

"Um, what time tomorrow?" I asked.

"Linc will be by early, like around seven. I can have him pick you up at six forty-five, then you can help him load his truck with supplies for the day."

"Perfect," I said, and then looked at the male super-model standing in front of me. "I guess, lead the way then."

Jake winked at me, and I seriously felt my knees go weak. God, this was going to be an interesting tour.

EIGHT

JAKE

S ITTING ACROSS THE TABLE from Todd was the mystery man I'd all too briefly encountered the other day. The one who had sent all those funny feelings coursing through me. I couldn't help but stare, just like I had then, but this time, he noticed me and our eyes locked.

From the way he looked at me, intense and with lips slightly parted, I knew this wasn't a one-sided attraction. The thrill of that realization was enough to melt the butter in every butter dish between here and Nashville. Learning my mystery man–*Lance*–was Allen McCartney's brother, and would be staying in town while working for Todd, pleased me far more than I'd readily admit.

I'd met Lexie's friends for drinks and a movie at their place and liked them all from the start. Interestingly, the group included her ex-husband and his brother, who owned a fledgling construction company in the heart of

Nashville. My instincts told me they were reliable, and the one thing I'd learned since being kicked out of my home as a teenager was to trust my instincts.

The next day, I'd investigated the men a bit, contacting a few people Lexie and I both knew who'd hired them. The reports were all the same. Top of the line, strong level of professionalism, and more importantly, didn't cut corners. That's when I decided to invite them to Crawford City. I figured if Lexie's construction friends could take on some of Todd's workload, we could finally get the mercantile project rolling.

Todd was barely keeping his head above water and I knew a lot of that had to do with all the referrals I kept sending his way. Having too much work was the best kind of problem to have in business, but it was still a problem. I knew for a fact that if I didn't intervene, our project would continue being pushed to the back burner. That would've been fine under normal circumstances, but since I'd decided to move into one of the condos we'd be building, I wanted that project completed as soon as possible.

Of course, learning I had a little brother who was used to living in the country and who, like me, would probably feel more comfortable in Crawford City than a busy metropolis like Nashville only fueled my drive to move my home and business to the inclusive small town. The only reason I could imagine why our religious zealot of a father would ever kick one of his kids out would be because of their sexuality and if that was the case, Crawford City was the best option for both of us.

Lance and I walked along the streets of the little town, and I could tell by the way he quietly kept sneaking glances at me that he was probably shy. I found it sweet.

"How long have you been in town?" I asked, trying to draw him out of his shell a little.

"About a week, well, not quite. I got here Tuesday."

That was the day I'd seen him, so that explained his rush. "Cool, and what do you think of Crawford City?" I asked.

He looked at me strangely, like he was deciding how best to answer without offense, before he shrugged and said, "I guess it's okay."

I chuckled. "Not used to small towns, huh?"

He smiled at that, looking relieved. "No, I grew up on Long Island. Our father runs a large hospital over there. I've only ever lived in cities, so this is...very different."

I let the conversation lie as we walked around the corner and up to the mercantile project site.

The burned-out building had already been demolished, and we also owned the two empty lots on either side of it that'd been vacant since the nineteen thirties. Next to the project site stood a small block building that had once housed a feed store and the adjacent grain mill. Both belonged to me and would need to be torn down when the project started, but the former grain mill had structural issues, anyway. For now, I used the old feed store as my headquarters when I was in town.

I enjoyed Lance's look of surprise when I pulled out my key and unlocked the front door. I hoped I wasn't being too forward, placing my hand at the small of his back as I ushered him inside, but seeing his small smile in response eased any doubt. We walked over to the large countertop where the current architectural plans lay open.

"So," I began, "the empty lots next door used to hold a big brick building built in the eighteen hundreds. It was a focal point for the town that once housed a mercantile, and as the trains traveled through, they'd drop off most of the provisions that supplied the county. That's why everyone refers to this as the mercantile project."

"It's too bad such a historical building was torn down. It must've been past the point of saving?" Lance asked, sounding disappointed that he hadn't seen it for himself.

"The original building burned to the ground a while back."

Lance shook his head. "That happens a lot with old buildings. Let me guess, bad electrical?"

"Arson, I'm afraid. The former mayor didn't like Todd and when he'd gotten approval for building renovations, the man had the place torched."

Lance's eyes grew large, but he didn't respond. I guess I'd shocked him into silence. Not that there was much more to say about it. At least the authorities got his accomplice to talk, so the jackass had been held accountable in the end.

"So," I said, redirecting our conversation back to the project, "these are the original plans that were drawn up before I bought this building and the old grain mill."

I showed him the old mercantile's original blueprints as a frame of reference so he'd understand what we were hoping to create with the new construction.

"Cool," he said. "It's a shame the old building burned. Do you have pictures?" he asked.

I opened my phone, and I found the photos I'd taken before the fire, then handed it over to him. "The original beams had never been covered, and it had wall-to-wall hardwood with over a century of wear and tear. It was truly a beautiful building, inside and out. Todd had plans to preserve as many of its historical elements as possible in the renovation."

"I wish I could've seen it, although that probably would've made losing it to fire all the more painful," Lance said, and I could tell he really felt that way.

I moved the original plans to one side and showed him the latest set of drawings. "These are the new construction plans, at least as they stand now. You can see we kept the elevation of the previous structure but extended the building to encompass the two vacant lots."

Lance didn't really say much as he studied the drawings. I wasn't sure if maybe I had overwhelmed him with too much information. I tended to do that with projects I was passionate about, prattle on and on until people became glassy-eyed. I hadn't really spoken to him about his knowledge of blueprints either. I was just about to ask him when he turned the page back and forth a couple of times, like he was trying to figure out how the front coincided with the interior sketches.

"So, you're trying to recreate the look of the old building, but you're also wanting to maximize the square footage."

I nodded. He'd caught on fairly quickly. "The problem is that I want to incorporate my two lots into the design. The town council is balking at the idea of a massive wall of brick stretching along this entire downtown block, but they're not seeing the forest for the trees. Aside from bringing in new business, this building has the potential to become a tourist attraction of sorts. Knowing Todd, he'll create a thing of beauty that'll become its own landmark, assuming he's given the chance."

"Has your architect considered designing the exterior to look more like the downtown area? I mean, that's pretty common for infill commercial structures."

Although Lance might not know much about construction, he clearly knew a thing or two about architecture. Color me impressed. "Yes, but we want to maintain the industrial components of the railyard and honor that history. We don't want it to look like the rest of the town."

He pondered for a moment, then asked, "Do you have a pencil and paper I can use?"

I fumbled through the drawers still full of stuff from the previous owner and found an old notebook and a couple dull pencils.

Lance stared at the paper for a moment before he began sketching. I was tempted to watch him as he worked, brows furrowed and so deep in concentration that he probably forgot I was standing there, but I also didn't want to hover, so I scrolled through work emails on my phone while his pencil flew across the paper. Several dozen emails later, I noticed him look up, and he turned the pad of paper around toward me. "I think it's a matter of how you use the space. So, if you bring the main building up to the curb, like this building we're currently in, that will give it dimension. You can recess the buildings on either side and even add faux exteriors, making them look more like wood-clad buildings. That will differentiate the structure without sacrificing space."

He paused, tapped the pencil to his lips a few times as if considering something, then erased the top of the middle building and took it up a floor. "I'd raise the elevation of this building, the one you're trying to make look like it was here originally, which would add another set of rooms for your hotel. I'm guessing that's what you're putting up there, based on the plans."

When I nodded in confirmation, Lance looked pleased with himself that he'd gotten it right, then gestured back to his sketch. "I'd maybe put offices on this side if you have a need for commercial space and perhaps incorporate mixed-use on the other if you aren't wanting a larger hotel."

I smiled at him and his blush returned. "I think you might've created the perfect compromise for the town. I can almost see this in my mind's eye. It'll look amazing and still honor the past."

"Yes, exactly, the best of both worlds," he said. "Do you plan to put residential in these?"

I had been holding that little piece of information close to my chest as I hadn't yet decided how I was going to fill the rest of the partners in on my plans. I wanted the two lots to house my condo, which I intended to incorporate into the plans as my go-to place while here in Crawford City.

"It's a possibility," I said.

"I think I'd put residential here, on the inside," he said, pointing toward the left side of the sketch. "The part closest to downtown, and make them exclusive. I'd also give them their own separate entrance from the hotel. People who own here wouldn't want to share their building with tourists."

He sat back a moment and looked over his sketch. When he looked up and caught me watching him, his blush deepened. "Oh, um, sorry, I can get carried away. I've only played around with the whole architect thing as an amateur. You'll want to take what I'm saying with a grain of salt."

"I guess you could say I'm an amateur as well, but I know what I want and what you've drawn here is really close to what I want. It's hard to express to the other partners, though. This will help me do that."

His smile was sweet and held a level of innocence I wouldn't have expected from a guy who grew up on Long Island, New York. "I'm glad I could help. So, how do you know Todd?" he asked.

"He and I met shortly after we both moved to Nashville years ago. Well, I'd just moved out of my foster parents' home and he had just moved there with his friend Jen. We hit it off fairly quickly, and then next thing I know, he's my best friend."

Lance smiled. "That's cool. He seems like a nice guy."

"One of the best on the planet," I said. "You won't meet a harder worker or more genuine friend, and he's not afraid to call me out on my bullshit, which I appreciate...most of the time."

I could tell Lance wanted to pry, but instead, he pulled back and started looking at the plans again.

"Want to walk to my new favorite ice cream shop?" he asked. "Allen took me there yesterday. The shop is scary looking, but Allen says the ice cream's good. I can vouch for the hot chocolate."

I had to laugh. Who was this man who would visit an ice cream shop for hot chocolate? He was right, though. The building did look like it could fall down at any moment.

I locked up behind us and as we walked down the road, I chatted more about my friendship with Todd. Even though I was thrilled for my friend to have found his life partner, I admitted there was a time I would've liked my relationship with Todd to be more.

"Why wasn't it?" he asked.

"Well, mostly 'cause he was, and is, in love with his husband. Even when they were bitter enemies, he couldn't stop talking about him. There's no way to compete with that, let alone risk standing in the way of two men obviously meant to be together, even if they refused to see it for themselves at the time."

"Todd's husband, that's Ash?" he asked.

"Yeah, have you met him?"

He shook his head. "No, I just know he works with my brother-in-law, Gib."

"Well, you will, especially if you're going to work with Todd. He's a great guy and I'm really happy for both of them- now at least."

He chuckled. "You had it bad then?"

I smiled. "Well, probably not that bad. He's just always been such a great friend. Kind, caring, responsible...not to mention gorgeous. It'd be cool to fall in love with someone you are already friends with, like your relationship just naturally grows that way. Hell, it'd be cool just to fall in love, period."

Lance nodded and a far-off look came over his face. "I've not really been out long. To be honest, I haven't even told Allen or my dad. Not that my father wants to see me anytime soon, anyway."

"Really? Why?" I asked, knowing I was prying but unable to help myself. I'd already been more open with Lance than I was with most people I called friends, aside from Todd.

He opened his mouth to speak, then his expression suddenly shifted to looking mortified. "Oh, no, sorry, I shouldn't be bringing up my pitiful, sad story."

When I didn't say anything, just tilted my head in confusion, he sighed. "It's not a big deal. My father wants me to be a doctor, I want to be an architect. My father is an overbearing pain in the ass, and I'm just as stubborn as him." Lance chuckled at that, like he'd only just realized the apparent similarity.

"Well, I sorta like stubborn."

Lance looked over, then blushed. "You do?"

"Oh yeah, I like it when someone has conviction and fights for what they want."

We stopped right behind the enormous old yew that stood between the sidewalk and the town hall.

"You know, I sorta like you," Lance said and his adorable blush deepened.

"Do you mean me or the tree?" I asked, teasing him.

Lance laughed and pointed a finger at my chest. "Y O U, not Y E W," he said, and I took hold of his hand and pulled him close.

I bent down and kissed him gently on the lips as our bodies pressed against each other. I'm sure we'd have both taken the kiss a lot deeper had Ms. Beth not walked around the corner.

"Don't make me get the hose out, boys," she said, laughing.

"Well, some way to make a great first impression, huh?" Lance asked as we pulled apart.

"Don't worry, Ms. Beth is a very kind and open-minded person, just like most of the locals here. Crawford City is special and unique. There's a greater tolerance toward folks like us than the rest of Tennessee."

"Good to know."

"So, that ice cream?" I asked, and Lance grabbed my hand and pulled me toward the shop.

I smiled at the adorable man and was mentally flipping through my calendar for when I'd be able to see him again. The rest of the weekend was out, since I was sure my foster moms would want to meet and develop a strategy for how to help my newly discovered brother. The following week was also out, since I had to fly to Milan to meet with Jen about promoting the photoshoot she'd be doing with a famous photojournalist who was developing a book celebrating Black supermodels.

"Um, so, I've got a crazy week ahead, but would you like to maybe go out the week after next? I'm going to be back in town on Thursday before the party I've thrust on your brother. I could take you out to Nashville or something."

He smiled. "Like a date? I'd like that."

We were just about to enter the ice cream shop when I got a call.

I excused myself and answered just in time to hear my assistant freaking out. "We can't use the venue we scheduled for Lexie's gig on Sunday," Charlie blurted. "They had a massive plumbing issue. I'm not sure what to do."

Handling last-minute crises was a big part of my job so I wasn't easily rattled, but that didn't mean they caused any less of a headache. I racked my brain for an alternative venue. If it'd been a Nashville event, I could've picked from at least a hundred different spots, but since it was in Memphis, I had no idea where we could book a concert on such short notice.

"I tell you what, I'm going to head back to town. Why don't you start a list of possible venues, and then meet me at the office when I get back?"

When Charlie agreed and sounded sufficiently calmer than when I'd answered her call, I hung up and looked over at my handsome date and sighed. "Well, that was work and we're in a crisis. I'm afraid I'm going to have to take a rain check on that ice cream."

Lance just shrugged, although I thought I caught a flash of disappointment cross his face. "It's all good. Why don't you call me when you have time and we'll set up plans for that date and the party."

I nodded. "Perfect plan," I said before rushing toward my car. I'd be lucky to get back in time before my assistant blew another gasket. I also needed to get this resolved as quickly as possible so I could meet my foster moms this evening for dinner.

Dang, I thought to myself, *at least my life wasn't boring.*

"Anita, Claire, are you two here?" I yelled as I came through the front door.

"We're back here," I heard Claire say.

I put my bag next to the chair just inside the entry. I was excited to learn more about Derek. At first, it had been a total surprise to discover I had another sibling, let alone one who might be gay, but the more I thought about it, the more excited I'd become to meet him.

My birth family had ostracized me, even threatened me. I wasn't sure what hurt more, though—them treating me like shit or pretending like I didn't exist. I'd tried reaching out to my sister, the sibling I was closest to in age, just a few years ago and was ignored. So, I hadn't tried again. I didn't need my birth family in my life to be happy, but I wouldn't throw the chance away either.

"I've already ordered pizza," I yelled into the house as I took my shoes off. "So, Anita, you won't have to cook tonight." I walked into the living room and stopped short. There, sitting in Anita's old recliner, sat Derek. The guy from the picture. My brother.

"So, I see you didn't get our text," Claire said as she got up from the sofa and came over to kiss me.

A text from them had popped up, but in my rush to get here, I hadn't read it.

"No, um, sorry, I was already on the road, so I didn't look at my phone."

Anita stood up. "Jake, meet Derek, your brother. And Derek, this is Jake."

Just then, a woman came out of the back hallway. I'd seen her before, but it'd been years. She was a caseworker with children's services. She'd never been mine, but I'd seen her often in the group home when she'd met with the other kids.

"Jake, do you remember Mrs. Lidia?" Anita asked.

"I do. Mrs. Lidia, nice to see you again."

"Likewise, Jake. We've all been so proud of how well you've turned out. The kids at the home are sick to death of how much we brag about you."

I looked at Anita, who I knew was a big boaster, and blushed. "Thank you, ma'am."

I crossed the living room with an outstretched hand and took Derek's in a shake. "It's really nice to meet you, Derek."

The kid was hesitant. I could tell he was as overwhelmed as me. Maybe more.

"So, I didn't expect to get to meet you for a while."

Derek didn't respond. Instead, he looked over at Mrs. Lidia, who quickly said, "Derek was anxious to meet you, and when Anita told me you were coming tonight, I asked permission to bring him over. I apologize for the last-minute arrangements. We didn't get the okay until the end of the day."

I nodded. This was awkward for both of us, but seeing Derek was shy, I decided to take it one step at a time.

"Well, it's been a crazy day for me. But I couldn't think of a better way to cap it off than to meet my baby brother." Derek was looking down at his hands. "So, why don't you tell me about yourself? I read that you like video games. Which ones do you like to play?"

When he told me BattleGild, I leaned back and laughed out loud. "Dude, that's perfect. I am the master of that game. I'm so gonna kick your butt!"

Derek's face lit up. "No freaking way, I'm the champion! You, old man, don't stand a chance."

"Challenge accepted, kid. Don't go crying to Mrs. Lidia, though, when I cream you. As your big brother, it's my *responsibility* to kick your butt from here to next week."

"Man, you're so going down in flames. You're too old to keep up with me."

"Please, I'm not that old, but I'm old enough to have more experience at BattleGild than you. I bet you have to be in bed by six every night!" I knew full well the actual bedtime of the group home was nine o'clock, but I couldn't resist some good-natured teasing and, apparently, neither could my youngest brother.

Derek burst out laughing, and I looked over at the three women. All of them were shaking their heads, but clearly amused. "What? Surely you didn't think I was going to take it easy on him just 'cause he hadn't had the incredible pleasure to know my awesome self until now."

Derek rolled his eyes at that, which made me smile. Mission accomplished by getting the kid to relax, and bonus points for discovering we had gaming in common.

"So, when's that pizza going to get here?" he asked.

"I ordered it before I got here, so a few more minutes."

"Did you order enough?" he asked, sounding concerned.

Both Anita and Claire chuckled. "Trust me, that won't be a problem."

I gave my foster moms the eye. "I like to order extra so I have some left over for breakfast. Do you like meat lover's pizza?"

"Oh man, that's the only kind."

I fell back on the sofa, lifting my hands to the heavens. "Finally, God, thank you! Someone who knows how to eat pizza properly!"

Derek chuckled, then his face sort of fell. "I didn't know about you until..."

I sighed. "Yeah, buddy, we'll get into all that, but right now, let's just hang out, okay?" He nodded. "So, you like meat lover's, which increases your cool quotient significantly. You also like my favorite game even though I still plan to mop the floor with your avatar. What else do you like?"

I leaned back and just let my baby brother talk about his world. Mostly, it revolved around how he loved mechanics. Taking things apart and putting them back together. How Mrs. Lidia had become his old appliance supplier. She laughed when he said that, and I could see a genuine attachment between the two. That was rare for caseworkers, especially those who'd been around as long as Mrs. Lidia.

By the time the pizzas arrived, there was just enough time for everyone to eat before Derek and Mrs. Lidia had to leave to get back to the group home before cur-few.

As we stood in the doorway saying our goodbyes, Derek grabbed me into a huge hug. "I can't believe I haven't met you until now."

"That makes two of us, buddy. I promise I'll do every-thing I can to make sure we spend more time together, okay?"

Derek nodded into my shoulder and when he let me go, I saw the same look of vulnerability as when I first walked into the living room. "You promise?"

"Dude, you're my brother, and you're cool on top of that. You'll never get rid of me now."

His whole face lit up with a smile. "I'm so looking forward to killing you in BattleGild. You're gonna eat your words."

"Never gonna happen, kid!"

He left chuckling. Before she walked out behind him, Mrs. Lidia put her hand on my shoulder and squeezed. "Thank you. He really needed this."

I nodded, looking toward the car that Derek was climbing into, and the backs of my eyes burned with unshed tears. "I did too," I whispered.

I'd told Derek we'd talk about the particulars, and I knew the kid would eventually need to, but remembering how vulnerable I'd been when I was in his situation, I knew emotions were often just too big to deal with, and I wanted him to have a little time just to get to know me. No pressure, no expectations, no heavy conversations he wasn't ready for...just hanging out with his older brother who, hopefully, he'd come to consider as a trustworthy and dependable friend. God knows I'd needed that at his age.

Now that Derek was in my life, I'd be damned if I ever let that change. Every fiber of my being had gone into high alert now, wanting to protect my brother and keep him safe. It seemed a little strange to feel this protective of a kid I'd just met, but the feeling was real and intensely sincere. I couldn't change the fact our dad was a full-out piece of fossilized shit, or that our mom passively watched her children be tossed out like yesterday's garbage, but I could ensure from now on that my brother had someone in his life who loved him unconditionally.

NINE

LANCE

"**L**ance, can you bring me the reciprocating saw?" James hollered down from the second-story window of the house we were rebuilding.

"Sure," I yelled up, then said quietly to myself, "as soon as I figure out what that is."

I had just pulled my phone out to Google *reciprocating saw* when Linc came up behind me, chuckling. "Here," he said and handed me a strange-looking long machine with a tiny blade on the end.

"What the heck do you do with this?" I asked.

"Stay up there and watch him use it. That's the easiest way to learn," Linc said.

I rushed up the stairs two at a time and handed the saw over to James. "Thanks, dude."

"Welcome. Linc told me to hang out for a bit and watch how you use it."

"That works. This baby is the best tool for ripping things out," he said and slipped his safety goggles down over his eyes and went to work cutting through a metal pipe.

Within seconds, he was done with that cut and went after the bottom part next. When he'd completely cut through the pipe, he said, "Now, I'm gonna go downstairs and do it there as well."

"Why are you removing the pipes?" I asked, knowing I sounded ignorant. Todd and Linc had told me to ask about anything and everything I didn't understand, though, so I had already asked a ton of questions.

"'Cause these are galvanized and nobody uses those anymore. They get clogged up and rust. Here," James said, handing a different pipe to me. "See all that corrosion?"

I nodded. "So, we now use this." He handed me a small cut of a plastic pipe. "It's called PEX and it's cool stuff. Come on downstairs and I'll show you why."

The other guys didn't seem very interested in my help, probably because they'd already grown tired of babysitting the know-nothing intern, and Linc wasn't particular about what all I was doing either, so I spent most of my day helping James.

He led me down to the basement and showed me how the PEX plumbing had valves you could turn on and off. "This is called the Viega ManaBloc," he said, pointing at the contraption connected to all the pipes.

I studied it a moment. "It looks like something out of science fiction."

James chuckled. "Maybe, but it makes the plumbing a lot more manageable. The homeowner will be able to turn off the water to each part of the house. So, let's say they have a leak in the kitchen. With this little key here, they can just come to the section labeled *kitchen* and give it a turn like that, and the whole thing is shut off. Crisis managed."

I shook my head. "I have a lot to learn."

"Don't worry about it. We all did when we started. You'll catch on fast enough."

I wasn't sure that was true. It seemed like I was stuck on stupid when it came to all this. Every day this week, one or another contractor would take me under their wings and show me the ins and outs of the job and every night, I went home with more questions than answers. The realization of just how much I had to learn seemed to hit harder each day.

I didn't hear back from Jake until the weekend. I got a text from him saying that his friends had confirmed they could come out the following weekend for the get-together here at Allen and Gib's house. When he didn't mention our date, I decided not to bring it up.

I probably annoyed him or drove him off with my ideas about his building project. I had a tendency to do that. If it was anything to do with design or architecture, I was a total geek to the point of being overbearing. I'd had to sneak around to learn anything about it, so when I found someone I could talk freely with, I tended to overwhelm them. As it was, I was lucky my dad didn't discover I hadn't gone pre-med until after I'd graduated from college, or I'd have been screwed and not had my undergraduate degree finished. All through undergrad, it remained a dance, taking enough science classes to keep up that illusion.

"Uncle Lance?" I heard what sounded like Ruby's voice say outside my door.

"Yeah, what's up?" I asked.

"Uncle Gib wants to know if you wanna go with us to the café tonight."

"Come on in, Ruby," I said, now sure it was her.

She opened the door and came in, hopping up on my bed before asking, "Whatcha doin'?"

"Looking at colleges."

"Why you doin' that?"

I chuckled. "'Cause, you silly rabbit, I've got to figure out where I'm going to school."

"I'm not a rabbit, I'm a hawk!"

"Oh, is that so?"

"Totally. I hunt rabbits, like you, and I eat them."

The next thing I knew, Ruby had jumped on my shoulders. Getting into the game, I stood up while holding onto her, and hopped around the room, saying, "I'm a giant rabbit and you are now in my power, hawk!"

She giggled as I pretended to buck her off. Finally, she slid down to the floor. "So, you comin' to dinner?"

"When are you leaving?" I asked.

She shrugged. "In a minute?"

I looked over at my laptop, then back at the little girl I'd grown incredibly attached to, and sighed. "Sure, why not? But I warn you, when I start school, I won't have time for all this lollygagging around."

"Well, then you better come lollygagging around with us now," she said and hopped playfully out of the room. She must've forgotten she'd proclaimed to be a hawk now instead of a rabbit.

I glanced at my laptop and the page I had open to the Vanderbilt website. The school was almost as well regarded as the Ivy League one I'd dropped out of for med school, and I couldn't deny it being a great opportunity, but the cost was astronomical. Not that my other options were all that affordable, either. I would have to sit down with Allen and look at the budget.

I needed to start applying to schools soon, although the idea of submitting applications filled me with dread. As it was, I'd have a hard time convincing either Vandy or the University of Tennessee to take me—a medical school dropout with dreams of becoming an architect—seriously.

At least my grades were good enough, though. I had a four-point-one in my undergraduate studies, and managed to pull all A's in medical school, even though I hated every fucking minute of it. That's not because I was a stellar student, though. Anything less than acing my classes and Dad would've stopped paying. Nothing like poverty to keep a guy's motivation up. "Lance, if you wanna walk down with us, we're leaving now," Gib called up the stairs.

I sighed. Gib. My relationship with him—or lack there-of—was something else I needed to work on. I knew he thought I hated him. And why wouldn't he? I'd been a jerk since we'd met, even refusing to go to his and Allen's wedding. I'd been so confused. Dad had filled my head with what I knew now was a bunch of lies about my brother. For some reason, he'd wanted to keep Allen and me apart, and he'd succeeded in doing so for far too long.

"Gib, give me a minute and I'll be right down."

I closed the computer, then grabbed my jacket and dashed downstairs. Even in chilly weather, the family seemed to walk everywhere. Not that I minded. It was no colder here than it had been back home, and I loved that everything was so close.

Once inside the café, I sat with a twin on either side of me in the booth, and Chrissy and Gib sat across from us. Allen was working a late shift at the hospital, so he wouldn't be back home for several hours.

I hadn't been to the Crawford City Café for dinner, and so I eyeballed the absolutely stuffed buffet with curiosity more than interest. Every leafy green vegetable known to man had been boiled into some kind of...con-coction. Two varieties of cornbread, one sweet and the other blah, at least according to the girls, were cut thick and piled high. All manner of sides and salads, except the lettuce variety, filled the buffet line.

I wasn't used to that sort of food, and tended to eat what I could recognize. Normally at restaurants, I'd hit the salad bar and order a tasty soup or baked chicken. I may have to branch out from that tonight, though I had no plans to touch the heart attack fried chicken. Still, despite trying to eat relatively healthy, I never missed dessert.

"So, have you chosen a school?" Gib asked and I glanced at Ruby, knowing she'd given me away.

I shook my head. "No, it's hard to decide. On the one hand, the university Allen works for looks promising, but I'm guessing it's hard to get into, not to mention it costs a fortune. The only other option I found was Knoxville, which is really far from here."

Gib nodded. "Have you spoken to Allen about it?" he asked.

"No, not yet. I'm still trying to figure out what to do."

"You might be able to benefit from Allen working for the university hospital," Gib said. "It's possible you could get a family discount on tuition."

"Really?" I hadn't thought of that. "But I'm not his kid or anything."

"I don't know any details, but it's worth discussing with him."

"Thanks, Gib, I will. Um, I wanted to say thank you for letting me stay with you. I know it's probably strange having me around..."

Gib put his hand up to stop me. "No, Lance, it's not strange at all. In fact, it's amazing and Allen is really enjoying you being here."

Out of the corner of my eye, I caught sight of Chrissy squinting at me. Gib nudged her arm and shook his head. Then he added, clearly for her sake, "I know you and

Allen struggled growing up, with getting to know each other. It's so awesome you're working things out now."

Chrissy made a low noise in her throat, almost like a growl, but didn't respond. Instead, she ignored us completely and started talking to the twins.

I looked at Gib in confusion and he shook his head and shrugged. I guessed I needed to have a one-on-one with Chrissy soon to clear the air. But first, I needed to find out what Allen and Gib knew about her feelings toward me. Seeing as I was already on her bad side, the last thing I wanted to do was make the situation worse.

Ten

Jake

SOMETIMES I THINK HOW crazy it is that I travel to far-flung places like Milan, New York, Paris, and Singapore, and never have time to do anything but attend a meeting, make deals and plans for future meetings, and then leave. This was one of those trips.

Jen was in a terrible mood when I called. The famous photographer had wigged out on her and wouldn't be arriving for two more days. In an industry where time is money, and schedules often left little room for flexing, my client was understandably pissed.

"Jen, please don't leave," I said.

"Give me one good reason why I shouldn't?" she asked.

"Because I'm on a flight to Milan to meet you."

"Ugh," she moaned. "Okay, but you're taking me out to eat and we're putting it on that jackass's tab."

"Agreed. I've got a layover in London, then I'll be in Milan tomorrow morning, okay?"

"Yeah, okay, but I'm so going to drag your butt all over Milan as soon as you land. I'm not about to just sit around waiting for that man to show up when he's already late."

"Whatever you need," I said, and cringed at the piles of paperwork I needed to finish before I got back to Nashville.

Upon landing in London, I decided to hang out in the business lounge during my two-hour layover and get some work done before my next flight. I opened my international messaging app and, seeing I had a text from Lexie, I opened it. It was confirmation that her friends were free the following weekend for the get-together at Allen's house. "Yes," I said to myself, hoping the planned introduction to Lexie's construction worker friends would lead to freeing Todd up so he could get the Crawford City project moving forward.

It was still early in Tennessee, so I quickly texted Lance that the party was a go.

As I scurried down the long hallways of the airport, I thought of Lance and how much I was going to enjoy getting to know him. Shit, I forgot to text him about our date.

Just then, I got a ping from my foster mom.

Claire: *When will you be back? We need to talk to you about Derek.*

Me: *Planning on Wednesday but late. Why? What's happening?*

Just as I was walking into the lounge, my phone rang. "Hey, honey, sorry to bother you," Claire said.

"No, it's no bother. Is Derek okay?"

"Well, not really." She hesitated, and I was beginning to get concerned.

"We got a call from Lidia wanting to know if our license is still good. Derek has a bully at the group home, and he beat Derek up pretty bad. I guess the bully was jealous he got to come hang out with you. Anyway, they're wanting to move him into a home and..."

I heard Anita talking in the background, but couldn't make out what she was saying.

"Anita is worried about how you're dealing with all this."

Their concern made me smile. "I'm doing fine, you guys. I told you, I don't care to spend time with my homophobic family, but Derek doesn't seem to be like them. Or at least, I hope he isn't."

"No, he isn't. Lidia told us he's been wanting to come out at the group home, but he's afraid...and clearly for good reason."

"Clearly," I said with a sigh. That, unfortunately, confirmed my suspicions of why our birth parents had kicked him out. "If I remember correctly, it wasn't a very friendly place for me either, when they found out I was gay. Do you still have your license?"

"Yes, but not for full-time foster care. We are respite providers."

"Do you want to take on another teenager?" I asked. "I mean, you are both sort of retired."

There was a pause, then I heard Anita say over the speakerphone, "We're not retired from family, Jake. We'll talk about it, but if it's okay with you, and you don't think it'll be too much for you, I think we'll take him as respite care this week. We can discuss long-term solutions later."

"I know he'll appreciate that, y'all, and so do I. I know a little about how he's feeling, and it's not a good way to feel."

"We know, sweetheart. We'll call Lidia back now and tell her to bring him over. In the meantime, we'll let you know how things progress."

We hung up, and I collapsed into a seat facing the tarmac and airplanes. I didn't know what was going to happen next. Anita had retired last year from the group home, mostly because her doctor told her he was concerned the stress of her job was causing her high blood pressure. Claire had put her foot down, saying Anita's health was too important to ignore. I'd been involved in those conversations and had supported Claire, which is why Anita finally caved.

How would having a sixteen-year-old around, one who had to be struggling with anger and all kinds of other emotions they didn't know what to do with, just like I had back then, affect Anita's health? How would it impact both of them?

A tidal wave of raw emotions crashed over me. Fear, concern for Anita, protectiveness for my baby brother, anger at our birth family... Then, as I stared absently at the busy tarmac, an idea struck. *Maybe I could help care for Derek.* I was his next of kin, after all, and I probably understood a lot of what he was going through more than most. Although there was no way in hell I could take care of a sixteen-year-old and manage my busy work life.

I looked around the Heathrow business lounge and sighed. My life was anything but consistent and nurturing. I prided myself on being available to my clients at the drop of a hat any time of the day or night, and they'd cashed in on that promise more than once. I never really considered my lack of a work-life balance because most of the time, work *was* my life. And damn, that sounded depressing as hell now that I thought about it. Still, I couldn't take on the full-time care of my brother even if I wanted to, not right now. If I had any hope of helping him, it'd have to be in a partnership arrangement between me and someone else. Someone like Anita and Claire.

"Excuse me," I heard someone say, and looked up and into the eyes of a particularly handsome man. "Are you going to use that port?"

I glanced at the charging station next to me and then quickly scanned the room, noting there were at least three others he could've used. I smiled at him and said, "No, you're welcome to this one."

Normally, I'd have seriously considered a quickie with this obviously interested and very attractive man, but I truly did have a lot on my plate that needed doing, and I would very much like to keep any sort of romantic focus on Lance anyway.

"Shit. Lance…," I whispered to myself.

Giving the stranger a friendly head nod in goodbye, I stood up and found another empty desk in the lounge. After unloading my laptop, I pulled my phone out and was about to finally text Lance to arrange our date when I realized it had zero battery power. *How the hell?* I'd just been on the phone a minute ago. With my phone off for the first time in I can't even remember when, I plugged it into my laptop to charge and got down to business.

I was so engrossed in my work for Lexie, I almost missed my boarding call. I quickly emailed my assistant Charlie what I'd gotten done, and hastily packed up in my rush out of the lounge. I had just enough time to see the disappointed look on the face of the hot businessman who'd tried flirting with me earlier. I couldn't resist giving him a playful wink as I made a dash for my gate.

The flight from Heathrow to Milan was only two hours, but the plane was significantly smaller and even in business class, I didn't have room to pull my laptop out. So, I decided to lay back and relax as best I could. I had slept horribly since finding out about my brother.

Worrying about how to deal with Derek was a whole new level of stress I'd never dealt with before. At least not in this way. I still didn't know much about the kid. There was so much more we needed to talk about beyond just pizza and video games, like his wanting to come out, dealing with having to leave his friends behind when our parents threw him out, and sifting through the pack of lies about me I'm sure our family fed to him his whole life.

I did know Derek had a bully, and Mrs. Lidia wouldn't have mentioned it if it wasn't a serious concern. That the little shit had apparently roughed up my brother was proof enough of that. I'd had more than my share of bullies while living in the group home, but none had gotten overly violent with me. But then, I wasn't one to back down either. One kid in particular was always spoiling for a fight and eventually, we got into it. Once, I punched him in the nose and he busted my lip, though, we sort of accepted an uneasy truce between us and nothing more came of it.

I already knew Derek was more sensitive than I'd been. That just made me worry about him more.

I woke up as the plane hit turbulence and sat up in my seat. I could tell by the way we were descending that we were approaching Milan. Minutes later, the captain came over the intercom and asked the flight crew to prepare for landing. Of course, the captain spoke in Italian and while I wasn't fluent, I'd picked up bits and pieces of many different languages in my travels.

After navigating through the airport and counting my blessings that my luggage was among the first to shoot down the baggage carousel, I was finally in a taxi headed toward my hotel. It was already late, and I was still tired after my mini-nap on the plane. I somehow made it off the elevator and into my hotel room before collapsing from exhaustion. Hopefully, I'd get at least a few hours of quality sleep tonight so I could be fresh enough to entertain my frustrated friend and client Jen while we killed time together waiting for her photographer to show.

ELEVEN

LANCE

"**W**HAT THE HELL DO you mean it'll cost twenty grand?!"

The man was screaming at Linc. I was standing behind him, trying to disappear.

"Well, Mr. Crouse, you've changed the plan multiple times. First, you wanted the gourmet kitchen we hadn't budgeted for. We were able to take off your sunroom to cover that cost. Then you wanted exclusive fixtures, and we removed the upstairs laundry room to accommodate that. Now, you want a finished basement with a sauna, but there isn't anything else to substitute. At this point, if you want more, you'll have to pay more."

"Why don't I just fire you and hire someone who can do it all and stay on budget?" the irate man bit out.

Linc took a deep breath. "Sir, I would highly recommend you not say that where my boss Todd can hear you, or else you'll *have* to find another contractor to finish the job."

The man looked shocked. I could tell he wasn't used to someone standing up to him, and I immediately thought of my dad.

"Listen, I am happy to tack on the job, but there is no way we can do it for less than the quote I gave you. It's a very fair price. If you wait and hire someone else, you're likely to pay even more. Why don't you talk it over with your wife tonight and let me know tomorrow."

I expected the guy to lose it, but instead, he just nodded. "I don't like it, but I'll let you know."

"That's works," Linc said and smiled before taking Mr. Crouse's hand in a firm shake.

I followed Linc out of the house and climbed into the truck next to him.

"Wow, that was...nuts."

Linc just laughed. "That's pretty much every build we do. That actually went pretty well. Every one of these builds costing over a million bucks starts out with the owner changing everything and wanting to nitpick. Of course, we build that into the costs, and I remind them time and time again that the later they make changes, the more it'll cost. But they always wait to the last minute to add big-ticket items."

"Do they all blow up like that?" I asked, appalled.

"Yep, pretty much. Par for the course in our line of work."

"Would Todd really have dumped that guy as a client?"

Linc chuckled. "If he'd have kept running his mouth about firing us, maybe. We've come close with other clients but it's never come to that, at least not yet. We have a bottom line too, and on every build, the owners want to force us into breaking that bottom line. This project is already four weeks overdue and the longer our crews are tied up here, the less work we can take overall. It also puts us behind on our other projects, so yeah, if he pushed too hard, we'd have to step away."

"Good to know. I wonder if clients act like this with the architects?" I asked, mostly to myself.

Linc cackled next to me. "You rethinking your career choice?"

I smiled. "No, but I've seen my dad act like Mr. Crouse back there and very few people have stood up to him. I'm not sure I'd have the strength to stand my ground like you did in that situation."

"You learn to have thick skin and even stronger boundaries when you deal with the entitled wealthy. You'll go out of business if you don't develop both of those survival skills."

I thought about what Linc was saying. Did I finally have a thicker skin and stronger boundaries with my dad now that I'd stood up to him? The more I considered it, the more I thought I did. The man was a bully when it came to what he wanted, and like Mr. Crouse, he expected to get his way come hell or high water.

My burgeoning sense of pride for standing up to my father slowed a bit when I realized that Mr. Crouse didn't have his finger on every penny in Linc and Todd's name. They'd never be beholden to the man for their financial security, in business or otherwise, and therein lies the difference. Or at least, it used to.

For the hundredth time, I thought about how my brother had stepped up for me. Opening up his home, heart, and wallet for me with no questions asked other than for me to dream big and work hard. I just couldn't imagine what I'd be facing right now if not for Allen's support. I may have only just gotten to know him as a person, but I could see clearly now that my big brother had been there for me all along.

TWELVE

JAKE

AFTER SPENDING AN INCREDIBLE day with Jen touring all the sights in Milan, then hitting the bars that night, the photographer finally showed up the next morning.

I'd tried calling Anita and Claire all day with no luck. I tried not to let that worry me too much, knowing they probably had a lot going on with arranging to help care for Derek, and Jen's photoshoot provided me with a welcome distraction. I got a text from them at midnight, which was about five o'clock in Nashville, telling me Derek was safely tucked into my old bedroom. I quickly decided I needed to be in Nashville more than I needed to be in Italy and changed my flight to the following afternoon.

Luckily, it only took a few hours to wrap up all of the business stuff for Jen. So, I packed and rushed to the airport, leaving her with an extremely apologetic photographer.

My trip home wasn't exactly restful, and with lengthy layovers in Amsterdam, then Minnesota, I didn't get back to Nashville any sooner than I'd originally planned. Maybe flying halfway around the world when my little brother needed me back home hadn't been the greatest decision, even if my work life demanded it. Although I didn't suffer much jet lag since I was only in Europe for a short time, my overall lack of sleep caught up with me.

Despite feeling completely exhausted by the time I arrived home late Wednesday night, I was also chomping at the bit to see my brother. Not that Derek would appreciate being woken up at this hour just so I could see for myself he was alright. There was no way I could muster up the energy to attempt it anyway. I didn't even shower or unpack before crashing on my bed. The only dreams I remembered were those of flying forever and not being able to get to where I wanted to be. Yeah, clearly this whole thing had me messed up.

When I arrived at my foster moms' house the following morning, Claire was home and Anita had just left to take Derek to school. I sat down at the counter as Claire bounced around her kitchen like she used to when I was growing up.

"You seem chipper this morning," I said.

"And you look like the walking dead."

"Oh, thanks," I said, trying to be sarcastic, but in truth, I did probably look like shit. Twenty hours to Milan, then sixteen back, was tough on the body.

"It was a long week. So, what's going on with Derek?" I asked, unable to hold back any longer.

"Why don't you wait for Anita? We can all talk about it then," she said, smiling over at me. I should've known she'd want to wait. Anita and Claire never talked over one another. It's just some weird respect thing they had.

Claire finished cooking and slid a plate of pancakes in front of me before pulling out my favorite maple syrup.

"You're so good to me," I said after swallowing the first bite. Anita couldn't cook to save her life, or at least she hadn't been able to until recently. Claire, however, was a natural. She didn't cook often, but when she did…heaven.

"You didn't tell me why you're in such a good mood."

Claire winked at me. "I forgot how much fun it is to have a young person in the house."

I winced. "If I remember right, it was a lot of *not* fun for a long time. At least when I first got here."

She sighed. "You'd been through a lot, sweet boy. Don't be so hard on yourself. Derek, he's not as damaged as you were when we got you. He's sad, of course. But he's also pretty well put together."

I nodded. "The drama could still come later," I said, remembering the feelings of happiness I'd initially had moving in with Anita and Claire, then the confusion, major upset, and depression that soon followed.

"It could, and if it does, I think we can handle it."

I wanted to argue. On the one hand, I really hoped they could take Derek in for the long haul. On the other,

I was more than a little worried about Anita and the stress raising a young man would bring into their lives.

Anita arrived back home a few minutes later and kissed my head as she walked into the kitchen. "You guys bring your breakfast into the dining room so we can sit down and chat."

"Two days in less than a week eating at the table? Are y'all turning over a new leaf or something?"

Anita gave me an eye before shaking her head. "Pun intended?"

I chuckled. She always got my bad puns. I only used them here because they were wasted on my friends and clients.

When we sat down, Claire and Anita were without food. "What, you aren't eating?" I asked.

"No, honey, we ate with Derek."

"Oh, cool," I said. "If I'd known what time he got up for school, I'd have come over sooner."

"There'll be plenty time for that."

I stopped eating and looked up. "Will there?" I asked, knowing they were telling me something.

Anita nodded. "That boy is family 'cause you're family, and Claire and I've decided to take him in."

"But your..."

Anita stopped me before I could say it. "I'm aware of my health, Jake. But I can't let that stop me from livin' or doin' what we think is right. That boy needs a home and people around him who care, and we can give him that."

I pushed my plate back and sat up straight in the chair, preparing to launch into the serious discussion I'd been mulling over for days.

"I had a lot of time to think on my flight back from Europe. I don't think you should do this on your own. I mean, I can't take in a sixteen-year-old boy, even if I had my license, but I can take a lot of his care off your plate."

When both women looked at me, confused, I pressed on. "Derek can spend most weekends with me. I can also help with homework and getting him to and from activities. I mean, I still have to work and that could pull me away a lot, but that doesn't mean I can't help. I want to be in my brother's life, as much as possible."

Anita and Claire turned toward one another, and I barely caught the wink they shared before turning back to me.

"We were hoping you'd say that 'cause that's exactly what you and your brother need right now," Claire said.

I sighed. "So, this is going to happen, huh?"

"Looks like it," Anita replied.

"Well, I better finish my breakfast then. Teenagers take a lot of sustenance. For the adults, that is."

Both women laughed and nodded in agreement. This was going to be quite an adventure for all of us.

THIRTEEN

LANCE

M Y HEART WAS SLIGHTLY broken when Thursday came and went with no word from Jake. He'd texted me about the house party several days ago, but nothing about our date. I really had fucked it up somehow. Oh well, no surprise given my track record, but still a hell of a lot of disappointment. I had never been as attracted to someone as I was Jake.

He was smart and, if appearances were correct, he was successful in business. He had confidence and a great sense of humor. And I found him as sexy as a man could be. It was my loss that he apparently didn't think I was worth the trouble.

I came downstairs Friday morning before Allen left for work and plopped down at the counter across from him.

"What's got you looking so gloomy?" he asked.

"I sorta got stood up."

"Really?" Allen asked. "By who?"

"Oh, well... it probably wasn't being stood up as much as a tentative plan didn't work out," I quickly said, remembering that Jake and Allen seemed to know each other, and I didn't want to come between them.

"Is this about Jake?" Allen asked.

I startled, shocked that he figured it out so fast. "Yeah, but how did you know?" I asked.

Allen laughed. "'Cause, little brother, I have eyes and could see the looks you were giving each other when you met."

I sighed. "Well, I seem to have chased him off fast enough."

"I seriously doubt that. I don't know Jake well, but he doesn't strike me as someone who is easily put off."

I shrugged. Allen's comment didn't make me feel better.

"I might have succeeded. We were supposed to have a date last night, but when he confirmed the weekend get-together, he neglected to bring up our date. Like either he'd forgotten or hoped I had."

Allen stood up and put his cereal bowl in the sink, then came around the counter and squeezed my shoulder. "Give him time to explain. I'm sure he didn't intentionally stand you up."

"It doesn't really matter. I shouldn't be dating anyone right now, anyway." Then it dawned on me what our whole conversation had been about, and I sucked in a sharp breath.

When Allen looked concerned, I chuckled nervously. "I realize I just came out to you. Umm...surprise?"

It was Allen's turn to chuckle. "I picked up on that when you were undressing Jake with your eyes at the café."

"Yeah, but I should've told you. I'm gay, just so you know."

Allen surprised me when he drew me into a hug. "I love you no matter what, Lance, and thanks for telling me. Oh, and don't think if Jake *did* intentionally hurt you that I won't make his life miserable. You know he and I are going into business together, right?"

I hadn't thought about that. "The commercial development downtown?" I asked.

"Yep, and I'm sure Mom can whip up on him, too, if you need her to."

I laughed. "I'll let you know, but for now, let's just assume he didn't call 'cause I geeked out on him."

"Again, I doubt that, but we'll see. For now, I need to get to work. Hey, maybe tonight when I get home, you, me, Gib, and the girls can celebrate your coming out."

I smiled. "I'm not sure that requires celebrating."

"Of course, it does," Allen said. "This is a big milestone in your life. Besides, I've wanted to throw a welcome party for you since you arrived. We'll make it a combined celebration."

I shook my head as my brother grabbed his keys and headed for the front door. "I'll arrange it all with Gib. Just make sure Linc drops you off before six tonight, okay?" he asked, but was out the door before I could respond.

"A coming-out party," I said out loud just as Gib walked into the kitchen.

"What's this?" he asked. "Who's having a party?"

"I am, I guess. I just officially came out to Allen and now he's wanting to have some crazy party to mark the occasion."

"That's a cool idea," he said as he opened a cabinet and pulled out a protein bar. "When's this party happening?"

"Allen said tonight?"

Gib smiled and, slipping on his coat that had been hanging in the little closet at the back of the kitchen, said, "I'll have Jamie at the donut shop make us a cake. It'll be fun."

I was chuckling as Gib walked out the back door. I had just enough time to rush up the stairs and brush my teeth before Linc would be here to pick me up. Today was one of the rare occasions we didn't start at the crack of dawn, so my nieces were the first ones out the door to school this morning.

"You seem in a chipper mood," Linc said as soon as I shut the truck door.

"Oh, yeah, my brother is planning me a coming-out party."

"Coming-out party? Like you just told him you're gay?"

"Yeah," I said, glancing at Linc warily. "Why? Is that a problem?"

Linc leaned his head back and laughed. "Um, no. I came out when I was sixteen."

"You're gay?" I asked, unable to hide my surprise.

"Yeah, why?" he asked.

"Let's just say my gaydar didn't ping on you."

Linc laughed again. "So, you just told your brother then?"

"Well, he knew. I'd been flirting with a guy and Allen noticed, so I just stated the obvious this morning and now my brother is throwing a party. Not that it matters, but the guy sort of stood me up."

"Really? Around here?" Linc said and quickly glanced at me before looking back to the road. "The only out gay person I know who's single and local is me. Unless maybe you ran into Jake."

My face blushed and Linc caught it. Damn, I needed to work on my poker face. "Wow, Jake stood you up?"

"Well, sort of. We were supposed to go out last night, but he never called to set it up."

"He's an idiot," Linc said, which caused me to blush deeper.

"I really geeked out on him. He was showing me the building designs for the commercial property downtown and I sort of let myself rattle on and on. I'm sure he thinks I'm a twit."

"My God, seriously? He can't shut up about the project. Why would he care if you geeked out? I'd have thought you being so interested in it would've piqued his interest in you even more."

I shrugged. "He probably never liked me that much to begin with. Anyway, I'd rather not think about that right now. Let's go back to laughing about my coming-out party," I said.

"So, is that what's happening this weekend? I heard Todd and Ash were asked to host it, like they have time or energy with three little ones at home."

"No, my brother just dreamed up my coming-out celebration this morning, but there is a get-together at my brother's house this weekend. Are you coming?"

"Didn't get an invite."

"Do you need one? I thought this was pretty informal. Jake is bringing some friends of his from Nashville, and Todd and Ash told me they've got a babysitter so they're coming. I'd say you're invited if you wanna come."

"Well, I might just take you up on it. It'd be fun to do something besides work for a change."

"Then I'll let everyone know you'll be there. Besides, maybe one of Jake's friends is gay and looking for a handsome construction worker."

Linc laughed, and I wondered for a moment if I'd like to date him. He was at least ten years older than me, if I had to guess, and gorgeous. Older men did make great lovers, or so I'd heard, since I couldn't speak from my own meager personal experience. Unfortunately, the chemistry wasn't there between Linc and me, at least not like it had been with Jake.

And there I was, thinking about him again. I shook my head to get the man out of my mind. I wanted to enjoy the final day of work this week, not spend it pouting over our non-date. I was beginning to realize as I worked with Linc that I did indeed enjoy construction. I remained about as clueless as anyone could be, but damned if I didn't love all the hands-on work it entailed.

Fourteen

Jake

I DIDN'T HAVE MUCH on my agenda today, considering I originally figured I'd need a day to crash after returning from Europe. I kept my work schedule light, heading in early and helping tie up a few loose ends, including getting all the YouTube links up from Lexie's mini-concert at the children's hospital. I made sure to reach out to all my contacts so they'd mention it on their social media sites and give Lexie as much exposure as they could.

I checked the hospital's fundraiser feed and was pleased to see the donation numbers were climbing there. This really was a win for everyone.

I left the office at noon and stopped by the store to pick up a few things to make Derek's move to Anita and Claire's a bit more fun for him. I grabbed a huge storage bin, too, then stopped off at the thrift store to find some cool old appliances that he could take apart since that's what he said he liked to do. I'd see if Anita and Claire minded if he set them up in the room behind their garage. It used to be their laundry room, but since they'd moved the laundry inside, it'd become a makeshift closet. Luckily, the room was heated because of the plumbing and I couldn't think of a better workshop space for a boy to do some mechanical tinkering.

When I got to their house, both Anita and Claire were sitting in the living room chatting on speakerphone with Mrs. Lidia.

"So, it's no problem to switch your license back from respite to regular foster parents. You'll have a couple classes you'll need to finish within sixty days, but they aren't too time-consuming."

"That's fine," Anita said. "We've done those before."

"In that case, I've already inspected your home when I came to visit with him the other day, and if you decide you're up for it, I can move his case file under your care today."

Anita and Claire looked over at me and all three of us were smiling from ear to ear. "Lidia, Jake is here too. He'll be taking Derek on some as well, so does he need to take classes or get licensed?"

"It wouldn't hurt, especially if you're going to be doing more than occasional care, Jake. But as you know, letting a foster child spend the night with family or friends is completely normal."

"Mrs. Lidia, I want to do this right, so if you have classes for me to attend, let me know."

She chuckled. "I'm so happy you're going to help out, Jake. I'll be coming over next week and I'll bring all the paperwork with me."

"Thanks, Mrs. Lidia," I said.

Anita chimed in then. "So, we'll meet with Derek as soon as he gets back from school, and if he agrees to these arrangements, we'll let you know."

"I'm sure he will, Anita, but I'm glad you're going to let him be an active part of deciding. I'll get the paperwork started and will check in with him before I bring anything over to sign."

When Mrs. Lidia hung up, I asked about converting the room behind the garage to a workshop for Derek.

"That's a great idea," Anita said as Claire nodded.

"Okay, I'll go start cleaning it out. What do you want me to do with the stuff?" I asked.

Both women looked at each other and laughed. "You know it's all your stuff in there, right?"

"What? I thought you got rid of all that."

"Jeez, boy!" Anita grumped. "It's not like we haven't told you a million times to come clean it out."

I chuckled. "I honestly don't remember, but you know I have a sieve for a brain for anything not work-related."

"Like you know what a sieve is," Claire said, laughing. "Okay, I'll pull my car out of the garage, and you can pile all the stuff there while you sort through it."

"Thanks. The space already has a lot of shelves but I think I'll put a desk in there too."

She just smiled. I knew I was being overly enthusiastic about all this, but damn, my brother was coming to stay with my foster parents and I was going to get to be a part of his life. Of course, he'd have to agree to it all first, but I was pretty confident he would. I remembered how important it was for Anita and Claire to ask me and respect my decisions. I didn't want to take that away from him.

I pulled out the boxes full of all the stuff I once treasured. Model cars, games, and piles of magazines. It was like my teenage years had been stored away for posterity. I decided to let Derek go through it all before I hauled it off.

I spent the afternoon organizing the new workshop, rearranging shelves and installing drawers I was able to get at the local hardware store. I also found a desk for him at the thrift store. I'd thought about getting Derek a nicer one, but seeing as this was meant to be a work-space and he'd likely bust it all to hell in the end anyway, secondhand would do for now.

When Derek got home from school, we all gathered in the living room. I was so excited, I was literally shaking. The poor kid probably thought something was wrong.

"So, Derek," Anita said, taking Claire's hand. "We'd like to offer you a place in our family. We've spoken to Lidia, who said our license can support us letting you move in, and you can keep going to your same school since we live in the same school district as the group home."

Derek looked stricken. I was feeling sort of alarmed too. Is this not what he wanted?

"I'd like that, but I..." Derek shook his head.

"Honey, I can tell you're concerned about something. It's best to be honest, especially if we're going to try to be a family."

Tears ran down Derek's face as he sat with his hands in his lap. I'd never wanted to give someone a comforting hug as much as I did in that moment, but the kid needed to get something off his chest. I just hoped I was prepared to hear it.

"I know it's silly, but I was just hoping my mom would change her mind. Like maybe she'd realize she missed me and wanted me to come back home."

Anita got up from her recliner and sat next to Derek on the sofa, taking his hand in hers.

"We went through your file the other day when Lidia dropped you off for respite. Your mom has been contacted but, as of yet, she hasn't responded to their outreach. We don't want to replace your family, Derek, we just want to become a part of it."

"I never told anyone I was gay. It's like they decided for me, then punished me for it," Derek croaked out as another torrent of tears started rolling. The full brunt of our parents' rejection was only now hitting him, and I knew from experience that it hurt like hell and likely would for a very long time.

"It doesn't matter to us if you're gay, straight, or otherwise. You know Claire and I are gay, and you know your brother is too, but it's perfectly fine if you're not. All the adults in this room will love you, just as you are."

"That's the way families are supposed to be," I said to him.

He looked over at me then and nodded. "They never came back for you, did they?"

I shook my head. "No, Derek, they never wanted me back. In fact, Dad told me if I ever came back, he'd kill me."

"Yeah, that's what he said to me too."

"Do you mind if I ask how all that happened? If you never told our parents that you're gay, why did they assume you were?"

Derek wiped at the tears with his shirtsleeve, but more continued falling as he took a moment to gather himself. I knew whatever he was about to say would be painful to hear, for all of us.

"We were at a revival meeting summer before last. The preacher was a man we knew from a neighboring church and they were having a 'purge the devil' prayer. Supposedly, a couple boys in his church had been caught together, and they sent them to one of those conversion camps. The preacher was walking around the sanctuary testifying when he stopped next to me. He started yelling for the devil to get out of me and the next thing I knew, I was being hauled up to the stage to be purified. After the service, Dad and the preacher met, and then they put me on a bus to that camp." Derek's hands shook as much as his voice as he recounted the story, clearly reliving the trauma in his head. "I kept telling them I wasn't gay...or at least, that I hadn't said I was gay. But they didn't believe me. I spent two weeks in pure hell."

"Derek, those camps are outlawed in most states. You know that, right?" I asked.

He shook his head. "What does that matter? It's not like I had the choice to stay or go. Besides, the bus only came and went at night so I don't even know for sure where the camp was located, other than out in the backwoods somewhere. When the bus dropped me off at home, I went in thinking everything would be fine now that they'd cast out whatever demon they thought lived inside me. But Dad was now convinced I was a 'faggot.' That's what he kept calling me."

Derek looked up briefly and then back down at his hands, which were a little steadier now, before he finished his story. "I was walking home from school and my friend Louis was walking with me. I mean, Louis has a girlfriend and is on the football team and everything, so it wasn't like anyone thought he was gay, except Dad."

The tears flowed from him again. When he got himself back under control he said, "Dad beat me up really bad. He'd never beaten on me before. Not like that. Mom ended up taking me to the hospital, and I was taken into custody. That was the last time I saw anyone in our family."

He looked over at me and swiped at his tears. "Until I saw you," he added.

I smiled. "Well, Dad never beat me up, but I always thought he could, and probably would have eventually. Derek, I'm sorry that happened. Had I known...well, I don't know what I could've done, but I'd have tried."

"They didn't ever talk about you. Kimmie once told me we had an older brother, but you had the devil in you so Dad wouldn't let you come around. I never knew what they meant."

I laughed but it came out sounding more bitter than I'd intended. "Well, if you ask me, it's Dad that's got the devil in him. Normal people don't throw their kids out, especially just because some whack job preacher decides someone is gay."

Derek shook his head. "So, Mom isn't coming for me, is she?"

Anita and Claire cast their eyes downward but I looked my brother in the eye. I knew this pain firsthand, and I also knew there was no way to deal with it except head-on. "No, I doubt anyone in our family will. But, Derek, you'll learn, just like I have, that family isn't necessarily those you're related to by blood. Most of the time, it's who you learn to love."

I glanced at my foster moms then and met their eyes. "These two women here, they are my moms, more like my real mothers than our birth mom ever was to me. When things went to hell, these two women stood by me and never stepped away."

Both Anita and Claire wiped tears and as much as I wanted to hug them both, I needed to stay focused on my brother. "Family sticks by you through thick and thin and cares about you with no strings attached, and if you want to be a part of that, I'd love to welcome you into mine."

Derek's eyes had cleared, although Anita and Claire's hadn't, and he nodded. "Yeah, I know you're right, although I didn't want to admit it. I want to be your family, too, Jake. I really do."

Relief washed over me and soon we were all crying. Derek and I both stood up, and he launched himself at me in a tight hug. We remained like that for several moments until we both got ourselves back together.

When he finally pulled away, he turned to my–now our–foster moms. "If you're serious, I'd like to learn to be your family too."

Anita got up and hugged him first, then Claire did the same.

Once we'd passed around the tissues and cleared up our faces, I announced I had a surprise.

Derek looked at me warily and I chuckled. "Come on! No more tears, I promise."

I ushered them all out back, first stopping by the garage to show Derek all my childhood crap sorted into piles. He was clearly trying to be nice, even asking me some questions about the car models, but I could tell he had no interest in any of it. "Anything you don't want, we can take to the thrift store," I said to take the pressure off him. "But this is the real surprise..."

I opened the door to the new workshop and led him inside.

"There are plenty of places for you to put the gadgets you're working on without Claire hollering at you to clean your crap up. I got you a storage bin to keep all your stuff organized, and a desk if you want to do your schoolwork out here. Which you will have to do. Anita and Claire may be the best moms in the world, but they are wicked tough about school. Trust me on this one, don't even push that button."

I heard snickers behind me and knew the two women were listening.

Derek wandered around the room. "This is my space? Just for me?"

I nodded. "It's heated, too, so you should be comfortable. Claire is a neat freak, so you'll have to keep it organized, but yeah, it's all yours." I looked over at our foster moms who were both nodding.

"Cool," he said. The kid may not have much to say about it, but his beaming face told me I'd gotten it right.

When he came back out of his new workshop, he took another long look at my jumbles of stuff littering the garage floor. I almost laughed at his conflicted expression.

"Dude, you don't have to take any of that. It was all being stored in the room I turned into your workshop. But you do have to help me load it and take it away." He grinned and nodded. "Anita, do you mind if we use your jeep?" I asked. "All this won't fit in my car."

"Sure, we'll help you load it up."

We later found out that Derek loved Mexican food, so after a donation run to the thrift store, I took the entire family out to dinner.

"What's your plans for tomorrow night?" I asked Derek.

He laughed. "I have literally just started living here. Do I have plans? I don't know...homework?"

We all chuckled. "Doing homework on a Saturday night? As your big brother, it's my duty to put a stop to that. But seriously, if you don't have plans, I'm having a party at a friend's house in Crawford City. Why don't you all join us?"

I looked around the table and Claire and Anita were shaking their heads. "Thank you, but we've got plans to play with the Bunko Gals tomorrow night," Claire said. "Unfortunately, it's girls night out so, Derek, why don't you go with Jake. You can spend the night at his place, then we'll meet up for breakfast together Sunday morning."

"Cool, can we go to The Springy Biscuit?" I asked. That was my favorite breakfast place in all of Nashville. It'd been around forever and as a teenage boy who'd had a hollow leg when it came to packing in food, I loved the buffet style that allowed me to get my fill. I figured Derek would appreciate it too.

Anita smiled. "You pick this time. But only 'cause I know you're trying to impress your brother."

"Impress him? Please, I just want all you can eat biscuits and gravy." They all laughed, and I turned to Derek. "So, that reminds me, I totally need to kick your butt in BattleGild."

"Sooo not going to happen," Derek said with a smirk. After we got back to the house, I set up my old game console, and he and I battled the evening away.

Between our pretty even wins and losses and plenty of trash-talking, I texted Lance, telling him I was bringing someone else with me to the party. I knew it was probably tacky to add another person at the last moment, but I'd already agreed to supply the food and drinks. Besides, how much more does a sixteen-year-old boy really add anyway?

FIFTEEN

LANCE

M Y HEART DROPPED WHEN I read Jake's text saying he was bringing a plus-one. Fuck, my stomach hurt at how stupid I'd been. He was probably married for all I knew...well, except Linc already confirmed he wasn't. It also confirmed that my streak of crappy luck with men–or more like my complete lack of getting lucky–continued on as usual.

Other than that mood killer, my Friday night wasn't half bad. Allen, Gib and the girls threw me the promised coming-out party, complete with rainbow streamers, rainbow balloons, a rainbow-colored cake from the donut shop...and lots and lots of glitter. Were the rainbows overdone? Yes. But did I get a kick out of my family making a big fuss over me? To my surprise, also yes. I do think the glitter had more to do with my nieces wanting an excuse to make a complete mess of the house than it did celebrating me, but at least they were enthusiastic and had fun.

The next day, I helped the girls clean up around the house to get ready for Jake's party. How the hell so much glitter could get into nearly every nook and cranny of that place–even rooms none of us had gone in last night–remained a mystery. I was thankful we only had to provide the space, since Jake was bringing all the food.

Of course, the girls were beyond excited about tonight's get-together. Even Chrissy managed to smile at me a couple times before she caught herself and remembered she didn't like me.

Around noon, I got a call from Jake.

"Hey, we're headed your way. I'm going to pick up pulled pork, and I already have some hors d'oeuvres. Can you think of anything else I need to bring?"

"Alcohol," I said.

"There's a little winery down the road from you that makes amazing wine. I thought I'd run by there to grab a few bottles. Do you think I need something more boozy?"

I smiled despite still feeling the disappointment of being cast off by him so easily. "We have kids here too. Do you want me to run down to the store and grab some sodas?"

"Yeah, that'd be great. Thanks for remembering that."

"Allen and Gib both worked this morning, but should be home in a bit. I'll head to the store when they get home. We'll see you when you get here," I said quickly and hung up. I was looking forward to meeting new people and being at a party not full of stuffy New York elites I couldn't relate to. The sort of parties my father frequented and hosted himself, and basically made me attend. Still, I'd be glad when tonight was over and I wouldn't have to plaster a smile on my face around Jake and his plus-one. I'd already decided I was going to pretend like everything was fine and just enjoy the night, even though it was bound to be awkward as hell, at least for me.

Gib got home a few minutes after Jake called, and I grabbed my empty backpack. "Girls, you wanna go with me to the store to pick up a few things for tonight?" I asked.

Chrissy was the only one not completely engrossed in some movie, so she and I walked to the grocery store located in one of the larger downtown buildings.

Thankfully, Allen had given me an advance on the trust money he was transferring to my name. It wasn't a lot of money, but it was enough to allow me to splurge a little for tonight.

"So, can you help me choose some snacks for you and the twins?" I asked.

Chrissy nodded. "We like root beer and chips. But since it's a party, we should have cheese dip and maybe sour cream and chives."

I smiled at how grown-up Chrissy was in her assessment. I basically just followed her around the store, letting her put stuff in the cart. When we got to the checkout, I paid and loaded the heavy things in the backpack, then we both carried shopping bags of chips back toward the house.

"Why didn't you come to Uncle Gib and Uncle Allen's wedding?" Chrissy asked as we walked past the donut shop.

I sighed. I knew this conversation was coming, but I'd still been dreading it. "Well, that's a hard topic. Why don't we stop in here and I'll get you a donut or ice cream while we chat about it."

She nodded and led the way into the shop. She wanted a single scoop of Rocky Road, and I just got a cup of coffee. We sat at the same corner table that Allen and I had my first time here.

"You already know Allen and I have the same dad, but different moms." I paused until she nodded.

Resisting a sigh, I continued on. "Growing up, I was jealous of Allen because of his mom. Mine doesn't really want much to do with me. Dad could also be hard on us, and when Allen got to go home to his mom after visiting us, I was stuck with our dad."

Chrissy sat staring at me, not giving me an inch. The girl was tough as nails.

"So, Allen and I weren't close. I thought he hated me, so I wasn't very nice and I avoided him."

"When did you decide he didn't hate you?" she asked.

I shrugged. "Just recently. I wasn't being fair to him. Now I regret that."

Chrissy nodded. "I heard Uncle Gib and him talking at the wedding. Uncle Allen was sad you didn't come. It was hard to see him sad on his wedding day."

I looked down at my hands as shame and remorse twisted in my gut. I'd just been called out by a no-nonsense tween and totally deserved it. "Chrissy, even adults make mistakes, and that's what I did. I will always regret not going, and not being Allen's friend all those years. If you want my advice, never let anything keep you from being friends with your little sisters."

Chrissy stopped eating her ice cream as her mouth turned down into a deep frown, and I knew I'd somehow struck a nerve.

"I didn't want them when they were born, but after Mom and Dad died..." She fiercely wiped a tear from her face as if it had annoyed her. Chrissy didn't like to be vulnerable, that much was obvious.

"When you lost your parents, it was good to have your sisters, wasn't it?" I asked, and she nodded. "I've sort of lost my dad too, in a different way, but he's still gone. Being around Allen has helped, though. I'm really happy I've got my brother."

"So, you won't make him sad again?"

I chuckled. "I can't promise that. I'm his brother and I love him, but I'm not perfect and I still make mistakes. I might accidentally make him sad, but I'll try to fix it if I do and I won't let him out of my life again. He means too much to me for that to happen. You all do."

She nodded, apparently satisfied with my answer, causing me to smile. "Now, we best finish up here and hustle back. We've got a big party to attend."

Sixteen

Jake

DEREK AND I GOT to Crawford City a little after four, and he helped me unload the car. I met Gib and Allen's girls and after I shook their hands, they pretty much took over showing me where to put the food and helping set it all up.

Lance had met us at the door, and shortly after, excused himself to go get ready.

I could tell he was significantly cooler toward me than he had been before. I was confused as to why.

I didn't have much time to ponder on it, though, before our guests started arriving. Linc came in first and although I was surprised to see him, I was ecstatic he'd been invited. If he met and liked Lexie's construction friends, he'd help move Todd closer to hiring them. That was, after all, the reason we were all here, even if only I knew it.

Lexie arrived next with some of her friends. "Hey, sweetheart," she said when she saw me. "You remember Zach and his husband, Lane."

I shook their hands. "Yes, thanks for coming out. When do you expect the others to arrive?"

"They're about a half-hour behind us. Bethie is notoriously late to everything, and therefore, Randy is late as well. But don't worry, Cliff and Kris will get them here," Lexie said.

"What about Renee and Fiona?" I asked.

Lane shook his head. "No, one of their girls is sick, so they had to rain check."

That was too bad. I liked the fiery Irish woman, and I figured her and Renee's twin daughters would get along with Gib and Allen's girls.

"Damien got out of going to dinner with his parents, so he's going to come too," Zach said with a smile. "But not until later, I'm afraid."

"That's perfect," I said and steered them all toward the drinks table.

Todd and Ash came in a little later, both looking exhausted. "You two look like you've been runnin' over hell's half acre," I said with a smirk, as I poured both men a drink.

"You know we have," Todd said, taking the offered glass. "Chasing children around all day is no joke."

I played the part of dutiful host, introducing Lexie and her friends to my friends and brother, while Gib and Allen's girls introduced themselves. Luckily, Lexie was a natural with kids and immediately let them pull her into some female bonding time, talking about hair styles or some such, while I ducked out to do some quick food prep.

The kitchen was off the back of the house, so I couldn't really see anyone, but I could hear their voices as everyone mingled. I hadn't been in the kitchen long when I heard someone come down the stairs, then heard Lance's voice.

Knowing he'd joined the party sent happy shockwaves through my system. I was so looking forward to getting to know him better, which I planned to do starting tonight.

Once all the food was out, the rest of the Nashville crew arrived and I went around introducing everyone.

"Todd, Ash, Lance, Linc, these are my new friends, Bethie and Randy, and Kris and Cliff. Randy and Cliff are brothers and own a small construction company in Nashville," I said and gave a meaningful look to Todd, whose eyes grew bigger as he shot a quick glance my way.

"It's a pleasure to meet you all," Todd said and proceeded to make small talk with the brothers while I mingled.

Allen and Gib's house was big, and even though a sizeable crowd had shown up for the party, we were able to comfortably fit in the front room. I was pleased that everyone in Lexie's group pulled the girls and my brother into their conversations. Derek, who had been super shy throughout the many introductions, seemed to be enjoying himself now.

When Damien arrived, that completed our guest list, so I escorted everyone into the kitchen to get food. As people ate and chatted, forming small groups in the kitchen, dining room, and front room, it was particularly fun watching Linc meet Damien. I didn't know Damien all that well, since he'd been quiet when I'd gone over to Lexie's place, but the chemistry between him and Linc was palpable. Linc said something I couldn't hear, causing Damien to blush so brightly, he could've lit up the room if the lights went out.

I took a seat next to Lexie, who looked at me funny when she caught me staring at the two men.

"Playing matchmaker or hoping to join in the fun?" she asked, giving me a playful wink.

I barked out a surprised laugh. The woman didn't have a shy bone in her body. "You are so naughty," I said, returning her smile.

"Would you have me any other way?" she asked, and we both chuckled.

The seat on my other side was empty, and I assumed, stupidly, that maybe Lance would sit next to me. But when he came into the room, even though I know he saw the empty seat, he turned the other direction and sat about as far away from me as possible.

I must've looked really perplexed because Lexie elbowed me and asked, "Boy troubles?"

I shrugged. "I didn't think so. We really hit it off the other day when we planned this party and our date...*fuck*," I said, catching the attention of several people sitting near us. "Oh, sorry about that, don't mind me."

After everyone had returned to their conversations, I leaned in to Lexie and admitted I'd stood Lance up. Accidentally.

"You are an idiot because that is one fine piece of man right there," she said.

"Um, that's my brother you're talking about," Allen said quietly, sitting down next to Lexie and causing us both to chuckle.

"You have eyes, Allen," I said, teasing him. "You have to know he's cute."

"Well, he didn't look so cute when someone didn't show up on Thursday. He looked pretty upset, actually."

"Damn, I need to apologize for that. I've had a lot going on the past week, and time got away from me." I looked over at my brother, who appeared to be warming up to Lane and Zack because they were all laughing about something.

"I gained a family member that, until recently, I didn't know existed. That sorta threw me for a loop."

Both Allen and Lexie looked over toward where Derek was sitting and back at me. "Wow, that's a lot," Lexie said.

"Yeah, it has been. Family is exhausting, but it's been amazing too," I said. "That doesn't mean I don't have a lot to clean up with Lance, though. I really did space out on our date."

"Well, my brother is the king of holding grudges, so all I can say is good luck."

I sighed. "Yeah, thanks. Luckily, I'm good at groveling."

The party was a resounding success, and I could sense several new friendships had been made. Todd, as I'd hoped, took an immediate liking to Randy and Cliff, and the three had exchanged numbers without me having to get involved. Linc and Damien were stuck together the entire night.

Making amends with Lance had proven less successful. I tried several times to connect with him, but each time, he'd disappear with some excuse of needing to go do something.

Around nine o'clock, the girls went to bed, and we pulled out the wine from the local winery. It really was top-notch stuff. I was hoping to eventually offer them a storefront in our new building to sell their wine, but doing so now seemed a little premature.

Gib and Allen pulled out folding chairs and invited us all into the main sitting room. I was just about to go with the group when I saw Lance begin to collect plates and take them to the kitchen. This was my opportunity, so when everyone had gone, I followed Lance into the kitchen.

"Hey, I need to apologize," I said as I came in behind him.

He literally jumped and almost dropped the dishes he was putting in the sink.

"Um, no need. I know you were probably busy."

"More than you know," I said. "But that's not an excuse for standing you up."

Lance began to rinse the dishes and put them in the dishwasher but didn't turn around or say anything.

"I just learned this week that I've got a baby brother. Well, not a baby anymore, he's sixteen, and now living with my foster moms. You met him earlier tonight. Anyway, it's been intense but wonderful, and between that and flying overseas and back for work and this party, I just blanked on our date."

Lance stopped rinsing dishes and turned to face me. "So, you really did just forget?" he asked.

"Yeah, I would never stand you up. I really want to get to know you better."

Lance smiled. "I was worried I'd chased you off with my over eagerness about your new project."

That caused me to laugh. "Lance, I hate to tell you this, but no one is more eager about that project than me. I'm chomping at the bit for it to get started so we can finish it."

He let out a long sigh. "I'm glad. I'm so new to being out. I've only dated a couple of guys and they were probably more hookups than dates, so I don't really know how to read things yet."

I stepped closer to him, nearly chest to chest, and said, "No one would know how to react to how this worked out. I think you're perfect, and I really am sorry."

Lance blushed. "Thanks, Jake."

I was just about to lean in and kiss him when I heard someone clear his throat behind us. "Sorry to interrupt, but they wanted to know if you had another bottle of wine."

I chuckled at the embarrassed voice of my brother behind me. "Sure, let me get it," I said and winked at Lance before I stepped away.

I led Derek to the dining room to show him where I'd stashed the other bottles.

He whispered another apology as soon as we were out of earshot.

"No need to be sorry," I said, draping my arm around him in a half hug. "Lance and I are just getting things started. You probably prevented me from chasing him off by coming on too strong." Derek smiled and winced at the same time. "You okay?" I asked.

He nodded. "It's good to see all these happy gay people. I just haven't been around many until now. Except at that stupid camp. All the adults were scary and mean."

I cringed at the thought. "Yeah, best to stay away from closeted gay people. They can be dangerous."

He nodded. "You know I'm gay too, right? I never told anyone, but I am. It helps to see it's not..."

"Not weird or evil?" I asked, knowing where he'd been going.

"Yeah," he said as he nodded.

"Listen, little brother, from now on, you're going to meet a lot of healthy and happy openly gay people, and you're going to find out that we're just like everyone else. That's the thing that helped me the most, learning that people are just people, no matter their orientation."

Derek nodded and smiled before leaning over to me and whispering, "Lance is really cute. Good luck!"

I literally laughed out loud. "You ain't shittin' me. He really is," I whispered back. "Now, let's deliver this wine before the guests come looking for us."

Seventeen

Lance

I BLUSHED A BIT as I listened through the butler's pantry door as the two brothers talked. I didn't mean to eavesdrop on a private conversation, but I was intrigued to hear what Jake would tell his brother about me.

I was about to leave when Derek admitted that he was gay. From what I could discern from the conversation, maybe his parents had sent him to conversion therapy. God, if that was the case, I really hated that for him. We studied that in my undergrad psychology classes and how much damage those camps could do to the kids subjected to them against their will.

I was sick at the thought of Derek there, when I heard him whisper that he thought I was cute. My cheeks really glowed then, and hearing Jake agree sent my heart soaring into the rafters. In a lot of ways, at least as far as being comfortable and confident in my own sexuality, I was just as awkward as Derek.

My father had made such a stink about Allen coming out, I was terrified to even consider it myself. I had dated a couple of women and, in truth, I didn't hate kissing them. I probably fell somewhere in the middle of the Kinsey scale, but the few times I'd kissed a guy showed me just which side of that scale I really tipped toward.

Kissing men just plain turned me on and the thought of kissing the incredibly handsome Jake Hudson had me burning with lust. He'd been so close to kissing me in the kitchen, and I crossed my fingers in hope that it wouldn't be his only attempt at doing so tonight.

After the guests started filing out, we all agreed we would do this again. Even though I was new to the group, I felt like these people could easily become my tribe.

Todd and Ash had left a full hour before the rest of the party, saying they had to go relieve their fathers from babysitting duty. Another gay couple I had yet to meet. It almost seemed like the entire town was gay, although I knew that couldn't exactly be true. I remember Jake telling me Crawford City was a special place, and the locals were generally very tolerant, though, so maybe there was something to that.

Just before Jake left, he pulled me into a hug, and I relished the feeling of being pressed up against the man. He kissed my temple as he let me go and said he'd text me in a little while. I'd been so sure just a few hours earlier he didn't want anything to do with me. But between his plus-one turning out to be his little brother, and his apology for ghosting me about our date, I now felt some hope about pursuing more with Jake.

I emptied and reloaded the dishwasher, and then helped Allen and Gib put the leftover food away. I also rearranged and wiped down the furniture to ensure there were no wine stains or anything that might do damage, a secret I'd learned watching my father's clean-up crews after his swanky parties.

Then we all retired to our beds. I was just about asleep when my phone dinged. Looking at it, I smiled when I noticed it was from the man I couldn't stop thinking about.

Jake: *Hey, just got home. Can you talk or should we wait until morning?*

Lance: *I'm free now.*

Luckily, my bedroom was across from the girls' room, so I didn't run the risk of waking them by talking on the phone. I'd still need to be relatively quiet, though.

I switched my phone to vibrate and answered on the first buzz. "Hey?" I said, feeling a bit awkward and groggy.

"Hey, I just wanted to thank you for tonight. It was a major success."

"Yeah, it was fun. I think Linc and Damien really hit it off."

"No doubt. I'm assuming you're the one who invited Linc, so thanks for that, too."

"Of course. He's become a good friend...well, boss. Um, supervisor? Anyway, he's been great."

"Glad to hear it. So, about our would-be date, I'd really like another chance."

I sat up in bed, not knowing how to respond. I didn't want to sound too eager and risk scaring him off for real this time, but then again, he wouldn't be asking if he wasn't interested, right? I nearly got lost in thought imagining being held by him again and getting that kiss that'd been interrupted.

"Lance? You still there?" Jake asked, snapping me back to the here and now.

"What did you have in mind?" I asked.

I could hear the smile in his voice. "How about tomorrow? I'm having breakfast out with my family, then I've got the afternoon and evening to do as I please."

I thought about it for a moment. "Yeah, I don't have plans. What time?" I asked.

"Well, I'm guessing midafternoon, maybe around three?"

"Ok, that works. Are we going somewhere nice or just hanging out?"

"Dress warm. I'd like to introduce you to the owners of the local winery. The farm they're on is beautiful and has some good hiking. It's located just outside Crawford City."

"It's supposed to be cold tomorrow," I said, feeling a little apprehensive.

"Yeah, but trust me, it won't be that bad. If you get cold, you can just snuggle up to me. I tend to run hot."

I couldn't hold back my laugh. "That you do, Jake. But to be on the safe side, I'll borrow Allen's ski coat and gloves. My driving gloves probably won't be enough."

"Sounds good. I think you'll like where we're going."

I smiled. "I'm looking forward to it. Good night, Jake," I said, unsure if the fluttery feeling in my stomach was nervousness over him possibly canceling again or nervousness that he wouldn't.

"Good night, Lance. Sleep well."

EIGHTEEN

JAKE

I WAS SO PLEASED Lance was giving me a second chance that I dashed into my brother's room and jumped on his bed. He was in the bathroom, so I hollered that I was in the room. I didn't want to startle him when he came out.

"Hey, what's up?" he asked, coming back into the room a few minutes later in his pajamas.

"I've got a date!" I said and fell back on the bed, covering my face like I was the teenager.

He laughed. "So, he's giving you another chance after all?"

"Looks like it," I said, coming out from under the pillow. I'd told Derek on the ride home how I'd nearly screwed things up with Lance by not showing up for our date on Thursday.

"Where are you taking him?" he asked.

"Well, I know a couple guys who own a winery not far from Crawford City. One is an artist and has a beautiful studio on the second floor of a nineteenth-century mill. I figured since Lance is wanting to become an architect, he'd enjoy seeing the old building restored."

"Cool, but not very romantic," he said, sitting in the chair across from the bed.

"No, but they have great hiking trails, and a beautiful chapel up in the woods that's next to a mountain stream."

"Now that sounds romantic."

"I hope so." I sighed. "I really do like him. Like, really like him...a lot."

Derek chuckled. "I think he likes you too, just don't be too pushy. I can tell you might be even if you don't mean to."

I sighed again, considering whether or not I needed to pull back a little with Lance. I probably was pushing him a little too much too quickly. I wanted to make Lance feel a lot of things, but uncomfortable wasn't one of them.

"You are perceptive, brother, too freaking perceptive. I'll try to play it cool. You've not told me, is there anyone you're interested in?" I said, catching myself once again being pushy. "But hey, if you'd rather not talk about it, that's cool too."

He shook his head. "No, I've been too busy keeping that part of myself a secret to actually explore it much."

"Yeah, Nashville is open, but I'd imagine high school might not be as accepting."

"We have an LGBTQ-plus club at school, and several of the members know I'm gay, but they aren't the kind to out me or anything until I'm ready."

"That's cool, and it sounds like you've got some good people around you at school. Most people weren't as accepting when I was in high school, teachers or classmates. I'm glad you're having a different experience than I did."

I looked over at Derek and could tell he was tired. "Okay, well, I'm gonna hit the sack so I'm at my best tomorrow. We'll leave here around eight. Claire will blow a blood vessel if we aren't at the restaurant by nine. The woman is nothing if not serious about punctuality."

"Hey, little brother, thanks for going with me tonight. It was fun to have you there."

"It was fun to hang out, even though y'all are old."

I laughed. "Okay, next time we do a party, you should bring a friend or two."

"Deal," he said, and I wished him a good night, wondering if he had a friend to bring. There was still so much we didn't know about each other. Hopefully, that would change soon enough.

It was clear, though, that Derek and I weren't going to have any problems being family. That was something that'd been missing in my life. I had Anita and Claire, but there was nothing like having a sibling to connect with in your life.

I'd missed that after I'd lost my birth family all those years ago, not that I'd been especially close with most of my siblings. I guessed maybe Derek hadn't been either.

I could totally feel that connection forming between us now, though, and the thought made me happier than I'd been in a long time.

After finishing breakfast with the family on Sunday morning–which I'd nailed, having turned Derek into a fellow fan of The Springy Biscuit–I texted Lance that I was headed back to Crawford City. I wanted to spend as much time as possible with him.

I also texted Logan and Matt, asking if it would be okay to hike around their vineyard, and immediately got a text back from them saying we were welcome, and to come by the old mill to see Matt's most recent exhibition.

On the drive, I stopped at the store to grab some snacky foods that would complement the wine I intended to purchase at the winery. Although it was too cold for an actual picnic, I wanted to be prepared in case Lance was hungry.

By the time I pulled up in front of Lance's place, I practically vibrated with nervous energy. I liked this guy more than the men I usually pursued. Lance seemed different, a good kind of different. Maybe a little innocent, but also reserved, and very passionate about the things that interested him.

I'll also admit, Lance had a bit of a lost boy vibe about him, which heightened my caregiver instincts. I longed to hold him and keep him safe. Not unlike how I felt about Derek, but with my brother, I wanted to be a part of helping him grow and then take flight. With Lance, I wanted to fly with him.

I texted Lance I'd arrived, and he came down the front steps a few moments later and got into my car, laughing. "It's so cold I almost called to invite you to come in for hot chocolate and to just hang out here instead. The only reason I didn't is because the girls are still so wound up after last night's party, it's almost impossible to hear yourself think."

I smiled and winked at him. "No problem, and we're going to be inside some, too. If you don't want to hike, we can head into town instead. I'm hoping you'll let me keep you late 'cause after the winery, I'd like to take you out to dinner." Lance nodded but looked concerned. "You okay?"

"Yeah, I'm just not sure about dinner. I have to be ready for work very early tomorrow."

I recognized that look, and it wasn't about needing to be home early. It was about finances, or more accurately, a lack thereof. I knew that expression so well because I wore it myself more often than not the first few years after moving out of Anita and Claire's. I needed to tread carefully here and not embarrass the man, but I also wanted to put him at ease.

"Either way is cool. I'd love to treat you, though. If not this time, maybe next."

He still looked unsure, but our conversation soon shifted and we chatted about the party and Lexie's friends as we drove to the winery. When we pulled up to the old mill, Lance's eyes grew wide. "This place is beautiful!" he exclaimed.

"Yes, it is. Now you see why I wanted to bring you here."

We were greeted at the front door by Lia, the woman who handled the winery's marketing and ran the gift store.

"Hey, Jake, Matt and Logan told me you'd be coming."

I smiled at the woman I'd already begun to think of as a friend. "Yep, and this is Lance, my date."

"Date? Well, it's an honor to meet you, Lance. Welcome."

I smiled at Lia and escorted Lance through the door. The place was so cool. It still smelled of the wood that Todd's company had so delicately restored. They'd made plenty of modern touches too, though, and it was now insulated, so it felt warm and cozy when we stepped inside.

I led Lance over to the wine display and grabbed a couple of bottles. "If you keep buying all our stock, you're gonna need to become an investor," Lia teased. Of course, I'd bought five bottles just the day before for the party, so I probably appeared to be quite the wine connoisseur.

Lia beckoned us up the stairs into Matt's gallery, and Lance's eyes went wide in surprise. He really wore his heart on his sleeve, and I enjoyed watching everything he felt cross his beautiful face. "I would've never guessed there'd be a gallery up here," he said.

"It gets better," I told him, taking him by the hand to the original preserved window that looked out over the stream.

"It's such a magical place," Lance said as he squeezed my hand and peered outside.

Lia left us alone then, and I sat back and watched Lance take in each of Matt's paintings. Matt really was talented and even though I didn't know much about art, I did know he was quickly rising in the art world.

I'd already purchased a couple of his paintings and had them hanging in my condo in Nashville. When his collection was featured in a small art museum in Murfreesboro, I knew it was just a matter of time before his artistic career blew up.

I also genuinely loved his art, and the two pictures I'd bought depicted this property. I could easily see why Matt would feel inspired by this place. One piece captured the mill's old wheel moving through the water, and the other showed the dilapidated log cabin that had since been taken down and reassembled on the hill behind the old mill.

To me, both paintings embodied this farm—its history and its revival—and maybe this part of the South.

After Lance had studied every painting on display in detail, he finally came over and sat next to me on the handmade bench in the middle of the room.

"This really is spectacular," he said, leaning into my side.

"I have one more place to show you, then we can go have some of that wine."

It was still really cold out, but I wanted him to see the beautiful chapel that had been finished just a few months earlier. The scene was even more breathtaking right now, with the leaves off the trees, because you not only had the view of the little stream that ran alongside it, but also the vineyard and land beyond for miles around.

As soon as we stepped outside, Lance picked up speed, walking faster to stay warm, and I began pushing myself to keep up with him. Before long, we were both running toward the part of the farm where the chapel stood and laughing the whole way.

When the glass structure came into view, Lance stopped and gasped, not unlike the way he had in the gallery. "Oh my god! Really?" he asked as we approached the chapel.

He began mumbling adorably about the building's features and the different architects who'd likely influenced its design. I recognized the name Frank Lloyd Wright, but the others Lance noted were lost on me. All I knew was it was a beautiful building, unlike anything else I'd seen in all of Tennessee, and that Lance would likely appreciate seeing it. Mission accomplished.

I stayed out with him for several minutes as he snapped pictures of it from every possible angle, but I got cold fast and decided to slip inside to hopefully warm up.

I was standing on the stage, looking out a window at the incredible view, when the door creaked open behind me. I heard Lance let out another gasp, and damned if I wasn't becoming addicted to the sound.

When I turned around, Lance held up his phone and snapped my picture.

Nineteen

Lance

THE BUILDING WAS AWE-INSPIRING, appearing like a shimmering mirage at the edge of the surrounding forest. I'd seen photos of chapels like it made by an Arkansas team and strewn around different areas of the Midwest. What I hadn't expected was to see a building like that here, in the woods, in rural Tennessee.

The straight lines and play with angles were definitely something that made my artistic heart sing. Maybe even more than the art we'd seen in the gallery, although that had been incredible, too.

When I stepped inside the building, all the angles were directed forward and seemed to be focused right on Jake. The man had his back to me when I walked in, but as he turned around, the light behind him caught his blond hair and looked just for a moment like a halo.

Without a second thought, I used my phone to snap a picture of him. But that was about all I could do because the sheer beauty of this magnificent place, and of the man looking at me, nearly overwhelmed me.

I stood transfixed by Jake's intense gaze as he walked across the building toward me. The moment he reached me, caught up in the emotion of the moment, I immediately pulled him into a kiss.

Passion, born out of all that I'd seen and felt here in this special place he'd taken me, flowed out of me and into that kiss. Jake moaned and wrapped his arms around my waist, and that just propelled me further.

When he pulled back, both of us panting for air, only then did I think about what I'd just done.

"Oh..." I said and felt my cheeks blush. I shuddered a bit, but he just tightened his hold on me. "I'm...I...Jake, I'm not usually so..."

He chuckled and kissed my forehead. "If you're about to apologize for kissing me, keep it to yourself because that was amazing."

Emotions were still swirling through me and I tried to blink away the burning at the back of my eyes. Jake released his hold, and I moved over to a pew and sat down. He sat beside me.

I turned to face him but couldn't quite meet his gaze. "I don't know why I did that, Jake. I don't usually throw myself at someone I've just met."

He brought his hand to my chin and lifted it so my eyes met his, then he smiled. The sweet gesture caused my tears to break free. Mortified, I wiped at them with my coat sleeve.

"Sweetheart," Jake said, voice full of concern, which just made me feel worse.

He slung his arm around my shoulders, pulled me into his warm body, and let me weep as all the emotions I'd held inside for so long worked their way out. Quitting medical school, the blowup with my dad, feeling uncertain about my future, knowing I'd been a horrible brother to Allen and feeling undeserving of his kindness. I knew this wasn't the time or the place, but I was as incapable of stopping my flowing tears as I was at stopping the flowing stream that ran down the hillside next to the chapel.

When I lifted my head, Jake cupped my face in his hands and wiped away my tears with his thumbs. "You okay now?" he asked.

I sniffed and couldn't help but chuckle, mostly from embarrassment. "I'm such a silly emotional wreck," I said, and Jake tutted.

"Oh no, baby, it's fine. You're fine. I can understand if a spectacular place like this feels overwhelming, especially for someone as artistic as yourself."

"Yeah, that and just...life, you know? Mine was a shitshow before moving here, and it's still a struggle sometimes, but being here with you, in this majestic place...it all just hit me. God, I'm sure you'd like to take my overly emotional ass back to town and be done with me now, huh?"

"No, dear God, please don't think that. Just being here with you has made me see this building–and you–in a totally different way. Believe me, I like what I see."

"Really? You don't want to get away from me?"

"The opposite, actually. All I want to do is kiss you again," he said, and slowly leaned in before capturing my lips with his.

Jake was right. This place really was spectacular. But so was the man holding me in his arms.

TWENTY

JAKE

M

Y DATE WITH LANCE hadn't gone the way I'd expected, but I wouldn't have changed a thing as we sat cuddled into one another, staring out the chapel's windows at the beautiful landscape.

I'd thought his breaking down had to do with feeling overwhelmed by our surroundings, him being an artist and all, but apparently he'd been releasing months, if not years, of pent-up emotions in that moment. As much as it pained me to learn he'd been hurting, I felt privileged to be the one holding him as he cried.

Even as we pulled apart and began our walk back to the car, I knew this spot would always be special to me. No matter how things worked out with Lance, this would now be a sacred space.

He remained quiet as we walked along the trail leading back to the old mill, and when we reached my car, he apologized. "I'm sorry, Jake. You must think I'm a total loser."

I laughed, unable to stop myself. "You are far from a loser. No, if anything, I'm happy you took me along for the ride."

Lance looked at me strangely. "Took you along for the ride?" he asked.

"Yeah, I'm here for whatever you need from me, even if it's literally a shoulder to cry on. I know we just met, and I'm really trying not to come on too strong here, but please don't feel like you can't be honest with me about however you're feeling," I said.

I nearly reached for him again when I noticed his chin tremble, but he bit his bottom lip and managed to pull himself together without shedding more tears. It'd been an emotional day for both of us in different ways, and I still needed to learn when to give him some space.

"I'm also no artist, so I don't naturally see things the way you do. Like the chapel, or even the old mill. The buildings are impressive, and I can appreciate the crafts-manship that went into constructing and restoring them, and I could even feel how the chapel is a sacred space, but I don't *feel* their beauty. Not like you do."

I smiled over at him, expecting to see understanding, but I only saw confusion.

"Lance, you do see that you're an artist, right?" I asked.

He chuckled and rolled his eyes. "No, I only see I'm an overly emotional ninny."

I walked around to the passenger side of the car and took his hand in mine. "No, baby, that couldn't be further from the truth. People don't have that kind of emotional reaction to something unless they see it and feel it on a soul-deep level. I know you said some of that had to do with letting go of past mistakes, and I believe it, but I also saw the effect this place was having on you since the moment we arrived. In my experience, artists often have that sort of instant and profound connection with whatever they're most passionate about."

Lance took a long breath and held it for a moment before letting it out slowly. "I guess I've never seen myself that way. I've always been pushed to become better, more productive, more focused."

He gave my hand a little squeeze to reassure me he was okay, then we climbed into my car. He stared out the front window while I started the car and began driving in silence, giving him time to come to terms with everything I'd said.

We drove for a long time before Lance spoke up. "So, I've always been told not to allow myself to follow fanciful thinking, like pursuing architecture or the arts in general. I mean, even in grade school, my teachers would tell me I had a natural talent for drawing, but my father frowned upon it. This past year, I've felt more and more confined. Medical school was tough, harder than anything I'd done before, and the whole time I felt like my life was being decided for me." He let out a sigh, then turned to face me and smiled. "Thanks for helping me back there. I was embarrassed, but you helped me see that feeling like I did, like I do, is okay. For some reason, I'm even starting to believe you."

I winked at him. "One more thing. I work with a lot of artists, mostly in the music business but also with painters like Matt, who owns the vineyard and chapel, and I can tell you that your abilities are just as unique and worthwhile as theirs. In fact, I've created an entire career out of helping people like me relate to people like you."

"Really?" he asked, perplexed.

"Yeah, really." I would've loved to have kissed him again, but driving prevented that. Not that I didn't have every intention of kissing him as soon as we arrived at the restaurant, provided he let me.

Twenty-One

Lance

J AKE BEWILDERED ME. THE emotional outburst I had in the chapel embarrassed me, and I'd have easily crawled into a hole if I could've found one. But instead of letting me hide, Jake pulled me out. Encouraged me to be...me. Even my own father had never done that.

I took in our surroundings as we drove through the beautiful countryside between Crawford City and Nashville. Now that Jake had called me an artist, it was like suddenly the world refused to stay hidden from me, and I drank it all in. The light, the shadows, the colors, the shapes, everything around me seemed more vivid.

That's more fanciful thinking than I'd ever dared to have. I chuckled to myself, and Jake looked at me, smiling.

"What's so funny?"

"Oh nothing, I'm just being sentimental and a little out there. It's like you calling me an artist has given me permission to be overly...observant, maybe? Overly something."

Jake reached over and took my hand. "I'm glad to have given you that permission, not that you need it from me."

I shrugged. "Maybe I just needed it from someone. My life really has been restricted to getting good grades, thinking scientifically, and making boring conversation at swanky New York parties. There was no room for anything artistic or creative in any way. I know I keep using the word fanciful, but that's what my father would call me when he'd catch me sketching. Needless to say, he didn't approve."

Jake glanced at me, then back at the road, and sighed. "My parents were...*are* religious zealots. They were okay growing up, loved me in their own way, as long as I toed the line. Which, to be honest, wasn't hard. I loved going to church, taking part in the youth groups, and we had a nice choir. Even though I don't have a really great voice, it felt good to be a part of something."

He drifted off for a moment, eyes still fixed on the road but his hand never leaving mine, and I could tell he was deep in thought. "But they were so rigid," he continued. "I wasn't able to be anything but what they thought I should be. So, when this kid I went to high school with caught me looking at male models instead of researching for our project in English class, he announced to the world that I was scoping out naked men. Incidentally, looking back now, I think he had a little crush on me.

Go figure. My parents heard the rumors and never gave me a chance to explain. They just kicked me out. The die had been cast."

Jake took a deep breath and shook his head. "They did the same thing to my little brother, Derek, the kid you met last night. Sixteen years old and they tossed him out on his ass like he was nothing. So, yeah, I get it. You had a dad who kept you from seeing and being yourself, and now you're free to be the person you've always been but never had the chance."

"Yes, exactly," I said, trying to sound encouraging since it seemed like Jake had more he wanted to say.

"It was hard when I was still a kid trying to survive on the streets," he said. "But even then, even when I was hungry, dirty and afraid, I was still happier being myself than trying to be a perfect kid in my parents' eyes."

I squeezed his hand. "Thanks for sharing that with me, Jake. It's awful you had to go through that, but it helps to talk with someone who understands."

"Yeah, it does. Now, on to the really important topics. Tell me, do you like seafood?"

"Oh my god, I love seafood! I haven't had any since moving here."

"Okay, Jeff Ruby's it is. Best seafood place in town."

I felt my face turn pink at what sounded to me like an expensive restaurant. "Um, Jake, I'm broke. Really, I'm fine with going to a burger place. I don't need anything fancy."

"Dude, I asked you out. Give me the chance to be a gentleman and buy his date dinner. Dessert included," he said, giving me a wink.

I blushed even deeper. "I don't like taking things from others."

"Not even a gift?" he said, sounding incredulous, but the smile never left his face. "I promise, I don't expect anything in return, except your amazing company. Come on, Lance, let me treat you. I remember being broke too and I know it's hard, but I want to do it."

I shrugged. "Okay, but just this once. After this, we go Dutch."

Jake's smile lit up even more. "If that means I've already scored a second date before the first one is even over, it's a deal."

The upscale restaurant was an experience in and of itself, with a beautiful Art déco interior and luxurious chandeliers, and the food was delicious. The sushi even rivaled some of the finer New York restaurants my dad frequented. But the best part was being there with Jake.

Not only was I attracted to him, but he made me feel like my feelings were important, that *I* was important. I hadn't had that in my life, and I was soaking it up as if I was drinking water for the first time after spending years in the desert.

TWENTY-TWO

JAKE

FTER A FANTASTIC DINNER, we drove back to Crawford City, and I dropped Lance off at his home. I wanted to do more, go further, but I could tell he wasn't ready. I recognized so much of the lost boy innocence in him that'd once been a part of me and that I now saw in Derek.

Sure, Lance was an adult, not a kid, but the pervasive sadness was still very apparent in them both. As my little brother had advised, I needed to keep my pushiness in check with Lance. If more happened between us, which I really hoped for, it needed to be on his schedule, and I respected that.

I spent the next week running between work appointments and managing things for Derek and our foster moms. I texted Lance at least a hundred times a day, mostly sending little updates or silly gifs I thought might make him laugh, to the point I finally got in trouble.

When Todd's name popped up on my phone, I immediately took the call. "Hey, dude, what's up? Did you finally get the blueprints for the new construction?"

"No, I'm calling 'cause you've got to stop texting my new gofer so much. He's got work to do."

"Gofer?" I asked.

"Yeah, Lance. Stop texting him every three minutes. It's leading him to distraction."

I laughed. "How did you know?"

"I was just over at the site where he is supposed to be helping Linc, but he can't, because you're blowing up his phone. Apparently, he feels the need to respond to every single text you send."

"Okay, I'll slow down," I whined, feeling appropriately chastised.

Todd chuckled. "You really like him, don't you?"

"Yeah. He's pretty great."

"Like, more than anyone I've seen you with in a long time."

"Hey, I might be crushing hard on Lance, but don't get ahead of yourself. We've only been out once. Let us have time to get to know each other before you start sending out wedding invitations."

"Yeah, once he gets to see how over the top you really are, he'll probably run the other way."

"God, really? You're gonna rain on my parade like that?"

"Oh yeah, you so have that coming."

"Hey, have you heard from Jen?" I asked, hoping to steer our conversation elsewhere now that it was feeling too close for comfort.

"Wow, changing the subject. You really do have it bad."

I ignored him and just waited for him to answer, even though I knew perfectly well how Jen was doing. I remained in fairly close contact with all of my clients, especially when they also happened to be one of my best friends.

"Yeah, she called yesterday," Todd said. "The photoshoot seems to have gone well, and she's back in New York."

"I've decided I'm gonna try to get her to come home," I admitted. I'd been thinking about it since Lance sketched his ideas for the residential side of the building project. I, of course, still wanted the upper floor for myself as one big condo, with visions of the roof acting as my upper deck. Maybe even including access to a pool and a pool house to be on the roof of the adjoining building. Since the rest of the building would only house a couple more condos, I thought those units could be combined into one large condo instead, and who better to live there than Jen?

"Really?" Todd asked, and I could hear the humor in his voice.

"Yeah, really, and I think I'll hook her with the new design on the build downtown."

"Seriously, have you met Jen? She has no interest in coming back to Crawford City. She hates it here."

"Not if she had a remarkable condo to call home," I said.

"Jeez, not this again. What? You're going to turn part of the building into a condo for you and Jen?"

"Well, two condos, but yeah, that's the plan."

"And what about the hotel and the offices and all the stuff we already have planned?" he asked.

"See, that's the beauty of it. With my purchase of the other two lots, we can integrate residential, commercial, and the hotel all in one spot. It'll be magnificent."

"You're nuts. When do you plan on fleshing out these new ideas with me?"

"Tomorrow?" I asked and Todd snort-laughed into the phone. At least my friend could forgive me for continuing to change my mind on this, but it's not like we'd broken ground yet, anyway.

"And I'm assuming we're hosting you at our house?"

"Yes, and maybe a plus-one?" I hedged.

"Really? You want to bring a date?"

I hesitated for a moment. Did I want to toss Lance's name into the mix as the would-be architect behind the condo idea? I figured I'd test the waters and see how Todd took it.

"Well, I want to bring the person who came up with the plan in the first place. He has a really good eye for design."

"I'm guessing this is Lance?"

"Yeah, damn, here I thought I was being sly about it. Is that okay, though? I mean, I know he's sort of interning with you..."

"No, he's great and Linc thinks he's made for the job. He can't stop talking about how Lance has taken to construction like he was born to do it."

The surge of jealousy that swamped me at the idea of Linc fawning over Lance for any reason took me by surprise. I forced myself to smile, though, lest Todd read anything into my reaction even if he couldn't see me.

Damn, that wasn't like me at all. Love them and leave them, that was usually my motto. If a guy found someone else more interesting than me to be with, easy come and easy go.

But that wasn't how I felt about Lance. I felt protective and needy at the same time. I couldn't imagine losing him, even though he wasn't even mine yet. *Fuck, I'm the needy one.*

"Hey, Jake, you okay?" Todd asked.

"Oh yeah, sorry, just got caught up in something. Hey, I'll call you later and set up for tomorrow. As usual, I'll bring dinner, okay?"

Todd confirmed, and I quickly hung up. Staring down at the park from my office window, I mulled over my feelings. To be honest, I didn't know how I'd deal with it. Lance was different. He'd got under my skin and I hadn't even realized it.

I quickly texted him about tomorrow night before remembering that I'd promised to text him less.

I chuckled to myself, knowing that both Todd and Linc were probably shaking their heads right about now. To Lance's credit, he didn't respond this time.

Needing to refocus on work, I called my assistant Charlie into my office, and we finished the projects that needed wrapping up before the end of the week. Then I rushed over to spend the evening with Anita, Claire, and Derek.

After one of my clients had been in a horrific car accident because of distracted driving years ago, I'd installed an app on my phone that mutes text messages and phone calls while driving. My client survived but the distracted driver hadn't, and I decided then and there that taking calls while on the road just wasn't worth it. So, the moment I put my car in park at Anita and Claire's, I started getting the dings.

I looked down and immediately opened the one from Lance.

Lance: *Hey, sorry I couldn't text earlier, but Linc and Todd were giving me the mean dad look.*

Me: *No problem, Todd called and fussed at me too.*

No sooner had I hit send than a reply popped up. Had Lance been waiting for me to text back? The thought made me smile.

Lance: *Yeah, so I heard.*

Me: *So, doing anything tomorrow night?*

Lance: *Todd already told me about dinner at his place. He said you wanted me to show them the plans you and I came up with.*

Me: *You mean the plans* you *came up with? But yeah, is that okay?*

Lance: *It's weird. You know I'm not a real architect, right?*

Me: *You will be, and since it's your idea, you should be the one to show them.*

Lance: *If you say so. Anyway, are you picking me up?*

Me: *Why don't you have Todd take you to his place after work, and I'll just plan to meet you there.*

Lance: *Cool.*

I could sense that I'd somehow made him nervous. I probably shouldn't have thrown him to the wolves like that. I was just about to text him back when I got a call from one of my clients.

"Hey, what's up?" I asked, sounding cheerful but cringing inside. This was my weekly call from the client who freaked out constantly when anything negative about her appeared in the press. Par for the course in the PR world, but definitely one of the less glamourous aspects of my job.

By the time I finished talking my client down from her usual dramatic cliff, I needed to get inside. Claire had already looked outside and waved at me like five minutes ago, which meant they were ready to eat.

I would've rather called Lance to make sure he was okay, but I decided to stop being so overprotective. Lance worked for Todd and, as far as I knew, they were on friendly terms. If Lance felt uncomfortable at the prospect of having dinner at his boss's house or discussing building plans with him, he'd have told me.

TWENTY-THREE

LANCE

U NEASY? YES. FREAKING OUT? Totally. Todd was my boss, even if I was an unpaid intern, and I had just begun to feel accepted by my co-workers. What would they think of me going to dinner at his house? And showing up on the arm of his business partner?

In the past few weeks, I'd been enjoying life more than I ever had before. I loved the constant movement that construction demanded. The workers coming and going. The instant changes from day to day. There was always something more to do, something new to learn, and all of it hands-on. I loved everything from demolition to reconstruction, and it seemed like most of the crew had finally warmed up to letting me help.

But now here I was, being invited to dinner with the boss. The owner of the freaking company.

When Todd mentioned it to me, I noticed three or four of the wallboarding guys look over at us. They weren't rude or anything, but I could tell they were curious. So much for fitting in.

That being said, my heart raced at the thought of spending more time with Jake. He was so sweet, patient, and accommodating. He liked nice things, like upscale restaurants, but he didn't shove that in my face. That felt right, too.

At the end of our workday, I climbed into Linc's truck for the ride home. We'd usually chitchat about work on the drive, but I had bigger things on my mind today. "So, I'm meeting Jake at Todd's tomorrow for dinner, and some of the guys overheard the conversation. Do you think that'll keep me from fitting in?" I asked.

Linc smiled over at me. "No, not really. They all know you're interning here and most of them know you want to be an architect. To be honest, I've been surprised at how quickly they've let you in. But I think they understand why you're here and that Todd is less like your boss and more like a family friend, one who gets to tell you what to do all day."

I sighed with relief. "That's good 'cause I think I'd like to work for y'all for real," I blurted. "I mean, after I'm better trained, obviously." I hadn't meant to let that cat out of the bag, but I'd been thinking about how helpful this was to ultimately becoming an architect. I also didn't want to get back into the habit of packing down my thoughts and emotions just because I was nervous about voicing them. I'd done that for far too long already.

Linc nodded. "Yeah, you'll have to take that up with Todd, since he's why you're with us. But I can tell you now, I wouldn't object. You're a quick study, and you're a hard worker too. Even the crew seem to have picked up on that."

The compliment made me blush, and I couldn't hide my smile.

"I hope so. I'm trying, Linc."

He reached over and patted my shoulder. "Yeah, it shows."

I was positively glowing as I got out of the truck. By the time I got inside the house, I was grinning from ear to ear. It had been a long time since I'd felt confident about anything I'd done. Nothing was good enough for Dad. Even straight A's were looked down upon because they could've been an A+. "You can always do better, son," he'd like to say every time I handed over my report card. Thank God those days were behind me.

When Catherine came around the corner, I jumped. "Oh! Hi, Catherine, I didn't know you were here," I said.

"Well, I just got here," she said as she breezed past me, picking up the girls' discarded coats as she went. "This is Gib's evening shift at the clinic, and Allen called to tell me he was going to be late getting home, so I'm on grandma duty."

This news hit me like a ton of bricks. "Oh," I said, the smile dropping from my face.

I turned to head to my room when Catherine stepped in front of me. "Are you okay?" she asked.

"Yeah, I'm just curious why Allen didn't ask me to watch the girls. I guess he doesn't trust me yet. I'm going to head up and get a shower," I said and turned to go up the stairs.

"Lance, hold on for just a moment," she replied.

When I turned around, Catherine had just hung up the last of the coats.

"Have you told Allen or Gib that you're willing to help with the girls?" she asked.

I shook my head. "No, not exactly. I know I don't have a lot of experience working with kids, and I've been sort of AWOL all these years, so I shouldn't be surprised they called you instead."

"But you want to be more a part of the family, though, right?" she asked.

I sighed. "Of course, I do. I love the girls already, and we all get along pretty well. I've never actually babysat anyone before, but I could probably watch them for a while if Gib or Allen are going to be late coming home. It seems strange to have you drive all the way out here when I'm already living here," I said.

Catherine studied me for a moment. "Lance, I think Allen is still figuring out how to involve you, and he's unsure where the two of you stand. I think that's the case for you as well. Go get your shower, and when you come back down, I'll let you take charge tonight. If you feel comfortable, then maybe you can offer that to Allen from now on."

I nodded. I'm not sure why that excited me. Except maybe it felt like I would be doing my part as a member of the family. Like maybe my brother and I could get past all the crap our dad had done to keep us apart.

I dashed up the stairs, got my shower, and dressed as quickly as I could. I'd smelled food cooking when I came in the house earlier so, thankfully, I wouldn't have to worry about fixing them dinner. The girls had arrived home and were already eating when I came downstairs, and Catherine had set me a plate as well. I sat down and immediately got pulled into some argument the girls were having about a video by a singer I'd not heard of. Luckily, when I told them I hadn't heard the song, they went from arguing to Chrissy pulling the video up on her phone.

I had to force myself not to laugh at the strange video with some guy in the background and what looked like a trashcan on his head. I managed to say the right thing, and the conversation went on without me offending any of them.

The subject switched to kids they knew in school and Chrissy pretty much ruled supreme over that conversation since she was the oldest but still young enough to be in the same school as the twins.

Catherine and I only had to occasionally respond to questions or comments. When everyone was done eating, the girls got up to leave and Catherine looked at me. I'd been here long enough to know the girls had clean-up duties, and they were all experts at trying to get out of the chores.

"Hey, girls?" I asked as they began to walk out of the dining room. "Would you like me to help y'all clean tonight?"

"Yeah," the twins said in unison while Chrissy gave me a look that was a mix between knowing she'd been busted but also curious what she could get me to do. I quickly added, "So, why don't you two clean off the table and take the dishes to the sink. Chrissy, if you'll rinse them off, I'll fill the dishwasher."

This seemed to work for them and within moments, we were all cleaning up and the chatter we'd had at the table continued in the kitchen.

It took hardly any time to finish cleaning up, and I asked the girls if they needed help with homework. They all told me about their assignments, and no one had anything they were really concerned about. As they did their work around the table, I grabbed my laptop to finish filling out grad school applications.

I decided to apply both to Vanderbilt and the University of Tennessee because I still hadn't actually decided where I wanted to go. Plus, it was possible one would turn me down.

I only had to answer the occasional question from the girls, and it didn't take long for me to finish filling out the online application forms and submitting the fees. Since the girls were still working, I opened up my email that I hadn't looked at since I'd been here.

It wasn't like I ever received much email, which is why I rarely bothered to check it. Most of my friends would text me if they needed to reach me, and the university had stopped emailing me since I withdrew from medical school.

I clicked from my empty inbox to the spam folder as the girls worked mostly silently, when I came upon an email from Dad. He wasn't in my contacts, never had been, which is why his email had kicked to spam.

I looked up at the girls, wondering if maybe I should wait to open it when I didn't have kid duty, but decided it was best just to get it out of the way.

Of course, I regretted it the moment I clicked on it.

Lance,

It's completely unacceptable that you haven't returned my texts or that you haven't tried to be in contact with me since you left.

You may think because you're grown that it's okay to treat your father like he no longer matters, but I assure you, that isn't the case. You owe me for all the time and energy I've put into raising you. Surely even a selfish child, like yourself, can see that.

It's time to grow up. You need to contact me as soon as possible so I can get you enrolled back into medical school before it's too late.

I've spoken to the admissions office, and they assure me if we act now, we can enroll you for the fall term.

Don't throw your life away, Lance. Grow up and do it now before it's too late.

Your Father

"What's wrong, Uncle Lance?" Ruby asked, and only then did I realize I'd been gripping the sides of my laptop hard enough to break it.

"Oh, nothing. Sorry, I was just reading an email."

"From who?" Margie asked.

"My dad," I said and looked up just in time to see Catherine's frown before she quickly schooled her expression.

"You looked angry," Ruby said.

"Yeah, he makes me mad sometimes, but it'll be fine. Are you all done with your schoolwork?" I asked, hoping to change the subject.

"I am," Margie and Ruby both said at the same time.

Chrissy shook her head and looked back down at a math worksheet that was only half-finished.

"Girls," Catherine said. "Why don't you go up and get your baths. Chrissy, you can go take a quick break, then come on back down and I'll help you finish this homework."

The twins quickly packed their homework back into their backpacks as Chrissy dashed up the stairs to her room. Catherine didn't let the girls have their phones when doing homework, so I knew she was rushing up to text her friends.

The twins left shortly after, and when Catherine and I were sitting alone, she asked, "So, what did he say that had you looking like you could rip that laptop to shreds?"

I took a deep breath and let it out with an irritated sigh. I shook my head and was thinking of a way to discount the email, then get out of watching the girls so I could sulk in my room for a while.

When I looked into Catherine's eyes, I knew that wasn't going to work. Not if I wanted to be a member of this family.

"I probably shouldn't be telling you this, but I'm so frustrated with that man. I don't even know how to deal with it. He kicked me out and told me to never come back. He froze all my credit cards, even locked me out of my own trust fund and savings account, which included money I'd made myself. I literally had nothing when I got here, and now he acts like I was some disobedient child just because I said I didn't want to be a doctor."

"Your father has never been the best at apologizing," she said, and I had to tamp down my reflexive habit of defending him.

"No," I said instead. "He doesn't apologize because then he'd have to admit he'd been wrong about something."

"So, what is he wanting you to do?" she asked.

"Oh, the same old same old. He wants me to call him so he can get me re-enrolled in medical school. I'm guessing he's bribed the admissions office or something to hold my spot."

She surprised me by laughing. "He never changes. Well, son," Catherine said, the smile slowly falling from her face, "you are making something of yourself here. I've heard from Allen that you're working as an intern for Todd. I've never seen you look so happy." She thought for a moment before she shrugged and added, "Ever."

I nodded. "Yeah, it's true. I've *never* felt this happy."

"So, you don't have to feel guilty about that. I know you care about your dad and his opinion, but you are an adult, and you have the right to be, and do, what you wish. It's okay if that isn't what your father wants for you."

I stared out the window over Catherine's shoulder for a long moment, thinking about all the times I backed down and did what my father instructed. I'm guessing I'd be doing the same thing now if Allen hadn't offered to help me.

Finally, when I heard Chrissy coming back to the dining room, I turned to Catherine and quickly said, "Thanks for listening. It's just hard to navigate how to feel after all these years of cowering to what he demands of me. But he really doesn't have any control over me any longer, thanks to Allen."

Catherine patted my hand. "No, thanks to you."

Chrissy came in, plopped down at the table and, with a look of pure frustration, grabbed her pencil and began to work on her math problems once again.

"Lance, why don't you head up. I'll help Chrissy finish this, and you can sort out that email," Catherine said, giving me an out.

I nodded and went up the stairs to my room. I ended up just deleting the email before putting my computer away. It never did any good arguing with my father, in person or in writing. The man wasn't one to negotiate. At this point, it was simply better to ignore him.

Twenty-Four

Jake

THURSDAY NIGHT, I ATE dinner with Claire, Anita, and Derek. Derek was all excited about some guy who'd just started at his new school. Even though he wasn't admitting it, our foster moms and I knew this was a new crush. I had to wonder if maybe it was his first crush, at least the first he could actually consider pursuing as a boyfriend.

I smiled as he talked about how the guy was "muscular like a football player, but nicer than most of them." I wondered if the dreamy look on his face was how I looked when talking about Lance. Funnily enough, I did feel like a smitten schoolboy lately.

I left after dinner to get back home to finish some work on Lexie's account that was needed the next day. Her fundraising concert at the children's hospital had done what we'd hoped it would. Not only had the album sold so well the hospital was getting a nice wad of cash from it, but Lexie was beginning to explode on the country circuits.

Influential mainstream radio stations in Nashville and beyond had placed a couple of her songs on heavy rotation after they gained traction with listeners. Lexie had called me screaming and crying from her car as she listened to herself singing on the radio. That'd been a great day, and the first of many more milestones we needed to make happen for her in the next several weeks to maintain momentum.

Now, we needed to secure invitations to perform in the right places at the right times. Not to mention increasing her social media presence and whipping up excitement and interest in seeing her perform live. I almost wished we still had something like TNN when it was still The Nashville Network or the old TV shows like *Hee Haw*, where she could perform to their built-in country music-loving audiences, but those tried and true ways of promoting up-and-coming singers were long gone. Still, performing at the Grand Ole Opry remained a holy grail for most country music artists, and it topped my list of achievable goals for Lexie.

With my work done for the night, I texted Lance, but he didn't respond. I had to force myself not to think the worst. Once again, I'd pushed the poor man out of his comfort zone by asking him to dinner with his boss. I shook my head and sighed. Todd was right... would he run for the hills when he figured out I was too much?

I wished I could just pull back and let things progress naturally, but that just wasn't my way. It really never had been. I knew I was a lot to handle and there was no use feeling bad about that. I just had to hope that as Lance got to know me better, he'd just accept that about me.

Luckily, I was tired enough that I fell asleep quickly, avoiding the self-recrimination I was prone to while lying in bed, staring at the ceiling. It never did much good, but that, too, was a personality trait I didn't have much control over.

The next day, I rushed from one meeting and task to another. Bless my assistant Charlie's heart because she was the best prepared and most solid support a person like me could hope for. By the end of the day, she'd delegated all the work to the appropriate people, drawing more than a few sighs at having to work the weekend again. But we all knew this sort of business often demanded it. Long hours, tight schedules, and a heck of a lot of kissing butt while wearing a smile. I mostly loved it and knew everyone who worked for me felt the same, even poor, overworked Charlie.

To be honest, I almost expected Lance not to show up Friday night at Todd's. I hadn't heard from him at all that day, and I had to assume that meant the worst. So, when I walked into Todd's extremely loud home that evening, with my arms loaded with take-out bags, I was pleasantly surprised to see Lance sitting in Todd and Ash's living room, playing with their three kids.

When he looked up and saw me, a smile spread across his face and all the anxiety and fear that I'd somehow screwed everything up again vanished in an instant. Lance was so good-looking, but he was shy and unassuming as well. Everything about that man melted my butter.

I stepped over the barrier that Todd and Ash had put up to keep the ever-moving little ones in the room and walked over to Lance, planting a quick, chaste kiss on his mouth before one of the kids wrapped her arms around my leg.

"Hello, beautiful," I said as I scooped Ellen up into my arms.

She giggled, as she usually did when I picked her up quickly, and I tossed her into the air a bit before she settled into my arms.

Lynn and Jessica were busy playing with Lance, or playing next to Lance, as he sat on the floor with them.

I put Ellen down and plopped down next to Lance. "So, I'm glad you came," I admitted.

Lynn picked up a plastic hammer and showed it to Lance, who then had to help hammer several big plastic screws before responding to me.

"I'm glad you invited me. And I didn't know I'd have the pleasure of all this energetic extra company," he said, chuckling.

"Yeah, the triplets are a lot. Aren't you?" I asked Jessica just as she thrust a spit-covered block into my hand.

Lance smiled and seeing him so happy unraveled knots in my heart I hadn't known were there.

Donna and Louisa, the kids' aunts, came into the room a few moments later and took over babysitting duty, allowing us to excuse ourselves. Lance and I wandered back through the big room to where Todd and Ash were sitting across from their dads, Amos and Doc.

"Hey, y'all," I said as we came in. Everyone turned toward us smiling. "So, you decided to baptize Lance by fire, I see." All four men chuckled.

"Well, we never turn down a babysitter," Ash said and pointed to a couple empty seats. "You two have a seat. Do you want me to get you something to drink?"

We both opted for the iced tea everyone else was drinking. Of course, I doubted Lance knew it was sweet tea like everyone in these parts drank. When he took a sip of the syrupy liquid, I almost cackled at his expression. To his credit, he didn't say anything. I was particularly thirsty, so when I finished my glass I discretely switched mine for his and smiled when he blushed.

All four men across from us were debating the project we'd come to discuss. I chimed in occasionally, but for the most part, I was enjoying watching Lance as he absorbed the wrangling at the table.

"I think you need to plan how you'll expand in the event the boutique hotel does better than you assume," Doc said. I'd been thinking the same thing, but when I'd brought it up with Todd, he just laughed, saying I had big city thoughts and that going from a town with only a ratty motel to one with twenty upscale rooms was a big deal. One that wouldn't likely need an extension anytime soon.

"What did you have in mind?" I asked Doc before Todd could shoot down the idea.

"Well, you know the grain mill is in bad shape and the town is already discussing dismantling it. But it will be real costly. The town's budget certainly doesn't support that kind of thing right now, but it could in the future. Or, if the hotel's business is doing well, and you wanted to expand, I'm sure the town council would consider giving the land to you at cost if you disposed of the thing."

I looked over at Lance and smiled. "Well, that sort of plays well with how we want to build."

"Before we get going too much, I've invited old Tom to join us. I'm tired of having to be the go-between for Jake and him, so he agreed to come over and you can all hash this out."

"Wait, did you invite Allen and Catherine since they are investing too?" I asked.

Todd nodded. "Yeah, but they said at this point, they couldn't make it tonight. They'll look at the plans once Tom gets the next ones drawn up."

"Okay, well, as long as you let them know we were meeting. I'd rather not piss them off just as we're finally getting this off the ground."

Todd chuckled. "You mean piss them off 'cause you keep making more changes?"

I put my hands up and smiled. "I can't help it that the property next to it came up so cheap. It just makes sense to pull that into this build since it'll help us in the end."

Todd just shook his head, like he always seemed to do with me.

"Why don't you give Lance here a tour of the house while we're waiting for Tom? If he's going to be an architect, he might like to see how we redesigned and added to it," Ash said.

When I looked over at Lance, his eyes had lit up at the prospect. "Well, sure. You don't mind if I show him?" I asked, thinking maybe Todd or Ash would rather do the tour instead of me. Really, though, I suspected Ash had suggested it to give us all a breather before Todd and I launched into our typical arguments about the mercantile project.

"No, please do," Ash said. "You were involved from the beginning and can show him the things we take for granted now."

I knew a set up when I saw one, but I appreciated it, nonetheless. "Okay. Well, Lance, if you're game."

"Yes, I'd like that," he quickly said.

We left the men in the kitchen and I started out in the back, where Todd had built a large family room with cathedral ceilings and a stone fireplace overlooking the back of the property.

I showed Lance how the original home had been a typical Victorian design with separate sitting rooms for women and men and how they'd combined the two rooms in front where the kids were currently playing with their aunts.

As I took him through the house, his eyes continued to grow with fascination about the rebuild. It'd been a while since I'd walked through the property and I'd forgotten just how well done the renovation had been. Now, as I gave Lance the tour, I once again saw it with fresh eyes.

When I showed him the third-floor master suite, which currently included three cribs, Lance gasped. "This is beautiful. Was the third floor finished prior to this?" he asked.

I shook my head. "No, this had been unfinished attic space."

"Well, it's spectacular," he exclaimed. "I especially love how they've maintained the character from the era it was built."

"Yeah, I was pretty impressed myself. You should log onto Todd's website and see the before and after pictures and videos I took. They'll show you just how much the house changed."

By the time we got back down to the first floor, Tom had arrived. Before we rejoined everyone in the kitchen, I told Lance, "Tom is ancient, but he does good work. Just look at this house, although Ash probably deserves more credit than Tom does."

Lance looked at me questioningly, then asked, "So, Tom redesigned this house? Is that why you hired him for the commercial project?"

I laughed, and speaking quietly enough so no one would hear us, I said, "No, he was hired because he's the only architect around."

"I see," Lance said but I could tell he didn't fully understand.

"Just know the old goat might be a hundred years old or more, but he's still sharp. If you want to be an architect, I'd recommend you listen to him. I'm guessing he could teach you a lot."

Lance nodded and I hoped I'd given him something to think about. Before I knew Tom would be here tonight, I had already decided I'd try to introduce the old man to Lance. The little time I'd had with Tom had shown me just how shrewd he was. A young guy just getting started in the business could do well by connecting with someone like him.

As we came into the room, old Tom was already holding court. He was sitting in front of the old blueprints I assumed he'd brought with him. And Todd and Doc were both still talking about expansion, the same subject they had been discussing before we left.

"So, before you all go too far down this topic, why don't we let Lance share with you what he came up with the other day," I said, leading everyone to quiet down and give him their full attention.

Lance's face turned bright red, but he cleared his throat and said, "I'm not an architect, well, I hope to be someday, but I just gave my opinion..."

When his voice cracked, I jumped in and said, "And that opinion would make this whole project better. Wait just a second and I'll show you."

I rushed out to my truck and grabbed the sketches Lance had drawn weeks ago when I'd first shown him the project. When I came back in, I opened them up and let him explain about using insets on each side of the middle part of the building, increasing square footage but also alleviating the town council's concerns about it just being a flat brick wall.

He also suggested we switch things around a bit and put the condos on the street-facing side of the building and the hotel on the back. "That way, you force your guests to walk past all the commercial space to get to the hotel. And if you put the hotel back there, if you need to expand later, your hotel rooms are already on the side where the expansion could take place."

I put my finger against the side of my nose and smiled.

Todd just shook his head. "You are all getting ahead of yourselves. I can't imagine we'll ever need that much hotel space, but I guess it couldn't hurt to plan ahead, especially since we don't have to invest anything in that expansion now."

Tom nodded sagely before looking at Lance, eyes assessing. "You've got sensible ideas, young man," he said. "I hear you're doing an internship with Todd and Amos here. That's also very sensible. Nowadays, young architects don't really value the hands-on part of things. If you can understand the basics of the building process, it'll save you and your future clients a whole heap of trouble in the coming years."

Lance was blushing again, and I couldn't help but smile at his adorableness. I also felt proud of him, which I'll admit was a little ridiculous, and I hoped he felt as much pride in himself for winning everyone over with his ideas.

"You think Lance could sit with you as you hash out the plans?" I asked Tom, knowing I was so overstepping my boundaries and doing it anyway.

The old man chuckled. "Jake, son, you are a pain in the ass, but I was about to suggest Lance come spend some time with me, if he wants to anyway."

Lance looked excited, then resigned, shaking his head and saying he wouldn't want to intrude. Thankfully, Tom stopped that train of thought quick enough. "If you want to do this kind of work, it'd be good for you to spend some time with an active architect. Back when I started, it was common for young people to job shadow experts in the field, like an apprentice. Nowadays, it just seems you go through school and they want to dump you in front of clients. No, son, that's not the best way. You come on over and I'll show you what all I do."

Lance was smiling then, and as he and Tom worked out the details, Todd contacted Linc to make sure he could free up Lance's time when Tom was available. After they agreed on some days and times, we all gathered around the table and chatted as we ate the take-out I'd brought for dinner.

Doc and Amos left with Tom after dinner, saying it was getting late and they needed to get home. Then Ash went to help Donna and Louisa put the little ones to bed, leaving just Todd, Lance, and me in the kitchen.

Todd spoke to me about how we needed to distribute the financial commitments, especially if I was planning to live in one of the condos. It would be three times larger than my current one, and initially I'd thought I was going overboard with its size and scope. But one thing my friends Todd and Ash had taught me was life came at you fast and you never knew when much more space could be useful.

Already, I had a brother I only recently met and whom I believed would one day be living with me. And looking at Lance, even though it was way too early for such thoughts, I could imagine what it'd be like to have an architect husband like him working in a well-lit studio space the large condo could provide.

When Lance looked back at me questioningly, I winked and quickly pushed those thoughts to the back of my mind. I should probably go on a few more dates with the guy before I announced my undying love and invited him to move in with me. But then, it never hurt to plan ahead.

TWENTY-FIVE

LANCE

J AKE REALLY WAS A bit pushy. Some of it reminded me of my father, but the biggest difference was that Jake pushed me toward my goals, whereas Dad pushed me toward his own.

Things got really busy for me after that night at Todd's. Most days, I divided my time between Tom and the construction company. I found everything Tom was teaching me to be intriguing. I mean, he was old school, even proudly so. His software had been developed in the early two thousands and likely way outdated by now, but it did the job well enough.

Tom also taught me a few things about drafting, which he did longhand. I was certain some software program could do it a lot quicker, but I knew I'd learn about that in school. What I was learning from Tom felt important and relevant to my chosen profession, and I tried to absorb as much of his knowledge and experience as I could.

One day, Tom announced we'd be going on a field trip and then drove me around the county, pointing out examples of different house styles and even visiting a few buildings he'd designed himself over the years. I especially loved the old Victorian structures around this part of the country. Whether they be the huge plantation style homes like Todd and Ash lived in, or the smaller homes called dogtrots, which were basically long houses with a huge open breezeway in between, I found all of it interesting.

Meanwhile, Todd and Linc had begun pulling me into discussions that involved the utilization of the drafts and plans, letting me see what it was like to turn them into reality.

Jake and I were definitely getting closer, too. We went out almost every Friday night, sometimes to a nice restaurant or to a movie, but as the weather warmed up, we spent more of those Friday nights walking or picnicking.

When I finally received an acceptance letter from Vanderbilt that spring, I almost collapsed in relief. I'd done the budget over and over in my head, and although the money Allen had given me from his portion of our grandparents' trust would cover most of Vanderbilt's tuition, it wouldn't cover all the costs. I wouldn't have a choice in that I'd have to take out at least a few student loans.

I'd also managed to convince Todd he needed to put me on the payroll, so at least during the summer, I'd be making some money to supplement the costs of going to school.

It shocked me that the first person I wanted to tell when I opened my acceptance letter was Jake. I, of course, wanted to overthink that. But instead, I grabbed my phone and pushed the call button on his number and waited for him to pick up.

"Hello, Lance. Is anything wrong?" he asked, causing me to chuckle. I rarely called him and never during the day like this, preferring to text instead, so it made sense he'd be concerned.

"No, I just got some good news and wanted to share it with you."

"Cool, hold on for a moment and let me step outside."

I heard him tell someone he'd be back soon, and I immediately felt guilty for disturbing him at work. I was being silly. People got accepted into school all the time. Why did I think that justified pulling him out of a meeting?

I was beginning to regret my decision to call him when he came back on the line. "Okay, Lance, tell me your good news."

"Um, I feel bad for disturbing you now. I mean, it's probably not a big..."

"Sweetheart," he said, interrupting me and speaking with the sexy as hell Southern drawl he only used when either extremely tired or to calm down one of his overly dramatic clients. "Stop fretting and tell me your news."

"I got accepted into Vandy!"

"Whoo-hoo!" Jake hollered, and it sounded like he was jumping up and down too. "Baby, that's awesome. Let's celebrate. Want me to come get you?"

I laughed. "I'd love that, but I should probably stay close to home tonight. I've got to get up early to meet Tom, then I'm working with Linc on a project in McMinnville."

"Then why don't I bring dessert and Champagne to celebrate with your family?"

I had to think for a moment what he meant by my family. Allen, Gib, and the girls, of course. It was still too soon to admit, but I'd come to think of Jake as my family, too. "You don't have to do that, but if you're willing, yeah, I'd like to celebrate. This is a really big deal for me."

"Yes, it is, baby. I'll wrap up this meeting and then I'll head your way."

I'm not sure why I felt emotional, but I did. No one ever acted this excited about me or my accomplishments. Jake was nothing if not genuine, so I knew his excitement for me came from his heart.

"Thank you, Jake. It means a lot to me."

"Of course. Okay, I better get back in there and force my employees to stop droning on and get with it. Oh, do you mind if I bring Derek? He's supposed to spend the evening with me."

"That'd be great," I said. It would be. I liked Derek more as I got to know him. He was smart and witty and was actually quite different personality-wise from his brother. Jake was outgoing and extroverted in every way, while Derek was quieter and much more thought-oriented. He was good with people like Jake was, but he didn't seem to seek them out in quite the same way.

When I hung up with Jake, I was feeling a little nervous about telling Allen my news. I mean, I would never have made a big deal out of anything with Dad. I'd just mention something like an acceptance letter to him over dinner, as just some casual conversation. Mostly because Dad would just assume I'd get into any place I tried for, and why celebrate a given? Over the past few months, I'd worked hard to keep myself from feeling bitterness and resentment toward my father. But if I continued down my current line of thinking, I'd unravel all of that progress in mere minutes.

I also didn't want to paint my brother with the same brush as our father, so I dialed Allen's phone before I could talk myself out of it.

"Hello? Lance?" Allen said.

"Hey, Allen. Sorry to bother you at work but um, I just wanted to tell you that Jake is coming by tonight to celebrate." I had to swallow hard before I could continue. "Um, we're celebrating 'cause I got accepted into Vanderbilt..."

"Really?" Allen asked, interrupting me, not unlike Jake had a moment earlier. "Brother, that's so amazing! Yeah, we all should celebrate, unless you prefer it to be just you and Jake."

I chuckled. "No, if you are willing, I'd like my whole family to be there."

"Cool, I'll beg off and come home early. Hey, do you mind if Mom comes too? She was supposed to come tonight to watch some show she and the girls have gotten addicted to on Paramount."

I chuckled. I was addicted to it too. "Yeah, that'd be great," I said.

"Awesome. I am so excited you'll be going to school where I'm working. Maybe you can ride with me sometimes, too." His comment immediately made me worry about where I was going to get a car. I couldn't depend on Allen, who worked long and odd hours, to get me back and forth to Nashville. But I needed to shove that worry aside for another day. Tonight, we'd celebrate the first major accomplishment of what, in many ways, I considered to be my new life.

Before letting myself get too distracted thinking about tonight, I hopped into the shower to rinse the day's dirt away. Even though I'd spent the last couple hours working with Tom, I'd helped out at the McMinnville build site that morning, and had more than a little sawdust still in my hair. Then I got dressed and went downstairs, determined to plan for a celebratory feast that even the girls would enjoy.

Usually, at least when I had money, I'd have sprung for pizzas, but money wasn't something I had much of these days. Still, knowing how much the girls loved to make their own pizzas, I grabbed the pita bread they used for crust and began prepping the ingredients for everyone to make their own.

I had just put the sliced pepperoni and Canadian bacon back in the refrigerator when the girls rushed into the house. The noise and chaos of three girls getting home from school was the same every day. Always a mixture of laughter, arguing, and coats and backpacks being strewn around the house.

"Girls," I hollered. "Make sure you hang your coats and backpacks up. Do you have homework?"

They walked into the kitchen and, seeing the pizza fixings spread out on the counter, began to cheer. "Yeaa, pizza night!" Chrissy shouted.

I smiled. "Yeah, we're having a party tonight to celebrate my getting into Vanderbilt. So, if you have any homework, you need to get it done now, before everyone begins showing up."

Before I could get all that out, all three girls were squealing and jumping up and down in a circle around me.

"Yay, Uncle Lance got into Vanderbilt," they chorused.

I was shocked that even my elementary-age nieces knew how important it was to get accepted into that school. Or, at least, they knew how important it had been to me. Such perceptive little beings.

All three girls wrapped their arms around me in a huge bear hug. Emotions whirled through me, and I had to work fast to avoid tears leaking out of my eyes and causing them concern.

"Okay, homework," I said, swallowing around the lump in my throat. "Go on and get started." I didn't have to ask twice because, within a moment, each one sat down at the dining table with books and papers spread out in front of them.

I marveled at how quickly they had become my real family. Even Chrissy no longer looked at me with suspicion. Ruby was still my biggest champion, and she'd also become my little buddy. When we watched TV, or even when we ate, Ruby would sit next to me. Sometimes I think it was to steal my popcorn since she and I liked the same kind, but it felt good either way. Like I somehow mattered in a way I never had before.

The girls were just finishing their homework, and I was pulling the toppings back out of the refrigerator for the pizzas when Allen, Catherine, and Gib all walked in at the same time.

"Congratulations," Catherine said first and pulled me into a hearty embrace. I chuckled when she bear-hugged me, which she was doing more and more often these days. Allen hugged me next, and then Gib, both of them congratulating me too.

Not long after that, Jake and Derek arrived. Derek shook my hand in congratulations, which was a little awkward but very sweet, and as soon as he stepped aside, Jake pulled me into an embrace and kissed me softly on the lips. "Congratulations, honey," he said.

I felt overwhelmed by everyone's kindness and all the focus being on me. Unable to do anything else, I clung to Jake, and he tightened his hold as I lost the war with the tears that had been threatening since I'd called him several hours ago.

"Baby, are you okay?" Jake whispered in my ear, which caused me to lose it even more as I buried my face in the crook of his neck. I don't even know how many minutes passed before I felt ready to pull back from the warmth and safety of his arms.

"Yeah, I mean, I just didn't..." I got choked up again and had to take a moment to get myself back together. "It's just that I..."

"It's that you aren't used to people caring," Allen said with a sad expression.

I nodded but couldn't find the words.

Catherine came over and put her arm around me. "Well, sweetheart, we all care now."

"Thank you," I managed to say, and seeing the concerned look on my nieces' faces, I smiled to ease their worry. "Now, let's get this party started."

Twenty-Six

Jake

MY HEART BROKE FOR Lance. Even I had a family that cared, at least conditionally, before they kicked me out. Mom would always make a fuss over our birthdays and Dad would proudly tack our papers up on the refrigerator if we got a good grade in school.

I felt a surge of protectiveness for this incredible, sweet man, holding him as he wept at the positive attention he was getting. It hurt that he hadn't had someone ever show pride in his successes. I glanced at Allen more than once and saw similar emotions war across his face.

This father of theirs must really be a jerk.

Once the emotional moment had passed, however, it was a true party. Well, one with young kids and a teenager, anyway.

I'd stopped off and bought a huge Costco cake after work, then Derek and I had hit a party store and bought as many helium-filled balloons as we could fit in the car.

After everyone had made their pizzas, the girls pulled out some board games, and we all played and laughed until they had to go to bed.

I couldn't help but enjoy how quickly Derek and Chrissy connected. Not unlike siblings, they squabbled over how the games were played, but then they'd both end up laughing out loud over whatever rule they were trying to make up.

If tonight was any indication, my little brother had a natural ability to connect with kids. He'd said he wants to work with mechanical things as a future career, but his easygoing nature and friendly demeanor made me think he could also be a fantastic teacher if he ever wanted to go in that direction.

With the evening winding down, I asked Derek if he minded if I went for a short walk with Lance just to have a moment alone with him. He was in the process of helping clean up at the time, so he just shrugged and said sure.

I took Lance's arm in mine and pulled him outside into the chilly spring night, though not so cold that we needed to wear coats. I kept my arm locked in his as we walked up to Lover's Lane, as it was called, and sat at one of the benches overlooking the parkway.

When I put my arm around him, he snuggled in. "You still okay?" I asked.

"Mm-hmm," he responded, but didn't say anything more.

I kissed the top of his head and we just sat together, cuddling in the cool night air for a while.

"I don't think I ever knew what it meant to be a family," Lance finally said. "Or to have people who care about you and are genuinely happy for you when good things happen, with no agenda behind it."

I knew Lance was talking about his father. He cuddled back into my side, which I suspected had as much to do with seeking warmth as it did wanting to be close, and I relished the feeling of his body pressed against mine.

"You're getting cold, wanna walk back?" I asked.

He shook his head. "In a moment. Right now, this feels good."

"You know," I said after a little more time sitting silently together, "it doesn't matter where you were accepted, it only matters that you're pursuing your dreams and they seem to be coming true."

He pulled back and met my eyes. "I've never had anyone say anything like that to me before. It's always been, 'you have to be the best, the smartest, the hardest worker.' I don't even know how to process what you just said."

"I-I'm sorry, I didn't mean to offend you," I stammered a bit, suddenly afraid I'd gone too far.

He laughed and gave me a peck on the lips. "No, you didn't offend me. It's just shocking, all of this is shocking. I mean, I can intellectually understand how getting accepted to a prestigious architectural program when I didn't even major in art is a big deal, but growing up, achievements were simply expected of me. Nothing to celebrate."

I sighed in frustration. Not with Lance, but for all that he'd gone though as a kid that he was only beginning to unpack. Growing up with parental expectations could be beneficial, depending, but setting that bar impossibly high at every turn led to a lifetime of never feeling good enough.

"Listen, I don't want to overstep here, but accomplishments aren't something to be expected. Many people go their whole lives without accomplishing much more than getting out of bed and going to jobs they hate. That doesn't make their lives good, bad, or otherwise, it's just life. But Lance, you've not only surpassed that, you've bucked the life you were told you had to live and you're pursuing a dream. Regardless of if it comes true, which I have every confidence it will, that's something to be proud of. I'm certainly proud of you."

I waited until Lance made eye contact with me again before continuing. "Baby, just because you were raised without the kudos doesn't mean you didn't deserve them. And you deserve them now."

I hoped I wasn't making Lance feel uncomfortable with my frankness, but dammit; he needed to know how amazing he was and believe it. I stared out over the parkway for a few moments, collecting my thoughts before I carried on. "When I was kicked out of my parents' home, I lived on the street and, to be honest, it's a miracle I survived. I saw more than one kid my age get caught in the undercurrent and later found dead either from a drug overdose or violence. I don't talk about this very often because, frankly, it's painful to remember, but I got lucky. I was taken into custody and put into a group home that led to me being fostered by two extraordinary women. They saved my life, in more ways than one, and it took me a long time to feel worthy of their kindness and love."

I paused long enough to pull Lance back into my arms and also get my emotions under control. He gave my neck a gentle kiss and leaned his head on my shoulder, which I took as his support and encouragement to continue when I felt ready.

"There were lots of ugly nights when I would spin out of control, afraid of losing them, afraid of everything really. Then the next day I'd feel bad about what I'd done or said." I chuckled at the hard memories.

"I'll never forget what my foster mom, Claire, said every time I came out of those episodes. 'You've got to celebrate the small accomplishments.' Life is seldom the big things, Lance. For me as a teenager, accomplishments were things like not screaming at my loved ones when I was afraid. Or managing to talk about my fears instead of destroying my bedroom wall."

I looked down at Lance and kissed the top of his head again. "Baby, tonight was one of the big things, and, of course, we celebrate that, but you've got to celebrate the small things, too. Like standing up to your dad, reconnecting with your brother, going out on a date with me..."

Lance chuckled at that last one, causing me to do the same thing. "I think that's a big accomplishment, though, 'cause you know I'm all that *and* a bucket of chicken."

"Crispy or grilled?" Lance asked, teasing me. "And who knew chickens could have an ego the size of the state?" I quietly crowed like a rooster, and Lance barked out a laugh. God, I loved him like this, playful and giving back as easily as he got. Incidentally, the first time he ever teased me that way was also a small accomplishment, not just for him but for us.

Just then he shivered, and I stood pulling him up with me. "Come on, you need to get warmed up and I need to get my teenage brother back to Nashville so he'll be able to stay awake tomorrow in school."

As we walked back to the house, Lance continued to lean against me, and we held hands the whole way. When we reached the front porch, he stopped us from going inside. "Thank you, Jake. I've never had someone mean as much to me as you do. I mean, I like that we're moving toward whatever this is, but I like it even more that you are becoming my friend." He looked shy for a moment before he smiled. "You were the first person I wanted to tell about my acceptance into Vanderbilt. You matter a lot to me. Hopefully, that won't scare you off."

I cupped his face in my hands and kissed him gently on the lips. "You matter a lot to me, too, and I don't chase off easily."

His smile turned mischievous. "Um, that's not what I've heard, *player.*"

"What?" I asked and began tickling him as he jerked the door open and rushed inside.

I caught him before we got into the kitchen, where everyone else was, and pushed him gently against the wall. "I'm not going away, at least not until you tell me to. I *might* have been a player once upon a time, but it's 'cause no one ever meant much to me. This," I said, pointing my finger between us, "is more. Call it friendship or something else, but I'm not being a player with you, okay?"

Lance, still smiling, nodded before tilting his head up for another kiss. I obliged, intending to keep it as chaste as possible since we could have an audience at any moment, but I couldn't resist pressing my body into his as he sagged against mine.

I don't know what made this so different, being with Lance, but that's how it felt. I was over the moon for this guy and he seemed to feel the same way. He'd told me he was largely inexperienced, and aside from casual dating and hookups, this was completely uncharted territory for me, too. The idea of being in a real relationship, of calling a man my boyfriend and sharing all aspects of my life with him, excited and terrified me a little, but I wanted that with Lance.

TWENTY-SEVEN

LANCE

I WAS NOW OFFICIALLY on the payroll at Todd's company, working with him and Linc and spending some time with Amos, Todd's dad. My job hadn't changed much, though, and that was fine with me since I enjoyed it. Mostly, I remained the gofer, chasing down tools, providing an extra set of hands to hold things in place, loading and unloading rigs, and doing whatever else was needed to help keep projects on track and moving forward.

I was also working more with Tom, who'd begun to ask my opinion about design and included me as much as possible in his day-to-day activities. He even talked to me about running his own business, since I might be doing the same someday if I struck out on my own, and I soaked up every ounce of wisdom he bestowed on me.

The Fourth of July crept up on me and, with it, the opportunity to finally meet Jake's foster mothers. They were having a party at their home in Nashville and the plan was to walk down to a local park afterward to watch a fireworks display.

I liked the two older women immediately. Of course, when I first met Anita, I was shocked that someone so laden with tattoos would ever be allowed to be a foster parent. She looked intimidating, to say the least, but I came to realize in talking with her that beyond the tough exterior, she was a softy at heart.

Anita's wife, Claire, was her opposite. Claire made me think of a cuddly, younger version of Mrs. Santa Claus. She was slightly taller than Anita, had perfectly coifed hair, and wore a beautiful red, white, and blue dress for the occasion. Everything about this woman screamed *well put together mom*.

Derek seemed like he'd been theirs his entire life and he fussed with them like any teenager when they refused to let him shoot off the larger fireworks or leave to hang out with a group of teens I'd seen drinking wine coolers on our way to the park.

But he didn't seem angry, just annoyed like a typical put-upon teenager.

Jake lounged out by the grill with a group of other guys I'd been introduced to, but couldn't remember their names. All the men seemed to be about the same age as his foster moms and kept laughing at things Jake said.

I ended up helping bring stuff in and out of the kitchen as I got to know the hosts better and, more importantly, got to see where Jake had spent his formative years.

When we finally all sat down to eat, Jake forced his brother to scoot over so he could sit next to me. It was the smallest of gestures, but still made my heart skip a beat, and his winking at me as he pressed his leg against mine underneath the table had me blushing.

I'd never been to a backyard cookout before. My father was way too snooty for such affairs. His parties were usually organized by a professional party planner with the precision he exercised in most areas of his life.

This was quite the opposite. Low-key, welcoming, and without pretense. Everyone appeared relaxed, talking and laughing as they ate from paper plates and fished drinks out of a cooler. Even Derek was right in the mix, seeming at ease chatting and chuckling with people twice his age. Mostly, I sat quietly, watching all the activity and meeting new people as they came over to introduce themselves.

It's not that I felt overwhelmed. I mean, everyone was too nice and friendly for that. It's just I didn't know how to mingle and interact with everyone, not in this type of free for all. It reminded me of a frat party only with less drinking, not that I had other family get-togethers to compare it to.

As the party wound down, the entire group helped clean up. People helped put the kitchen to rights, and set trash bags out along the curb. Then everyone collected their lawn chairs as we all walked the three blocks to the park. It was all very strange but oddly comforting.

Jake hadn't really kept me close during the party, mostly hanging out with his friends while manning the grill, but he took care to touch base with me every so often. Occasionally, I would see him searching the crowd for me and when we made eye contact, he'd smile or nod. I knew that was his way of checking to see if I was okay. His keeping an eye on me felt good, like we really were there together even if not joined at the hip, and I had to wonder if this was what having a boyfriend was like. He stuck close to me as we walked to the park, and probably would've held my hand had we not been hauling our chairs.

When we found a space large enough for the group, we all set out our chairs and the party continued. Jake placed his chair next to mine and after we both sat down, he took my hand in his. "You okay?" he asked.

"Yeah, your family's great."

"They really are, aren't they?" he said, smiling, and I saw the genuine love he felt for them in his expression. My heart broke because I knew I didn't feel the same about my father. Hell, it'd been months since I arrived on Allen's doorstep and, aside from a few demanding texts and that one nasty email, I hadn't even heard from Dad. I wasn't exactly surprised by that, but it still hurt.

As a local school band began to play patriotic music, I thought about my brother, the girls, my brother-in-law, and even Allen's mom. In the time I'd lived in Crawford

City, they had become more my family than my father had ever been.

The friendships I'd developed made me feel like I also had an extended family. Todd and Ash, Doc and Amos, and, of course, Linc, had welcomed me into their lives without question. I considered Tom less of a friend and more of a mentor, someone I respected and felt gratitude toward for helping me learn about my chosen profession, something I'd only dreamed about until now. Working with him helped me realize beyond a shadow of a doubt that I wanted to be an architect.

And, of course, there was Jake. I might well be falling in love with him, even though I didn't really know what that was supposed to feel like. I did know, though, how I felt a jab of pain in my heart if I went a day without at least hearing from him. How even the slightest touch, like the way he held my hand right now, sent my heart soaring.

If someone asked, I'd say Jake was my boyfriend. But he was more than that. He made every day brighter somehow, and in matter of months, he'd also become my best friend. My person.

I lifted his hand to my mouth and kissed it just as the first burst of fireworks painted the night sky. The fireworks seemed to symbolize my feelings for Jake. Powerful, surprising, exciting, blazing, beautiful...all swirling together in a dazzling burst that lit up my whole world. As if this man, my boyfriend, was my own personal firecracker.

Once the fireworks show ended, we all dragged ourselves back to Jake's parents' house. The guests got quietly into their cars after saying goodbye and lots of *nice to meet you's* to me, leaving just the core group of us.

"Well, I don't know about y'all," Anita said, "but I'm plum worn out." She hugged Jake and then me and, after saying she expected to see a lot more of me now, headed to her bedroom.

"That woman has no tolerance for anything past her bedtime nowadays," Claire said, looking just as tired as her wife. We chuckled as she, too, wished us a good night and went up to bed.

Derek had already checked out, lying on the sofa in the living room and tapping away on his phone. I assumed to text his friends. Jake went over and ruffled his hair before telling him he'd see him this weekend.

"Yeah, sounds good," Derek said without even looking up.

Jake just shook his head but smiled as he walked toward me. "Night, Derek," I said, and he managed to look up at me and smile. "Night, Lance," he said, then quickly looked back down at his phone when it dinged again.

We headed out to Jake's car and when the front door closed behind us, Jake said quietly, "He was texting a boy I think he has a bit of a crush on. The kid just moved here a few months ago."

I chuckled. "I wish I'd had the nerve to date a guy back in high school. My dad would've had a fit if I'd even attempted it."

"Yeah, same here," he said, looking sad.

Jake appeared so cheery and playful most of the time, it was easy to forget the pain and rejection he'd endured growing up. But I knew all the hurt his teenage self had experienced remained inside him, just below the surface, because that's where mine lived too.

"But hey, there's a silver lining," I said, trying to lift the mood back up. "It's better dating now when we don't have anyone to force us to live by some curfew. We can do whatever we want, when we want."

He smiled. "Speaking of, wanna spend the night tonight?"

The question caught me off guard. Up until now, we'd not pushed things sexually. I mean, I had wanted to a few times, but the fact that Jake usually picked me up at my brother's place in Crawford City, and I'd never been to his place in Nashville, had put the skids on much of anything physical.

"Um, like at your condo?" I asked stupidly.

"Yeah," he said sheepishly. "At my condo...with me."

"That would be a heck yeah," I said, grinning wide. Jake laughed, sounding a little relieved, and he gave me a quick kiss before we climbed into his car.

As we drove toward his condo, I checked my phone as a way to distract myself from the nerves that had just begun to surface at the prospect of finally being intimate with Jake.

When I absently opened up my text messages, my eyes snagged on one from my father. It'd been such an amazing night, I foolishly thought maybe he was turning over a new leaf. Maybe he was texting to say he missed me, like any of the people I'd begun to see as my family would've done if we'd not seen each other for months on end.

Opening his text proved to be a massive mistake.

Dad: *I can't believe after all I've done for you, you'd treat me like this. You are worthless. From this point on, you aren't my son.*

I practically threw my phone into the console as my stomach churned. "Jake, can you please pull over?" I asked in a panic, trying to force down the bile threatening to spew at any moment.

He quickly navigated to the side of the road and as soon as he stopped, I flung the door open and barely had time to clear the car before everything I'd eaten at the cookout came back up.

I was bent over, still coughing and sputtering, when I felt a hand gently rub my back and an uncapped bottle of water appeared at the edge of my vision. "Oh shit," I said. "I'm so sorry, Jake."

"Don't be sorry, sweetheart. Are you okay?"

"Yeah, but I think I'd like to go home, if that's okay."

Even though I wasn't looking at him, I could tell he was nodding. When it was clear I wouldn't puke again, Jake escorted me back to the car, and I buckled myself in while he came around to the driver's side.

"Too soon?" Jake asked as we began to move along the road again.

"Oh, no. Sorry, Jake, no. That had nothing to do with you. It was something my dad just texted me that caught me off guard, is all."

"Oh," Jake said before we rode in silence for several miles. I let my head fall back against the headrest, closed my eyes, and forced myself not to cry. I'd rather not make Jake's night worse than I'd already made it by bailing on staying the night, so I didn't pay attention to where we were going.

When Jake put the car in Park about ten minutes later, too soon to be back in Crawford City, my eyes popped open and I looked around, startled.

"Where are we?" I asked as I stared at the newer-looking building.

"Well, we were almost at my place already, Lance. I'm happy to take you home, if that's what you still want, but I'd also like to just take care of you. I happen to know a little bit about how parents can rip your heart to shreds, and I can see how upset you are. We don't have to do anything. I just want to comfort you."

The tears that I'd barely held back but remained so close to the surface erupted. I hid my face in my hands, once again embarrassed by my reaction. I heard Jake's seatbelt unlatch and within moments, strong hands pulled me up against him and the console that separated us.

"Shh," Jake soothed as I sobbed. "It's all okay, baby. It'll all be okay."

It took me several minutes to get myself under control. Fuck my father for making me feel like this. *Fuck him.* If I was no longer his son, then he wasn't my father anymore, either. It was time to let him go.

That thought struck me again, and I had to shake my head not to burst into tears again.

Jake managed to get me up to his condo, pulled off my shoes, and laid me on his sofa. He disappeared down the hallway a moment and reemerged with a blanket in hand, then lifted me up and back down onto his lap before covering us both.

We remained fully clothed, and maybe we'd fall asleep this way, but it didn't prevent me from sinking into the warm, protective cocoon of Jake's body. He kept his word of only wanting to comfort me, and he did so for what felt like hours, tenderly running his fingers through my hair and whispering sweet, reassuring words.

I'd been mortified at getting so emotional in front of Jake, especially after spending such an amazing afternoon meeting his family and friends. My father's hateful text had unleashed a torrent of packed down feelings I'd been numb to for years that had nowhere to go but straight through my heart with barbs attached. But if Jake thought of me as the emotional basket case I felt like, it didn't show. If anything, my breakdown seemed to bring out the caregiver in him all the more. My boyfriend really was an amazing man.

I must've fallen asleep in Jake's lap because I woke up the following morning snuggled into him. I don't know when he had moved from holding my head to crawling next to me on the sofa but I was spooning him from behind, my nose tucked into his neck. Jake was breathing gently, still very much asleep.

Although I'd much rather have stayed there, feeling his chest rise and fall with each breath, my bladder demanded I get up to use the bathroom. Jake stirred and objected as I began to pull away, reaching for me with his eyes still closed, which caused me to snicker. He stretched and yawned as I extracted myself and began to climb over him.

"So, sleepyhead, where's your bathroom?" I asked and Jake popped an eye open and pointed toward the hallway to my right.

"You'll find new toothbrushes in the righthand drawer," he called after me as I quickly rushed down the hall.

When I emerged from the bathroom minty fresh, I found Jake in the kitchen making coffee. "Hey," I said as I walked in and sat on a stool at the counter.

"Hey," he said before he came over and kissed me. "You okay?" he asked.

"Um, embarrassed beyond belief, but otherwise okay."

That earned me a small smile. "No need to feel that way. I've been where you are. I get it."

"Yeah, but so much for our romantic night."

"There'll be plenty of time for that." Jake's fingers grazed my chin and lifted it up until I was looking at him. "When I broke down, I had two incredible women to help me pick up the pieces. This is my turn to return the favor. Thank you for trusting me to take care of you last night. That I got to cuddle with one of the cutest men in Tennessee made it extra worth it."

"You mean the biggest crybaby in Tennessee."

Jake didn't laugh. Instead, his soft expression didn't change as he continued to hold my face. "Baby, you have every right to feel the way you do. Parents aren't supposed to reject their kids. Trust me, years of therapy have taught me that healthy families don't toss their kids away. They love each other unconditionally. You might be an adult age-wise, but you're still the kid in this situation. None of this is your fault, Lance. Your father failed you as a parent."

Jake's blunt words hit me hard, and I thought of how he'd been abandoned as a teenager. I had at least finished college and had someone to turn to, even though I honestly didn't know my brother very well at the time. Jake had had no one. So, I wasn't even going to try to argue with him. Besides, I knew he was right. It was a parent's job to love unconditionally, and my father...didn't.

"Thank you, Jake. I hear you, and I understand. It's just I'm not used to breaking down in front of someone I'd rather impress."

Jake just shook his head. "I'd rather you be yourself. A man who works through his emotional crap is much sexier to me than one who stuffs it all down, then blows up when it gets to be too much."

I nodded. "Yeah, but that's probably what you witnessed last night."

"Baby, emotions aren't always front and center. Sometimes they have to marinate a while before you can confront them. And sometimes they blindside you and leave scars. The point is, you're dealing with things as they come now rather than running from your feelings, and that's admirable."

Jake kissed me, then went back to his coffee pot that'd finished brewing. "What do you like in your coffee?" he asked.

"Cream, if you have it. No sugar."

Jake prepped both our cups and poured us coffee, then asked if I minded having it out on his balcony.

He led the way, and I nearly dropped my cup as I took in the stunning view of downtown Nashville. The view alone must've cost him a fortune, never mind the sleek and spacious condo itself. I hadn't really thought much about Jake's financial situation until now. I knew he was investing in Todd's commercial property in Crawford City, and I knew he worked with celebrities, but I didn't really put two and two together.

I wished that realization didn't make me feel uncomfortable. Just because he had money didn't mean he'd be like my father. Everything I'd learned about this man and witnessed for myself indicated he was, in fact, my father's opposite. But I couldn't deny the precariousness of my own financial situation, which likely wouldn't change until well after graduating from Vandy, and I didn't want that to impact our relationship more than it already had.

When we sat down on the balcony, me on a patio chair and Jake on the outdoor sofa, I didn't try to hide my concern. "Um, Jake. You know I don't have two pennies to rub together, right?" I asked. I'd heard Ash say that to the girls, and feeling it was an apt description of me, I had adopted it as my own.

Jake looked at me, confused for a moment, then around at the balcony and the downtown skyline.

"I didn't either when I started out, Lance. In fact, I lived in a tiny apartment with three other people when I first moved out of my foster moms' home."

I nodded and took a deep breath. "I just don't want you to think I'm taking advantage of you or anything."

Jake laughed. "Baby, nothing about you indicates you are someone who'd take advantage of people. Remember, you're the one who won't even let me take you somewhere you can't foot half the bill."

"Well," I said, pouting, "I think it's important to be on equal footing." A memory came to mind of a college classmate who I'd thought might be interested in me, but he kept asking what my father did for a living and the size of our house. My stomach clenched at the thought that someone might compare me to that gold digger.

"We are and always will be equals, Lance. Now, I worked my ass off for this balcony and the view, and I'd like to enjoy it with my boyfriend, if you don't mind," he said.

Jake was smiling at me. His expression was all sweetness and affection. I sighed and crossed the space between us to sit next to him on his outdoor sofa, which, like his indoor one, was comfortable and built for snuggling.

We sat silently drinking our coffee and looking out over the incredible view. My fear of being seen as a gold digger quickly subsided. I knew I wasn't and, apparently, so did Jake. Besides, as he said, he'd worked hard for this, why not enjoy it with him?

When I finished my last sip of coffee, I stretched and moaned before leaning back into Jake. "So, I'm your boyfriend now, huh?"

Jake's body tensed, but when I turned around to face him, he was grinning wide. "Yeah, I mean, I'd like you to be. Is that okay?" he asked.

I nodded and then took a moment to work up the courage to say what I felt he should know. "It's too soon, Jake, but I need to admit to you that I'm having...I *have* feelings for you. Big feelings."

"Like love feelings?" Jake asked and I felt my face burn with embarrassment and had to look away.

"Well, honestly, I've never been in love so I'm not sure how it's supposed to feel. But if I had to label it, yeah, I think that's what this is." I met his eyes, so full of warmth and compassion, and I hoped he saw the sincerity in mine. "Jake, I think I might be falling in love with you."

He reached up, cupping the back of my head, and pulled me to him. His lips glided over mine, slow and sensual, as if Jake was pouring everything he felt for me into the kiss. "You know I've been feeling that for a while now," he said.

His declaration took me by surprise, and I leaned back against the sofa so I could look him in the eye. "Really? Since when?" I asked, curious.

"Since we went to the chapel together."

I was embarrassed all over again. "You mean the first time I wigged out on you."

Jake chuckled. "You see it as wigging out. I see it as you letting me in. Lance, you're the first romantic partner I've ever had who dropped any and all pretense at the door. You've let me see the real you, and that's who I've fallen for."

I stared at him dumbfounded. "I don't think I did that on purpose. Just, my emotions have been too close to the surface since moving here."

Jake leaned in and kissed me again and when we pulled apart, he pressed his forehead to mine. "Maybe it takes going through the hard stuff to force us to take down the walls long enough to get to know each other. Whatever the reason, Lance, I appreciate you trusting me enough to let me be here for you. You opening up, not being afraid to be vulnerable, is what led me to fall in love with you."

Jake kissed the tip of my nose, and I snuggled back into him. "I think your willingness to let me just feel what I feel, even when it's ugly and messy, has allowed me to fall for you, too. Emotions are strange things, aren't they?" I asked as his muscular arms wrapped around me.

Jake hummed and squeezed me a little tighter. "Strange, yes, but also wonderful."

Twenty-Eight

Jake

I'D NEVER BEEN WITH a man who felt so much like home to me as Lance did. Normally, I'd have been an emotional mess about professing the big L to a guy–not that I ever had–but with Lance, I didn't feel freaked out at all. It just felt right.

After the Fourth of July, when we'd officially become boyfriends, we began spending more time together, at least when our schedules allowed. I'd asked him a couple times to travel out of town with me on business trips but he'd turned me down, saying he wasn't ready for that quite yet. I also knew summer was one of the busiest times in construction and he didn't want to put any unnecessary strain on his coworkers by taking extra time off.

Although I'd love to have a boyfriend who was footloose and fancy-free, I admired his work ethic and keeping to his commitments more than I could say. He seemed to respect mine without question, too, even when I had to bail on our dates a few times to handle PR crises for clients.

After the Fourth, his nieces had made it clear that he needed to spend the next holiday with his family, which caused us both to laugh. One of the twins, Ruby, had been the most vocal. So, for Labor Day, we planned to take over the park near Allen and Gib's home for a big celebration that included my family, Lance's family, and probably most of Crawford City.

Lance's excitement about the event became clear as the holiday drew closer, so he took charge in organizing most of it. The last I heard, all of Todd's family, including Ash's sister and her husband and kids, were planning to attend. I'd also invited Lexie and her friends, as well as our friends who owned the winery, who then invited some of their family members.

Doc had reserved the park for us and as soon the RSVPs started rolling in, it became clear that the facilities wouldn't necessarily accommodate everyone comfortably. So, since this was going to be a potluck, Lance had convinced Todd and Linc to help him build buffet tables.

Then the café got involved. Somehow, our little family picnic had morphed into a full-on community event, which I found very cool. One of the biggest reasons I wanted to move to Crawford City was how friendly and inclusive the community seemed to be, and how much the townsfolk all seemed to like being together.

I'd fully planned to help out with the last-minute planning when the crap hit the fan with Derek. As July came to an end, our birth mother had contacted family services and requested to see him. We'd spent a great deal of time as a family discussing it with Mrs. Lidia, whom we'd all come to consider more as a family friend than simply Derek's caseworker.

Mom ended up taking any decision-making out of our hands, though, when her attorney petitioned the court for visitation. Understandably, Derek was an emotional wreck. As a teenager, the thought of seeing Mom again after being kicked out had messed me up, too. Only that day never came to pass. She hadn't come for me.

Two weeks before Labor Day, Derek was scheduled to visit Mom. I planned to hang out at Anita and Claire's during that time so I could work through my own emotions that had come crashing to the surface. My foster moms had always been my reassuring, safe place when the stinging pain of my birth parents' rejection flared up. It still did, even after all these years, and I didn't want my issues to spill out onto Derek.

I'd shown up early and had breakfast with everyone and purposefully teased Derek about our game rivalry, just to keep the mood light. I even teased him about his new boyfriend, whom he'd officially started dating just last week.

Before Mrs. Lidia showed up, though, he sobered and asked, "Are you okay with me seeing Mom?"

I ruffled his hair affectionately, like I did when I wanted to irritate him before saying, "I'm more than okay with it. I wish she'd come to her senses before putting you through all this."

He nodded. "I wish she'd come to her senses before she allowed Dad to hurt you."

"Me too, buddy," I said on a sigh. "Me too."

Mrs. Lidia arrived a little later and when the two of them had gone, Anita, Claire, and I gathered around the dining table. Like so many times before, when they'd helped me navigate through my complicated feelings about my birth family, they sat waiting for me to speak first. Until, of course, Anita couldn't stand the silence any longer.

"So, tell us what's going on in your head," Anita said. She'd long ago lost her therapist ways when it came to me. Now, she was Mom and just wanted to tackle any problems her kids faced head-on.

"Way to dive right in," I said, causing both her and Claire to chuckle.

"Well, we could beat around the bush if you'd rather."

I smiled. "You know I hate that."

"Not my style either," Anita said.

She did give me a moment, though, as I stared down at my hands while collecting my thoughts. "It's hard to see her connecting with Derek after she abandoned me. I mean, I'm happy for him, of course I am, and it might be the best thing for his healing if she's able to work it out. But I'll always wonder why she didn't do the same for me. She didn't even try."

Anita reached over and took my hand. The tears I had for my birth mom had long ago been cried out, but I still felt the hurt of my own mother not wanting me. The once searing pain of it may have dulled over time, but it remained a pebble-sized ache in my chest that I didn't think would ever go away completely.

I took a deep breath, and feeling that sore spot, rubbed my chest.

"Was I just not worth her love?" I asked. I knew the answer, that I was and am worthy of my mother's love, but I still warred with myself sometimes that maybe I wasn't. Anita had taught me years ago that those were the feelings of a hurt and mixed-up teenage boy, not the man I'd become, but trying to reconcile that as an adult still proved difficult.

"You are worth everything, but you know we don't have the whole story," Anita said before letting go of my hand. "More information will come after Derek gets home. But I suspect, when you were kicked out, she didn't feel like she could come after you. She had a house full of kids back then and if your father decided to reject her too, how would she have survived? What would've become of all your siblings?"

I shook my head. "You know I understand that, but it's hard to convince the little boy inside, the one who only ever wanted to be loved and accepted by his parents, that this wasn't personal. That Derek is somehow worth more to her than me. I know that's not fair to him, and maybe not even fair to her, but that's how I feel."

Both my foster moms nodded, accepting my emotions for what they were and not trying to change my mind. I knew they couldn't fix this, and that wasn't the point anyway. I needed to get this out, get it off my chest before it burned a hole there, and they listened without judgement.

Finally, after we'd sat around quietly for several moments, I took a long deep breath and let it out slowly, allowing my emotions to settle where they may.

My birth parents and my sisters and brothers may be blood relatives but they weren't my family, Derek being the exception. Like I'd told him, family is who you learn to love, and I believed that wholeheartedly because it'd been true for me.

The tears did fall now, but not for my birth mother. "My family, that's you two. You were there when they weren't. You didn't even know me, but you brought me into your home and embraced me like I was your own flesh and blood. Nothing she says or does now will change that."

I reached out and took both my moms' hands and just held them while the tears silently rolled down my cheeks. Nothing more needed to be said and Anita and Claire remained quiet but squeezed my hands, both offering me their support just like they always had.

By the time Derek got back home, I was in a completely different mindset. Although I'd worked through some of my own emotional baggage, I was at a loss anticipating the headspace my brother would be in after seeing our birth mom. I had no experience to draw from there.

Derek came in with Mrs. Lidia and immediately went to his room, not speaking to anyone.

"How did it go?" Anita asked as we all took a seat in the living room.

"I'd rather let Derek tell you, but he did say I could share some of it with you," Mrs. Lidia said, sighing heavily and turning toward me. "Melody was upset when she learned you were in Derek's life now."

That our birth mother disapproved of my connecting with Derek–or hell, even learning of his existence–didn't come as a surprise to me, or probably to Mrs. Lidia either. I'd imagine it was a tough pill for my brother to swallow in the moment, though.

Mrs. Lidia then let out a bitter chuckle and continued. "She spent the entire time trying to convince Derek that your lifestyle was evil and that if he agreed to give it up, he could come back."

"I'm sure there was talk of repenting too, huh?" I asked, and I was barely able to contain my anger.

Mrs. Lidia nodded. "Derek's naturally upset, and he's said he won't see her again, although I can tell that's hurting him, too."

Derek came downstairs then, sat next to me on the sofa, and leaned into my side. "I hate her," he said after burying his face in his hands.

I put my arm around him and said, "I hate what she's putting you through. I also still love her and resent her, and I'm sure you're already familiar with those feelings."

We sat like that for some time, my arm draped across my baby brother's shoulders and him working through his emotions.

Finally, he leaned up and, wiping his eyes, said, "I don't want her to be my family any longer. She doesn't want me back; she wants me to go back to pretending I'm her perfect baby." Derek looked me in the eye, a determined expression on his face. "You're my real family. You accept me for who I am and love me no matter what. That's what's real. What they want me to be, that's not. It's not love either."

I looked over at Anita, remembering when I'd come to that same realization years before. "That's right," I agreed. "It's not real, any of it. Love, real love, isn't conditional."

Derek took a long, deep breath, then sighed. "Okay, I'm done with that, done with them. Mrs. Anita and Mrs. Claire, I'd like for you to adopt me."

Of all the things I'd anticipated may happen, that wasn't it. I flushed because even after I accepted these two women as my parents, I'd refused adoption. I'd refused to give up that one tiny connection I still had to my birth family. Anita and Claire had asked all the way up until my twenty-fifth birthday before they gave up. Still, with me being an adult, they were willing to make me their own. I felt like I was now and honestly, did even then, with or without official paperwork.

"Derek," Mrs. Lidia said. "That would be hard to do. We'd have to get the courts to terminate your parents' rights."

"Then we can wait until I'm eighteen," Derek said. "Regardless, I see how the two of you and Jake are family. A real family, one I want…no, need to be a part of. That's important to me."

I looked at my baby brother, who clearly meant what he was saying, then over at my foster moms. The two women who, in every possible way *except* legally, were my mothers. Without even having to consider it, I said, "If Derek wants to be adopted, I'd like to be too. We can just make it official for both of us."

Anita and Claire were clutching each other's hands as they nodded and cried. I pulled my brave, smart brother up off the sofa and went over to our foster moms, and the four of us embraced in a group hug.

When we broke apart, even Mrs. Lidia was dabbing at tears.

"It'd be our honor to adopt both you boys," Anita said. "But Derek, honey, if you change your mind, you just have to tell us, okay?"

"I won't change my mind. I'm ready," he said without hesitation.

When he looked over at Mrs. Lidia, he said, "Please let the judge know I'll not be meeting with my birth mother again and that I've requested to be adopted by my new parents."

Derek may be a quiet kid, even shy sometimes, but no one could deny his inner strength. My brother had taken the emotional bull by the horns, and I couldn't be prouder.

Mrs. Lidia smiled and nodded in answer to Derek's request, telling us she'd be in touch again soon, and then took her leave.

The four of us ordered pizza and sat around the living room for a few hours watching Netflix. No one said much, I suspect because emotions were still running a little high, so we all just lounged around the living room, hanging out. Like a family.

As soon as I was back home at my condo, I called Lance and filled him in on the emotional upheaval the day had brought. I would've preferred he be here with me, to see and feel his support more than just hear it over the phone, but this being a weeknight meant he'd have an early start tomorrow. Still, none of it had really felt real until I'd told Lance, and I went to bed content in the realization that my brother and I would soon officially be sons of the two loving parents we'd always deserved.

TWENTY-NINE

LANCE

L ABOR DAY POTLUCK PREPARATIONS were more than I'd bargained for. When the nieces all ganged up on me about my not spending the holidays with them, I decided to plan a get-together at Allen's place. What began as planning to host a few friends for a house party had grown, though, into a huge neighborhood party. I swear the whole town had been invited by friends of friends because I'd received RSVPs from locals I hadn't even met yet.

Between work, mentoring with Tom, and all of the party planning, I had very little time for much else. That included being the supportive rock I'd wanted to be for Jake and Derek as they went through a mini-crisis. I'd done what I could do, mainly just offering a sympathetic ear whenever Jake called or texted, but not being there with him depressed me more than I could say. I hoped

I could at least give them both a nice party to take their minds off things and have some fun.

School had begun in late August, which piled on to my already busy schedule and added a huge new wrinkle in being able to see Jake. Luckily, I hadn't been assigned too much homework in my first couple of classes, so I wasn't falling behind. I still felt overwhelmed by everything I'd taken on, though.

By the time the big day arrived, excitement helped ease my exhaustion. Thankfully, as the event grew larger, more people chipped in to help.

Even as a potluck, at least originally, the Crawford City Café offered to donate some food and drinks and provide all the plates and silverware. The high school band teacher had taken over organizing the music, so I didn't have to manage that at all. The high school band had agreed to do a few patriotic numbers, and a few local music groups would be performing throughout the day. As mayor, Doc had volunteered the city's help for setting up and then cleanup afterward. He told me he thought I'd just created an annual city event, which I agreed with even if it'd all been by accident. He also said he took care of the permitting and arranged for some port-a-potties to be delivered, which hadn't even crossed my mind since I'd never organized anything like this before.

People began arriving at ten that Saturday morning and I went out to help the city volunteers set up the tent where the performances were being held. Then Linc arrived with the buffet tables he and Todd helped me make, so we set those up as well as the tables and chairs the local Methodist Church had allowed us to use for the event.

By noon, it seemed the entire town had descended on the park. What looked to me like hundreds of people were going through the buffet line, playing games they'd brought that I hadn't even thought to plan for, and milling around talking to each other.

I lost count of the number of people who stopped and thanked me for planning the event by the time Jake and his family arrived.

"How are you feeling?" Claire asked. "Do you need any help?"

I smiled. "To be honest, I don't know. It seems people who know what they are doing have taken most of the responsibilities off my shoulders. But if you wander around, I'm sure someone would put you to work."

Claire laughed. "I've planned a lot of events, and if you can get people to step up and take on some of the responsibilities, that's a sign you're a true leader."

I wasn't sure what she said was accurate or not, but I was feeling pretty good about the day so far.

Claire and Anita soon went in search of other volunteers to help, while Derek made a beeline for the buffet. Jake and I zigzagged our way through the park, hand in hand, and I noticed he seemed quiet and contemplative today.

"What's going on?" I asked when we reached the other side of the park, away from most of the activity.

He smiled. "Nothing, not really. I'm still reeling from the other night when Derek and I asked to be adopted by our foster moms."

"Are you regretting that?" I asked, concerned.

"No, no, of course not, but..." he said, then paused a moment before shrugging. "It's just there was some hope my parents–my birth parents–would one day see the light and at least apologize for what they put me through. It's silly, but even as an adult, I felt like that was a possibility. Now that we're moving forward with the adoption, it feels like that hope... for some level of reconciliation I'd secretly clung to since they kicked me out, has just died."

I squeezed his hand and leaned into him as we walked toward an area where someone had put up a badminton court.

"Obviously my situation is a bit different, getting kicked out as an adult rather than a teenager," I said. "I knew when I walked out that door, my father would likely never forgive me. I would be the ultimate embarrassment to him. Still, the pain of his rejection still hurts and maybe it always will. I mean, you saw that for yourself when I nearly threw up in your car."

Jake nodded and pulled me into a hug, creating a safe, quiet cocoon with his arms while activity bustled around us. "I'm glad I can talk to you about this, and that you understand," Jake said. "Anyway, I'm mostly happy about the adoption. It's like closing a difficult chapter of my life, and I want to focus on the future, not keep reliving the past."

I smiled at him, wondering if that future would include me. We were about to walk past the game of badminton when Sheriff Cross, a woman I hardly knew, called out for us to join her team.

"Wanna play?" Jake asked, and I shrugged.

"I have no idea how to play badminton, but I guess I could learn. Just keep your expectations very low, and by that, I mean don't have any."

Jake laughed as we took up rackets and joined the game. By the time it was in full swing, we were both laughing at the sheriff and her husband, who was on the opposing team. It was almost like they'd wanted to be on opposite sides just so they could taunt each other.

When I heard the bands start up, which meant it was two o'clock, I excused myself to go make sure everything was proceeding as planned.

Jake stayed to finish playing, and I rushed toward the performance tent.

Weaving through the crowds, I'd just about reached the tent when I ran into someone and almost fell to the ground. I grabbed the man to steady myself and apologetically looked into the face of the person I'd nearly toppled over.

My father's frown stared back at me. "Dad?" I asked as I stepped back. "Why?" I looked around the celebration as it registered that my father really was standing in front of me. Here, in Tennessee. At my event. On a great day, that was about to turn to shit. "Why are you here?"

"Because you won't return my texts or emails and your brother finally told me you were here to stop me from launching a missing persons case. I flew out this morning."

Just then, out of the corner of my eye, I saw Allen and Catherine closing the distance between us.

"Dad, I organized this event, so I've got a couple duties I need to attend to, then maybe we can all get together and talk," I said, trying to sound diplomatic and mask my shock at seeing him here. I really did need to go check on the music lineup but, honestly, it also provided the perfect excuse to step away and gather my thoughts before talking with him.

I turned to head to the tent when Dad's hand shot out and grabbed my arm, holding me in place. "You need to stop acting like a child and come back with me this instant. It's not too late to get you re-enrolled..."

"Dad, stop. I'm already in school, pursuing what I've always wanted to do. If you've come all this way to try to strong-arm me into doing what *you* want me to, you can just go back home."

I jerked my arm out of his grip just as Allen and Catherine reached us. "I need to go..." I said, trying to tell Allen I was going to check on the bands, but my voice cracked before I could get all the words out.

Catherine took my arm and led me away, just as my emotions were getting the better of me. Allen must've stayed back to block Dad from following us because it was never our dad's way to give up easily. If anything, my becoming emotional would've made him more insistent that I was in over my head here and basically incapable without his guidance.

Catherine didn't let me go until we'd gone all the way back to the house. When I complained that I needed to check on the bands, she just said, "Sweetheart, all that is under control. Come on inside with me and give yourself a moment."

I didn't have the strength to argue as Catherine deposited me in the formal sitting room and returned a few moments later with a glass of iced tea. Unsweetened, thank God, since I'd yet to develop a taste for the sickly sweet stuff favored down here. I drank the cool tea, thankful to have something cold after being outside in the sweltering humidity for hours.

Seeing my father had been a shock and brought back all the frustration and hurt that had led me to show up unannounced at Allen's door in the first place. Walking through the park with Catherine, though, had given me some time to collect myself and come to terms with having to face Dad now.

"You doing okay?" Catherine asked, sitting down next to me.

"Yeah," I said. "Thanks for getting me out of there and giving me time to get myself together. I just hadn't expected to see him...here."

"Well, I don't think Allen would've dreamed he'd come here."

"Yeah, so Allen told him I was here?"

"I didn't know the whole story, but when Allen saw him pull up and get out of his car, he immediately grabbed my hand and asked me to help find you before your father did. As we were searching, he admitted that your father had called last night saying he'd be filing missing persons papers on you. Allen didn't have the chance to tell you that with everything being so busy today, but it put your brother in a difficult position, and he felt like he had to inform your father you'd come to live here."

I sighed. "It's my fault. I'd told Allen I was going to tell Dad I'd moved to Crawford City, but I chickened out."

"Well, I can't say I blame you. Your father is a tough nut to crack."

"If you mean he's stubborn as a mule, that's an accurate assessment," I said on a sigh. "Anyway, I should get back. I've got a couple things I still need to be looking after at the party."

"Allen and I will try to keep your father occupied until you can talk to him alone," Catherine said as she winked at me.

"Good luck," I said but smiled because I had no doubt, if anyone could handle Dad, this woman could.

I finished the tea, then stopped quickly at the bathroom because I hoped to avoid using the port-a-potties around the park if at all possible. I saw my father talking to Allen as I approached the performance tent and although we made eye contact, I steered clear of him. That was new and different. In the past, I would've never been brave enough to avoid my father. His look of surprise indicated he hadn't expected it either.

After all these months away from him, out from under his thumb, I didn't feel like I really owned him anything. I wanted to focus my efforts and energy on things that mattered to me, positive things that could make a difference at least in some small way. Things like this event.

I rushed into the performance tent and found the band teacher. After verifying everything was going okay, I headed over to where the buffet was being closed down, and people's potluck dishes were being placed out for them to collect on their way home.

Mrs. Cole, who ran the café and more or less oversaw the food arrangements today, smiled and assured me that all was good and I let out a relieved sigh. I took a moment to relax and scan the happy crowd, pleased that things were still going according to plan. I had just spotted Doc and Todd talking on the other side of the performance tent when something caught my eye before I could head in their direction.

Derek was standing near the street that led up to the city hall, arguing with an older man I didn't recognize. Then the man took hold of Derek's arm and began to pull him toward the parked cars.

I sprinted toward them without thinking, hollering, "Sir, you need to take your hands off of him."

The man turned his head and looked back at me, but didn't stop pulling Derek toward what I assumed was his vehicle.

When I reached them, I grabbed Derek's other arm and tugged him out of the stranger's grasp. Within seconds, the man drew back a fist and planted it square in my nose. I didn't even have time to react before I was on the ground with the man on top of me, pounding me in the face.

I heard Derek yelling, pleading for the man to stop his assault, which must've caught the attention of the crowd. Before he could get in a third punch, someone had shoved the man off of me and several others soon pinned him to the ground. I heard someone say they'd fetch the sheriff, and another had taken off to find a doctor.

Several townsfolk crouched around me, asking if I was alright. I didn't know if I was or not. It'd all happened so fast, and the world seemed to move in slow motion now. Without moving my head too much, I looked around to see if Derek was still in jeopardy but the kid had vanished. That was good, it meant he'd gotten away from the man.

Before long, my brother-in-law knelt down next to me, looking over my injuries. I heard him asking questions, but I couldn't quite understand what he was saying.

I noticed the sheriff emerge from the crowd that had gathered and handcuff the man, then drag him away from the scene.

Gib's voice became more insistent, and it finally registered he was asking me if I was okay. "Lance, Lance...I need you to focus. Can you hear me?" he asked.

I nodded and immediately felt my injuries. My whole face throbbed and I could feel blood trickling down my chin. My nose felt like it was on fire.

I tried to get up, but Gib held me down. "No, stay there until we can get you checked out," he said.

"I dink I'b find, Gib, but my dose urts dike ell."

I could hear I was talking funny. *Did that son of a bitch break my nose?* I wondered.

I'd never been in a fight before, but I'd been hit in the nose when I was a kid playing dodgeball at school. That'd hurt and given me a bloody nose, but this felt worse.

"I dink my dose is broke," I said.

"I'd be willing to bet on it," Gib said. "Okay, y'all help him up and let's get him down to the clinic."

Luckily, Gib's clinic was just down the street, so there was no need for a car, and it had stayed open for the event. My head was beginning to hurt and my nose was still burning, but with two men who flanked me, I got there quickly.

We'd reached the front door when Jake came running up behind us. The guy to my left let Jake take his place as my boyfriend began peppering me with questions. "Are you okay, baby? We had no idea he was coming..."

"I'b okay. Just gonna have dis looked at." Jake was in a near panic, which in my partially incoherent state caused me to chuckle. "I'b da one who's urt. Why are you freaking out?"

Of course, if I'd been in my right mind, I'd have realized he was freaking out because some man had tried to abduct his baby brother, then pummeled his boyfriend. But, at the moment, my mind was still too muddled to work that out on my own.

Before Jake could respond, Gib ushered us inside and whisked me into an exam room. He then began prodding my nose, which hurt like hell.

When Gib looked up my nose with the nasal speculum, I winced at the pain. "That doesn't look good," he said. "I'm going to spray an anesthetic to help reduce the pain, but we'll need to have you taken up to Lebanon's ER for a CAT scan."

"Jit. Dat zucks. You jure, Gib?" I asked.

"I'm pretty sure," he said. "I'm not happy about how the break looks, and you may need surgery."

He left me alone then and seconds later, the nurse practitioner, a woman I'd only met once when I'd come to meet Gib for lunch, came in, I assume to monitor me while Gib got the spray.

One semester of medical school didn't make me an expert, but it did give me enough background that I understood why Gib would be concerned.

He returned a moment later and after applying the spray, we waited a moment for it to kick in before he tried using the nasal speculum again.

"Yeah, it's fractured. Okay, so Allen is outside and he's going to transport us to the hospital. Jake is wanting to come with us."

"No, de needs to stay wid Derek. We'll keep him idformed."

Gib nodded and once again leaving me with the nurse practitioner, left the room, I assumed to tell Jake what I'd said. When he reappeared, both escorted me back out to the waiting area, where Allen and Jake stood talking, concern etched on both their faces. Jake rushed over as soon as he saw me.

"Sweetheart, I'm not happy about you going without me, but I understand and respect your wishes. Just know that Derek is safe. He's shaken up, we all are, but he's okay and he's worried about you too," Jake said, then kissed me sweetly on the forehead.

Feeling relieved and with my nose thankfully numb, I let Jake help me into Gib and Allen's minivan. After I was strapped in, the three of us took off toward the hospital in Lebanon. I waved at Jake as we drove out of the parking lot and he placed his hand over his heart, still looking concerned, and watched the van until we disappeared from view.

THIRTY

JAKE

E'D JUST FINISHED THE last game of badminton. Sheriff Cross was harassing her husband, Danny, for losing even when we were one man short, when I heard Derek screaming for me. As soon as I heard him say the words *Dad* and *Lance*, I took off in the direction of my brother's voice.

I didn't hesitate, didn't even think, but my mind flashed to worst-case scenarios the closer I got to what appeared to be a crowd gathered near the parking area. Two things raced through my head as I ran. The first was that my dad had shown up to create havoc. The man was a hothead at the best of times and when he was angry, like when learning his youngest son wanted to be adopted by foster parents, it could get scary. The second was who the hell would want to harm my boyfriend and how badly was Lance hurt.

The sheriff had kept pace with me as we ran, and when we came over the rise, she took off with a burst of speed. When I reached the scene, I saw two people on the ground. One was Lance, lying flat and unmoving with Gib crouched over him. A group of men were restraining the other person. My father.

Sheriff Cross had already begun reading my father his rights as she pulled out handcuffs I hadn't even known the plain-clothed officer had been carrying. She cuffed him and hauled him up to his feet, then began marching him toward her parked patrol car. I assumed she'd soon be driving him to the county jail in nearby Mayville.

As far as I could tell, Lance was in bad shape. I saw blood running down his chin, and he winced in pain as Gib checked him over. I felt powerless to help, but I could at least give Lance my support and was about to go to him when someone wrapped their arms around me in a bear hug.

I looked down to see Derek clinging to me, hysterical. I knew Lance was in good hands with his brother-in-law, so I turned my attention to Derek. I needed to console my brother.

"Shh, it's okay. It's going to be okay now," I whispered to Derek, who was trembling a little as I held him.

"Is Lance okay?" Derek asked as we watched my boyfriend be slowly escorted toward Gib's clinic by some men I didn't know.

"I'm not sure. I'll go check on him in a moment, but are you okay?"

He nodded, but I could tell he was anything but fine. Sheriff Cross came over then and asked Derek what happened. As he began recounting how Dad had tried to pull him to his car and kept saying he was going to get the 'faggot' out of Derek, my heart dropped.

"Lance saved me. He rushed over and jerked my arm out of Dad's hand." Derek started to cry then, but kept talking. "Dad didn't hesitate. He just began popping Lance in the face over and over. I think he hit him three or four times before he was stopped. Is Lance going to be okay?"

"I don't know," I said helplessly, just as our foster moms showed up.

"Derek, are you okay to stay with Anita and Claire? I want to go check on Lance."

He nodded and wiped at his tears. "I'm going to need to ask you some questions, okay?" Sheriff Cross asked Derek, and he nodded.

"Is it okay if I go?" I asked the sheriff. She nodded, and I hugged Derek, leaving him in the care of our foster moms, as I dashed down the street toward the clinic.

I caught up to them just before they entered the clinic. When I saw Lance, I wanted to lift him into my arms and reassure him everything would be fine and tell him how much I appreciated what he'd done to help Derek. I wanted to tell him I loved him and that I was sorry my father had hurt him. I wanted to say so much, but I didn't get the chance to say any of it before Gib pulled Lance into an exam room.

I paced the floor, unsure whether I should be here or with Derek. But since my brother had the support of our foster moms, not to mention wasn't covered in blood like Lance, I decided I was right where I should be. Well, I'd have preferred to be in the exam room holding Lance's hand, but I'd have to wait for that.

Allen rushed into the clinic just as Gib came back out to the waiting room. "We need to get him to the hospital in Lebanon for CAT scans," he said. "He's got a broken nose but we need scans to confirm the extent of it."

"I'll drive," Allen said without missing a beat. "Mom is with the girls, and said she'd check in with Doc to make sure the event gets shut down properly."

"I want to come," I blurted. "I want to be there with Lance, at the hospital."

Gib nodded and went back into the exam room. I was just about to text Anita when he came back out and told me Lance would prefer me to stay with Derek. Gib smiled when he said, "Lance said Derek needs you more than him at the moment."

Just knowing he was thinking about my baby brother, concerned about his wellbeing when Lance himself was bruised and bleeding, struck me in the solar plexus and it's a wonder I didn't break down right then and there.

Gib ducked back into the exam room and brought Lance out a moment later and I rushed to him. Seeing my boyfriend's beautiful face, swollen and beginning to bruise, filled me with a rage against my father I hadn't even known myself capable of. Lance gave me a half-smile, even though it looked painful, and I assured him Derek was alright and I wouldn't argue about going with him to the hospital. I'd do whatever he wanted me to, even if that meant staying behind.

I helped Lance to the van and watched as he, Gib, and Allen set off for the hospital in Lebanon, having been assured by Gib that he'd keep me updated. Walking back to the park, I saw the sheriff, Derek, and our foster moms sitting not far from where the whole thing had gone down and headed their way.

Their demeanors had completely changed since I'd gone. Sheriff Cross had apparently finished asking Derek questions and instead, talked about what sounded like baseball. "They have been getting better, but they could use a coach," she said as I came closer.

I looked at her in question and she smiled. "I was telling Derek that he should consider helping me coach our local Little League team next season."

I nodded but was confused about what this had to do with anything. Maybe she'd just been making conversation while they waited for me to return. Derek didn't waste any time asking me about Lance. The look on my brother's face told me he wasn't in a place to absorb the news of Dad having broken Lance's nose, so I kept the injury details to a minimum.

"I think he's fine. His brother is driving him to the hospital to have CAT scans run just to make sure, but he was pretty concerned about you. Are *you* okay?" I asked.

Derek shook his head. "No, Dad was...well, he wasn't right. I've never seen him like that. Just so angry. I don't know what would've happened if Lance hadn't been there."

I took a deep breath, more to give myself a moment to figure out what to say. Inside, I was reeling. I wanted to go off and scream or go punch the old man in the face just like he had Lance. But that wasn't what Derek needed. He needed calm reassurance from his big brother.

"He's in custody now, right, Sheriff?" I asked.

She nodded. "I had one of my deputies transport him to the jail in Mayville. Booked him about a half-hour ago."

"Any chance he'll be released tonight?" I asked, trying to school my features while worry coursed through me.

"No, no chance. For one, he's been charged with aggravated assault and there were so many witnesses, my deputies are still collecting statements. On top of that, I've learned the court had a no-contact order in place for Derek, which your father just violated. So, he'll have to spend some time in jail."

"Is it possible he'll be released on bail? I don't want him showing back up."

"No, nothing is going to happen on a long holiday weekend. Besides, if he violates the order by coming after Derek again, he won't get a second chance, so I doubt he'd try. I'm guessing since he was three sheets to the wind, he wasn't thinking clearly, anyway."

"What? He was drunk?" I asked, surprised. In the fourteen years I'd lived with him, I'd never seen my father take even a sip of alcohol. He'd always been way too pious for that.

"He reeked of the stuff, so we planned on giving him a breathalyzer test at the jail. I haven't heard the results of that yet, but it's likely he'll be charged with public intoxication as well," Sheriff Cross said.

"Derek, have you ever seen Dad drink alcohol?" I asked.

Derek shook his head. "No, he said it was the devil's drink."

"Yeah, this is strange, Sheriff," I said. "It's basically unheard-of for him to even touch alcohol, let alone get sloshed."

She nodded. "I'm sure it'll all make more sense come morning. I'll be getting in touch with your..." The sheriff's words trailed off as her eyes flicked to Anita and Claire before returning to mine. "I'll contact his wife and your other siblings before the day is out, which may give us a better understanding of the whole situation."

I gave Sheriff Cross my contact information, and Anita and Claire did the same with theirs. The sheriff told us that children's services had been notified as well and said she'd be in touch before leaving us to go talk with one of her deputies.

Both Anita and Claire had nodded in understanding, but I could tell this was overwhelming them. Until that moment, I hadn't noticed how much the two had aged since they'd taken me in all those years ago. I quietly resolved to pick up more responsibilities for Derek after today. Even if the adoption went through, they'd need the support.

Knowing Dad was in jail, I asked if Derek was okay to go with Anita and Claire. "I want to stay close and make sure Lance gets back okay," I said.

Derek nodded. "Yeah, and keep us informed, too."

"Of course," I said, and smiled at him. "Our boy Lance was a hero tonight, huh?"

Derek nodded, and I looked over at our moms. "I think we owe him big-time. Be thinking about how we can thank him properly for all he did tonight."

"We could let him win at BattleGild," Derek suggested.

I laughed out loud. "Nice try, but I'm gonna guess it'll take more than that. Besides, I don't think you'd be able to lose on purpose."

He nodded and smiled, trying to look sage. "That's probably true."

"Probably true? Oh, please. You're a freak when you play that game."

"Dude... I'm the freak?" he asked, sounding incredulous. I watched, pleased, as my teasing eased some of the worry lines from his face.

I drew him into a hug. "Don't worry, this will all work out, okay?"

He nodded into my chest and when he pulled back, he sighed and turned to our moms. "I think I'm partied out. Can we all go home?"

The women both nodded before I pulled them into a group hug. I could see clearly how I needed to visit them tomorrow. We still had a lot to process. Even if it was just quiet time spent hanging out together and watching bad TV and Netflix. My family needed me, and I needed them just as much.

Thirty-One

Lance

W ELL, TO NO ONE'S surprise, including mine, getting your nose broken isn't very much fun. Gib said I was lucky I didn't need surgery after all, but I didn't feel so lucky. After having my nose probed and scanned, then the fracture set back into alignment, I was done. I wanted the day to be over, to just take as many of the painkillers that I could and crawl into bed for the rest of my life.

It was late, and the party had ended by the time we got home. Not that I cared that much, or cared much about anything, because the painkillers were doing their thing.

I vaguely remembered being brought into the house and up to my bedroom, but the rest of my night consisted of fitful sleep, occasionally waking up when I accidentally brushed my nose on the pillow.

The next morning, I woke up and felt two arms wrapped around me. *Jake*. I naturally cuddled back into the warmth of his secure embrace.

"Mmm, you awake?" he asked into my ear, then gently nuzzled the back of my neck.

The pain was front and center, but I managed to moan a yes. "Good, 'cause I've had to pee for like two hours."

I laughed as Jake wriggled free of me and dashed into the bathroom. I found my pain pills sitting on the bedside table, thankfully beside a glass of water.

After popping a pill, I sat up, stretched, and about had a heart attack upon noticing three pairs of eyes staring at me from the doorway.

Despite my pounding headache, I motioned for my nieces to come into the room.

"Are you okay, Uncle Lance?" Ruby asked, biting her lip. I could only imagine how frightening I must've looked to them, all swollen, bruised, and bandaged.

I nodded gently and stood, then hugged all three girls at once. Chrissy was tall and when we hugged, her head brushed up against my nose, causing pain to rip through my face.

When I grunted, all three girls pulled back, alarmed. "I'm okay, bud dis still urts a lot," I said, pointing to my nose.

"You sound funny," Margie said, and I stifled a laugh. I'd have laughed out loud if I wasn't absolutely sure it would've hurt like hell.

"I'b guessing I'll soud funny for a while," I managed.

Jake returned from the bathroom and sat on the bed with me as the girls asked more questions. Fortunately, Jake played interference and answered most of them for me, so I wouldn't have to push myself too much.

Before too long, Gib came up and sent the girls outside to play. "How are you feeling?" he asked.

When the girls were out of earshot, I admitted I felt like crap and had just taken a pill.

Gib smiled. "Well, I suspect that's not going to change for a while. Can't go brawling and not expect consequences," he said, teasing me.

I glanced at the doorway to make sure the girls were nowhere in sight and flipped him off. Luckily, the painkiller was kicking in again. I had just enough time to go pee and climb back into bed before it hit full force.

Later in the day, I felt well enough to venture downstairs. Jake had left without waking me up, and Gib and the girls told me that Allen and Catherine had taken Dad to Nashville to give me time to heal.

I groaned before I could stop myself. "I fordot he was here."

"Oh, he's still here," Gib said, but winked at me. "Luckily, your brother is playing interference."

"Dank God for dat," I said.

I was about to fix myself a sandwich when the girls told me to sit back down because they'd fix one for me.

Sandwiches made by the girls were always a culinary adventure, with odd combinations ranging from peanut butter and ham to tuna with cheese. But they wanted to do something nice for me so I wasn't about to say no.

Besides, I was hungry, and my head hurt, not to mention I remained groggy from the pain meds.

I lucked out, though, because my sandwich ended up being plain ham and cheese with a splash of mustard, the way Ruby liked hers. I wasn't a mustard fan, but I figured I got off scot-free without the plethora of other ingredients they could've added.

I lasted a full hour before I ended up back upstairs with another painkiller to help me sleep through the night.

The following day, I woke up disappointed to not find Jake's strong arms around me. He had never stayed the night at my brother's house before anyway, so it had been a fluke that one time. I just had to assume it was because he'd been really worried about me.

I was feeling significantly better, thank goodness, because I'd taken my last pill around two in the morning and Gib had already told me they wouldn't prescribe me any more after those were gone. Not that I was a big fan of pills, but I was less a fan of pain.

I got into the shower and washed my hair from the back like I'd been told I'd have to, considering they didn't want me to get the bandages wet. Just being clean helped me feel almost normal again.

I went downstairs and found Gib and Allen sitting across from one another in the kitchen. The moment Gib saw me, he got up and poured me a glass of water and put two Ibuprofen down for me to take. "You'll need to take these every four hours if you want to keep the pain down," he said.

"Thanks, Gib," I said. I didn't sound quite as muffled as before, at least not to my own ears, and Gib and Allen assured me they could understand everything I was saying.

"You hungry?" Allen asked.

When I nodded, he went over and pulled out my favorite cereal and poured me a bowl, then put it in front of me alongside the milk.

"Where are the girls?" I asked.

"Mom and Dad have taken them to Nashville to see a matinee at the theater," Allen replied.

I looked at my brother like he'd just grown horns. Not that he could read my facial expressions through all the bandaging.

"You mean your mother and our father are doing something together that doesn't involve firearms?"

Allen laughed. "Yeah, I think your, um…circumstances had a pretty intense impact on our father. He's the one who recommended the day out."

"Wow," I said. "Did I get knocked into a parallel universe?"

"Maybe. Anyway, are you feeling well enough for me to change your dressing?" Gib asked.

"Is it going to hurt?" I asked

"Probably a little but not too bad."

"Yeah, I guess, after I finish my cereal," I said. "Unless you think it's going to hurt bad enough that I'll puke again."

"No, it won't be as bad as it was when you had it set."

I was on some pretty intense painkillers when the ER doc had adjusted my nose and reset it, but even with that, I'd thrown up twice.

"Okay, then I'll go ahead and eat, and if you hurt me, I can enjoy watching it all come back on you."

"Sounds fair," Gib said, chuckling.

"I haven't thanked you for coming to my rescue," I said as I poured the milk over my cereal.

"No need. It's part of the job."

"Well, you aren't my doctor, you're my brother-in-law, so accept my appreciation."

"Okay, taken," he said.

"I've got to run down to the clinic to speak to Ash about something and pick up more stuff to rebandage your nose. Can you stay up until I get back?" he asked.

"Yeah, not sleepy," I said.

Allen sat across from me after Gib left and said, "I know you don't feel like talking, but I wanted to tell you Dad felt bad for what happened, and how he confronted you beforehand. I think hearing you'd been beaten up and then rushed to the hospital woke him up."

"That's something good out of this, then."

Allen nodded. "Mom talked to him, too. I'm not sure what all she said, but I think he might be a little less in your face now."

"If that's the case, Catherine deserves a medal or something."

"That's true," Allen said on a chuckle as he got up to leave. "I'm gonna leave you to finish your cereal and try to get some paperwork done so I can enjoy the rest of the day."

I nodded at him, causing my head to hurt, although it wasn't nearly as bad as it had been.

Gib returned as I was finishing my second bowl of cereal. I was a lot hungrier than I'd thought when I came down. I hadn't eaten much on Saturday and only the sandwich yesterday, so my stomach was growling by the time I sat down to eat.

Replacing the dressing hadn't hurt at all. But I didn't tell Gib that. I got some perverse joy out of my brother-in-law not knowing if he was going to be upchucked on or not. Gib was in every way the perfect doctor, with the best bedside manner. I'm not sure why that annoyed me at the moment, but it sorta did.

I wasn't sleepy, but I was tired, so I got my schoolwork out and attempted to read my latest assignment. I made it halfway through before I gave up and tried answering the questions that went with the reading instead. I'd answered two-thirds before I had to give up. I would have to finish the reading later in the day and then attempt it again.

I had a paper due midweek, but I seriously doubted reading the stack of work required to write the paper would happen today or tomorrow. So, I snapped a selfie of my face and sent it to my professor, asking for an extension. I knew it would put me behind temporarily, but the workload was nothing like in medical school, so I had no doubt I'd get caught up. I was just about to fall asleep on the sofa when I heard a ruckus that could only be created by three pre-teen girls arriving home.

I laughed as they all came into the sitting room where I was lounging, all talking at once.

When they spotted me, all three dashed over, asking if I felt better. I hugged them because my nieces were about as huggy as anyone I'd ever met and answered their questions before looking up and seeing Dad and Catherine walk into the room.

"You three go take your stuff to your room and get ready for supper," Catherine said.

Without even a glance at their grandmother, they were gone in a flurry of arguments and laughter, leaving Catherine, Dad, and me alone in the sitting room.

"Well, I'm going to go put dinner on," she said. "I'll leave the two of you to talk."

Watching her leave, I couldn't help but smile. "She makes a great mom, doesn't she?" I asked.

Dad just nodded in his distracted way and the deep sigh escaped me before I could hold it back. *Might as well get this over with*, I thought. At least since my nose still hurt and talking was a pain, to say the least, I could get away without having to respond much.

Dad sat across from me, and I could tell he was searching for words. That gave me some hope. He seldom thought before he launched into his lectures about how worthless or unworthy I was.

"Son, I've made a mistake."

I jerked my head up to look at him so quickly it made my nose hurt, and I reached up to put my hand over the bandaging. "What?" I asked, not believing my own ears.

He managed to smile, another rare occurrence for my father, particularly when he was about to lecture me.

"Catherine reminded me that when I was your age, my father was pushing me to go into the Air Force. He wanted me to follow in his footsteps and to one day make general, a rank he'd gotten close to but never quite achieved."

"But granddad was a doctor like you," I muttered through the bandages, confused by what he was saying.

"Yeah, an Air Force doctor. He had other hopes and aspirations, though, until he got injured. Well, anyway, I had forgotten." He looked at me for a long while, clearly deep in thought, which unnerved me a little. "I made a mistake, Lance. A lot of them, apparently. I thought you were just throwing your life away, ditching a promising career you hadn't even started, and I didn't take into consideration your own goals. I was being my own f...freaking dad," he said. I assumed he was forgoing the cuss word since the girls were in the house.

I didn't know what to say. I mean, I wasn't that interested in forgiving him considering he'd taken away my home, my trust money and what I'd earned myself, and most damaging, his love. What I thought was love at the time, anyway.

We sat silently for a moment before he said, "Son, I apologize."

"That's a first," I said before I could think about what I was saying.

Dad chuckled instead of getting mad. "Yeah, I'm sorry about that too."

"Who are you?" I asked, looking at my father askance.

"Reformed. Your brother and Catherine have come down pretty hard on me. I...well, let's just say I see things differently now."

I threw my legs off the sofa and onto the floor.

"Dad, you left me homeless and penniless. If it hadn't been for Allen, I'd have been screwed. I love you, you're my dad, but it's going to take some time for me to forgive that." I looked him in the eye then, and said something I'd never had the balls to do during an argument before. "Assuming I ever forgive you."

I hoped that last bit would sting. I wanted to make him feel as shitty as he'd made me feel after texting me I wasn't his son anymore. I figured that would be enough to send him into one of his typical rages, but to my surprise, he nodded and looked genuinely forlorn.

I didn't recognize the man sitting across from me. My father had never been anything but confident and certain in everything he did. Maybe I really had landed in a parallel universe.

"Let's talk more later, okay? I need to go lie down for a nap before I have to deal with three very inquisitive girls."

That caused him to smile. "Do what you need to, son. I'm not going anywhere."

I cocked an eyebrow and wanted to ask about him about not being at work, but decided to wait. My father only took time off twice a year, once over the Christmas holidays and again during the early summer when we had our annual vacations. Besides that, he'd have to be on his deathbed not to be at work.

I nodded, more to take my leave than anything else, and headed up the stairs. The nap I now craved would give me time to think about what my dad was up to. He looked and sounded genuine, but I had to assume this was his next attempt to force me to do his bidding.

Not that he held any power over me any longer. My life was my own now, and that life was in Crawford City. With Allen and Gib's help, I'd made a home here. I'd enrolled in school, had a good job, and was determined to succeed. I had family, friends, co-workers, and a whole community who cared about me. And I had Jake. Nothing my father could say or do would change my mind about where I felt I belonged.

THIRTY-TWO

JAKE

I'D PLANNED TO SPEND the day with Lance and possibly bring Derek so he could say thank you in person, but that hadn't worked out. I'd gone to the house early to have breakfast with everyone before heading for Crawford City when Mrs. Lidia arrived.

She announced that an emergency hearing in family court had been scheduled for Wednesday. They were to consider how our father had violated the no-contact order, attempted to kidnap Derek, and physically assaulted Lance while also being drunk in public. I had to assume the rushed session was to assess if Derek was safe in his foster care placement. I was bound and determined to be a part of that discussion, even if I wasn't officially part of his case.

By the time Mrs. Lidia left, I could tell Derek was emotionally wiped out, so I didn't even suggest going to

Crawford City. Instead, we played some of our favorite games. Then he went to his room to hide out for a while and text his boyfriend.

Once he was out of earshot, I sat in the dining room across from Anita and Claire and talked about how best to ensure Derek's safety moving forward.

"Your father knew where we were yesterday, which means someone in children's services told him," Anita said, after I suggested he stay with me for a while.

"I hadn't thought of that. You're right, someone must've told him we were going to Crawford City. Who did you tell?" I asked.

"Just Lidia," Anita replied, "but she put it in her report that we were spending time with you that day. I had told her our whole family was going to a community event there."

"Dang," I said as my racing mind tried to connect the dots. "You don't think Mrs. Lidia..."

Anita shook her head before I could continue. "No, absolutely not. I've known her for years, and she's an honest person who genuinely cares about the kids in her charge. She wouldn't jeopardize the safety and welfare of any child, but that doesn't mean someone else in the department wouldn't."

Anita let out an irritated huff, although her face conveyed worry more than annoyance, before continuing. "We did have several cases a while back before I retired, where someone with access to internal information was leaking the whereabouts of kids in the system to local preachers. The department investigated, even had a couple of suspects, but never could fully trace the leaks before it all mysteriously stopped. Of course, Lidia was telling me they have a new system now that tracks who is in and out of each child's account. I don't think it'll be too difficult to narrow down who opened Derek's account Friday after I told her of our weekend plans."

Learning that someone, anyone, would knowingly put already vulnerable children at risk like that had me seeing red. Just thinking about what might've happened to Derek, or what might still happen to other kids who the system failed, turned my stomach.

"Thank God Lance was in the right place at the right time," I said, voicing what I'd thought a million times already. "The silver lining in all of this is, because Dad attacked Lance while trying to kidnap Derek, it's not very likely the courts will let him go with a slap on the wrist."

The three of us chatted a little more, then I went to check on Derek again before leaving. When I saw him curled up on his bed reading, I figured he'd be okay. "You think you'd like to go with me to Crawford City after school tomorrow? If Lance is free, I'd like to go say hi. But I'd like to run out to the winery too. I need to pick up a few bottles for my clients this week."

Derek looked up and shrugged. "I guess. Can I tell you tomorrow?" he asked.

"Yeah, that'd be fine. Hey, text me if you need to chat, okay? He's my dad, too, and I know a little bit about how you might be feeling."

Derek shook his head. "But you weren't the one he was trying to kidnap. It's not really your fault Lance got beat up, either."

"Woah, hold on, Derek," I said, stepping into the room.

"It's not your fault, either. That all sits on Dad's shoulders. You didn't invite him, and you were wise not to go with him. Especially if he was drunk."

Derek sighed, but stared at his book. "Listen," I said as I went over and sat on the end of his bed. "Dad fucked up. Like, *really* fucked up. I have no idea what legal punishment he's facing, but none of it is your fault."

Tears began to run down his face, and he swiped them away with the back of his hand. "If I hadn't asked to be adopted, he probably wouldn't have done this."

"No," I said, anger beginning to get the best of me. "If he wasn't a sorry excuse for a dad, dumping both me and you, then he wouldn't be facing any of this. I mean, face it, Derek, neither you nor I did any damned thing wrong. I didn't come out, I was forced out, *then* he kicked me out onto the freaking streets. You didn't even get the chance to come out before they were acting like total fools. I won't let you blame yourself for this any more than I'm gonna take responsibility. Dad is a grown-ass man and knows better than getting drunk, trying to abduct you, and then taking it out on poor Lance. If he hadn't wanted this outcome, he could have made a different choice!"

I took a long breath and tried to let some of the anger out with the exhale.

"It's hard not to think it's on me," he admitted.

I chuckled bitterly. "Listen, dude, you're preaching to the choir here. It took me a long damn time to stop blaming myself. That, and a heck of a lot of therapy with poor Anita in there."

Derek laughed, causing some of the tension to leave the room. "Yeah, Anita has a low shit tolerance."

"When it comes to misplaced emotions, she certainly does," I said, laughing myself.

"So, come with me tomorrow and we'll see Lance. He's crazy about dark chocolate, so we'll stop by the Chocolate Factory I took him to after his first day of school and buy him a bunch of candy bars."

Derek smiled. "Yeah, I love their chocolate and lemon."

"Okay, we'll stock you up as well."

I left my brother feeling a bit better, or at least I hoped he was. Sometimes looking at him was like looking in a mirror, and for the first time I was confronted with how frustrating it was to deal with someone who didn't share their feelings with you unless you pressed.

As I was leaving, I looked at Anita and Claire and, with a deep sigh, said, "I'm really sorry."

"Why?" Anita asked.

"'Cause I was a jerk kid, and you still loved me."

I saw understanding dawn on their faces and both of them broke into a smile. "Hey, I'll probably pick Derek up tomorrow afternoon to go visit Lance, if he's up to it. Do you have anything else planned?"

"No, honey, that sounds like a great plan," Claire said. "I know he's concerned about how Lance is doing."

"I'll call when I know more about the plans," I said as I headed out the door. As I drove home, I had to navigate my own anger with my father and his sheer stupidity. For the first time, realization dawned about how fortunate I'd been that my parents *hadn't* come for me. Who the hell knows what would've happened if I'd been back in Dad's clutches. I sure as hell wouldn't be the person I am now, that's for sure.

I decided to forgo going home. Instead, I went to the training gym between my office and condo. I texted my trainer to let him know I was going to spend some time blowing off steam and got a reply asking if I wanted him to join me.

I declined his offer, but appreciated the gesture. Larry was a sixty-year-old hulk of a man. He used to be a professional boxer, but after he'd almost been killed in a fight, he'd retired, went to school for physical education, and then opened the gym. I'd referred more than a few of my clients to him over the years because, just like now, he was pretty much always willing to come out if you needed him.

I pounded the punching bag until I thought my knuckles would bleed. Mentally, I wanted to punch it some more, but my body eventually protested. Finally, I had a shower and headed home. I'd texted Lance before hitting the gym and he said he was happy to hang out tomorrow, but warned me that his dad was there.

It didn't matter to me whether his dad was there or not, but I figured Lance might not want to be affection-ate with him around or something. In any case, I'd take my cues from my boyfriend when I saw him tomorrow. When I walked into my condo, I noticed he'd texted me again.

Lance: *RESCUE ME!*

I chuckled.

Me: *No problem. Shall I swoop in wearing a red cape or would you prefer a sexy Clark Kent to come running? Pretty sure I can find some glasses.*

Lance sent back a heart-eyes emoji and I grinned. I loved teasing him, and was relieved I'd read the situation right and he didn't actually need rescuing.

Me: *Oh, Derek is coming with me tomorrow, if that's okay? I think he needs to see you and make sure you're okay.*

Lance: *Cool, I'd like to see him too.*

Me: *How are you doing? Really?*

Lance: *Sore and grumpy and looking like I have raccoon eyes from the bruising, but physically I'm fine.*

That he noted his body was fine but not necessarily the rest of him didn't go unnoticed. But I didn't want to push. I'm sure his father being there had nearly everything to do with it.

Me: *Glad to hear you're okay, sweetheart. We'll see you tomorrow.*

I resisted the urge to call him, and to get back in my car and head for Crawford City to spend the night with him in my arms. Derek wasn't the only one who wanted to see with his own eyes that Lance truly was okay. I missed my boyfriend, and after seeing him hurt, I wanted to pull him close to me and never let go.

I collapsed on my bed a full two hours earlier than usual. It had been a stressful long weekend, and I was ready to be done with it. Visions of Lance, safe and secure in my arms, flashed through my mind as I dozed off. The fleeting thought of *it might be time to ask him to marry me* was all I remembered before sleep overtook me.

THIRTY-THREE

LANCE

THANK GOD I DIDN'T have to be back at school today. Gib had written doctor's notes to all of my professors, stating I wasn't in any shape to attend classes, and that bought me a little more time to complete my assignments, too.

My nose was feeling better, though, and I wasn't having to take as many pain pills. Gib had told me the internal stitches would dissolve on their own and I only had to apply icepacks two or three times a day now. He said it was remarkable progress, since swelling from a procedure like mine could sometimes take up to three weeks before it started to go down.

I still slept badly without as many painkillers in my system, so to entertain myself, I'd try to read and absorb a few chapters of my schoolwork at a time. Luckily, that seemed to work, and between naps, I'd study a little, then fall asleep again.

I was able to get around four hours of continuous sleep, though, just as light began to slip through the window. I don't know why, but whenever I'd have a hard night, mornings tended to be when I was able to sleep the best.

When I finally got up, I felt oddly refreshed and stumbled into the bathroom for a shower. I'd almost become an expert at washing my hair from the back and keeping the bandages around my nose from getting wet.

I'd woken up thinking about Jake, and knowing I'd see him later today probably explained my good mood. He had mentioned going to the winery with him, but I knew that would be too much for me, so I encouraged him to go alone and then come by here when he was done.

I went downstairs to the sight of Gib, Dad, Catherine, and my nieces all sitting in the kitchen eating breakfast. Allen must've left for work already. I was surprised to see Dad and Catherine here so early, particularly on a school day, but perhaps they'd be taking the girls to school. I wasn't too interested in the details, though, since I needed caffeine more than conversation right now.

"Hey, Lance," Gib said as he got up to check on me. "You looking for coffee?"

I smiled. "You've come to know me well."

Gib chuckled. "I just made a fresh pot, and your dad hasn't had time to drink it all yet."

"Hey," I heard my dad complain behind me. "I've usually had twice that amount by now."

Gib turned around and shook his head. "I don't need to mention to you, *Doctor*, how bad that much caffeine is for you, do I?"

Dad chuckled. "No, Doc, I'm pretty sure I'm aware."

"Okay," I mumbled. "Enough with the doc talk, I need coffee before a caffeine withdrawal headache takes hold."

"You're all addicted," Catherine said. "Girls, let these men be a lesson to you. Keep your coffee intake low or you'll end up just like them, barely able to function without it."

"I wanna be like them," Chrissy proclaimed.

I glanced over at Catherine, who was frowning. "I'll try my best to educate that out of you, granddaughter," she said. Chrissy didn't seem to understand, but the rest of us chuckled.

There was no hiding the fact that Catherine wasn't a fan of the medical profession. I think that's probably why she'd become my biggest supporter in having dropped out of medical school.

Medicine was a strange field of work. Sure, having a doctor in the family was great, but a medical career could also dominate your life to the exclusion of everything else. Somehow Allen and Gib had avoided that, but Dad never found that balance. It wasn't a life I'd wanted for myself, on top of having other dreams anyway, and Catherine must've recognized that.

Gib pointed at the barstool for me to sit down. After pouring me a cup of coffee and putting out the creamer I used every morning, he began looking over my bandages.

"You're a fast healer, Lance," he said proudly. "I'll change out the bandages after you finish breakfast, and I'll double-check, but it looks good."

I smiled at him. Gib had become my primary caregiver despite the fact that both my father and brother were doctors as well. I guess as a family care doctor, though, this was more in his wheelhouse. I don't think my father had actually practiced medicine in years and Allen was following closely in his footsteps.

Just since I'd been here, my brother had accepted a new position overseeing the university hospital's pediatric residency program after his predecessor stepped down. Ironically, the promotion came with more responsibilities, but had actually given him more time off than he'd had before. I looked over at my father, wondering if he was proud of all Allen had accomplished or annoyed he'd chosen Gib and Tennessee over a higher profile medical career in New York.

I knew it was just a matter of time before Dad and I had to address the elephant in the room, but once again, I felt like I'd dodged a bullet when it came to my decision to drop out of medical school. As much as Gib and Allen seemed to love what they did, that's how much I didn't. Working with Todd and Linc, however, had been eye-opening, and I missed the day-to-day construction work I'd done with them over the summer. Todd told me on my last day that I had a place working for him next summer, as soon as the school year ended, although I was already considering attending summer school.

"Hey, Uncle Lance?" Ruby asked, and I turned toward her. "Can you help me practice my pitch again after school?"

The girls found out that I used to play baseball when I was young and Ruby, the most athletic of the group, was obsessed with me helping her practice. She wanted to be a pitcher and had become dead set on improving her game since a couple of other girls on her softball team were currently better players.

"Uncle Lance needs to rest for at least three, maybe four weeks before he's out throwing the ball around," Gib said. "But I can help you later if you wish."

"I can help too," Dad said, and we all turned toward him. It's funny how I never thought of my father as being anyone's grandpa, let alone an involved grandparent. "I used to coach Lance's team when he was just a little older than you," he told Ruby.

How had I forgotten that? Thinking back, I vaguely remembered him being in the dugout for a few games, telling me all I was doing wrong, but he'd ended up being gone more than he was there. Our team's assistant coach had been more of a coach to us than Dad, but I didn't dare mention that.

Ruby lit up. "Thanks, Grandpa."

Dad's face shone as Ruby and the other two girls darted up the stairs to finish getting ready. Gib went into the utility room off the back of the kitchen and came back with a catcher's mitt in his hand. "You might need this," he said, handing the glove to Dad. "She's developing quite a good right arm, and that softball hurts when you catch it bare-handed."

I could tell Dad felt a little out of his element, although that was a rare sight. He'd never been particularly good at getting involved. Running the hospital had been his sole focus and concern for as far back as I could remember. Unless, of course, he was criticizing his sons. Baseball had been the only extracurricular activity Dad had tolerated or supported. To this day, I still don't know why it was the exception, especially since a good fastball could do more damage to my future surgical hands than a hammer. But I never questioned it...I never questioned a lot of things until now.

The girls came back down a few minutes later, carrying their backpacks. After saying our goodbyes, they left for school with Dad and Catherine, leaving Gib and me alone in the kitchen.

He began undoing the bandages on my face and once they were completely off, he examined the injury. "Yep, it's looking better. Much better," he said, then rebandaged my nose. "You'll need to keep icing it and you'll have times when it hurts and swells more than others, but as long as you keep that up, it should continue healing nicely."

I felt wiped out after breakfast, so I went back upstairs to try to get another hour or two of sleep. I grabbed my phone and sent a text to Jake asking when he thought he'd be here.

He texted back saying to expect him and Derek some-
time late that afternoon, and he'd let me know when
they were leaving the winery.

Perfect, I thought. I had plenty of time to take a nap.
I closed my eyes and, despite the two cups of coffee I'd
just finished, I dozed off quickly and slept hard.

Thirty-Four

Jake

W HEN DEREK AND I went to the winery, Lia took him on a quick tour of where the wine would be processed starting next month during the harvest, and also showed him the artist complex above the mill.

Lia had attended the Crawford City event, so she'd likely seen, or at least heard, about what went down between Derek, Dad, and Lance. I hoped she could talk to Derek about her own experience with hateful parents making a public spectacle. Hers had come to the winery's opening, and unceremoniously dumped all of her possessions on the ground as their way of kicking her out of the house. All because she and her girlfriend Millie had announced they were together.

I hadn't planned it, but maybe Lia would be able to offer Derek some words of comfort. The rest of Lia's family, namely her girlfriend and the winery's owners—her cousin Matt and his partner Logan—had helped her then, and my friend was happier now than she'd ever been. I hoped hearing that everything would be alright from someone besides me would help Derek see that things do get better.

While they toured, I wandered over to the chapel where Lance and I had our first date. I still remember his visceral reaction to its beauty, and how being overcome with emotion had brought us so much closer. For me, the chapel would forever be our special place.

I hadn't been back since then and it was incredible how the forest had filled in around the building to create a feeling of being embraced.

The smell of the forest permeated the air, and I noticed a lot of muscadine vines growing high on the stand of oak and hickory trees around the perimeter. Lance had probably never experienced the amazing smell of ripe muscadines as they fell, and I wanted to share that with him. I would have to make note of when the vineyard fruit ripened so I could bring him back then.

I sat in the chair behind the lectern because it gave the best view of the valley and stream below, and thought about how much things had changed since I'd met Lance.

It's true that I had been a player before, and never really pictured myself in a serious relationship. Lance forever altered that. He brought out the protective instincts in me, and I just wanted to hold him and keep him safe. But he was also his own man, one who I respected, who had just needed a little love, support, and encouragement to go after what he wanted in life. And hopefully, that included me for the long haul.

My thoughts shifted then from a happy future with Lance to his beautiful face, battered and bleeding. The murderous rage I'd felt toward my father returned in an instant. But no, I couldn't let that coward taint this special place I shared with Lance. My father–even as a thought, even as a whisper of memory of a parent I once loved–didn't belong here in this sacred space.

I closed my eyes, intent on calming myself, and opened them to the sight of a goldfinch outside the window, sitting just on the other side of the glass. It looked like the bird was staring at me, and I smiled at it. Watching the beautiful creature preen itself, then look back to the window before darting off, eased my tension and soon my anger subsided.

It's almost like it was saying, *everything will be okay. Just wait.* Sometimes nature had the best cure for what ailed you.

I leaned back in the chair, letting the peace that this place embodied embrace me. It was then I decided I was ready to make a lifetime commitment to Lance. The next time we came here, with the fruity aroma of ripening muscadines in the air, I'd ask him to be mine.

THIRTY-FIVE

LANCE

J AKE AND DEREK CAME by so late Tuesday afternoon that they ended up staying for dinner. Jake kept apologizing, saying time had gotten away from him at the winery, but that didn't matter. I just wanted to see my boyfriend, hear how things were going, and be able to talk to his little brother.

Derek stayed pretty quiet all evening, and I'm sure seeing all of my bandages and bruising didn't exactly convey I was alright.

Jake, for his part, asked a dozen questions about my nose and how it was healing, most of which I just let Gib answer for me. He took great care being affectionate while keeping it PG-rated and not accidentally bumping my nose. We held hands under the table, as was becoming our custom, and a few times I caught him looking at me with such love, I thought I'd melt on the spot. I was reluctant to let him go that evening, but knew he wasn't far away if I needed him.

The rest of the week flew by and both Gib and Allen agreed I was more than ready to go back to school. I'd been granted an extension for my paper due that week, thank God, and despite missing a few lectures, I wasn't really behind in any of my classes.

Dad hadn't flown back to New York like I thought he would. He'd found a hotel in Nashville and spent every night there, and although he came by the house when Allen or Gib and the girls were home, he wasn't a constant presence. I still dreaded the conversation that was coming, so I mostly avoided him while he was here.

I was able to hitch a ride to school with Allen every morning, since with his new position, he didn't have to be at work until nine, and my first class wasn't until ten. He tended to work late, but that was fine for me, too, since I always had plenty of schoolwork to do and the Central Library on campus was more than adequate for studying.

Only a few of the other students gave me funny looks when I came in with a bandaged face. I'm sure they were all curious, but no one asked. Maybe they all thought I'd had some sort of accident and didn't want to risk hearing the possibly gory details.

On Wednesday, Allen texted me that he was headed home early because Chrissy had some last-minute event at school. I still had a class I needed to attend so I couldn't go with him, but he said Catherine had volunteered to drive me back to Crawford City.

It was strange and a bit awkward to have to accept a ride from Catherine, but beggars can't be choosers, and unless I wanted to take out more loans, I couldn't afford a car right now. So, I texted Allen back asking him to thank Catherine for me.

I began to wonder if maybe I should ask Todd about the house he owned close to the school. I knew he was using it as an Airbnb, but maybe I could stay there during the week, especially on nights like tonight when I didn't have transportation back home.

When class was over, I texted Catherine to let her know I was done and ready whenever she was. She texted me right back, asking if I'd heard from Dad.

Me: *No. Why would I?*

Catherine: *He wanted to come pick you up, said you both needed to talk.*

Me: *Thanks. I'll text him.*

I'd have rather slept in the library stairwell than deal with my dad's attitude all the way back to Crawford City.

I quickly texted Dad, telling him where to meet me, and went to wait for him in the quad outside the Arts building. That's where Allen usually picked me up because it was easily accessed, and I like the public benches for people-watching or for reading if I had to wait long.

Dad texted me back fairly quickly, saying he was on his way. I opened my art history book and was thumbing through to find the part I needed to read when my father pulled up in his rental car.

I took a deep breath, put the book away and, after tossing my backpack into the back seat of the white Lexus, I climbed into the passenger side. I steeled myself for what I assumed was going to be a lecture of some sort, since my father only ever volunteered to pick me up from something when that's what he had in mind. It was probably about how I needed to be an adult by accepting his apology.

Dad immediately asked if I'd eaten and when I glanced over, he was smiling. "Um, not since lunch," I replied.

"Good, I found a nice little Greek restaurant not far from here. It's small and quaint, but the food is better than you'd expect."

I nodded, not sure how to react. Dad never asked if I was hungry and usually by now, he'd be building up to a full rant. Not that he'd picked me up from school more than a handful of times in my life. One of the many nannies he'd hired to keep me under control would take me to and from elementary school. When I got a little older, before I got my driver's license, I'd ride the subway.

The times I rode with Dad to an event usually entailed either ranting or total silence. I hadn't experienced anything civil before, let alone polite conversation.

Of course, by the time he started with the small talk, questions about my day and how I was liking my classes, I was becoming so nervous, I would've rather had the yelling. I knew how to put myself into shutdown mode and survive that. I had no idea what to do with this person.

The restaurant wasn't far from the school, but unfortunately, I immediately knew I couldn't afford to eat there. "Dad, I'm sorry I can't afford this," I said, hoping we'd just head for Crawford City instead.

He looked at me funny. "Why would you assume you'd have to pay?"

The bitterness that came out even surprised me. "Because you told me you'd never spend another penny on my worthless self as long as you live.'"

He shook his head. "I was wrong to say that."

If I hadn't been shocked before, I was now. Usually, I'd have been dressed down for being disrespectful to him. Dad admitting that he'd been wrong, let alone about something that truly mattered, was straight out of the twilight zone.

"Dad, are you okay? I mean, you don't seem like yourself. Are you sick or something?"

When he grimaced, I felt the knots bunch up in my stomach. "Wait? You *are* sick? Is that why you're here?"

Dad shook his head. "I had a scare a few months back, but I'm in remission."

"Remission! What the hell? Dad, you have cancer?"

My father laid his head back on the headrest and closed his eyes. "I didn't mean to talk about this tonight. I came to clear the air with you. That's why I'm here."

"What, you've finally decided to let me live my life, and it's because you've got cancer?" I wasn't sure whether I felt more scared for Dad or pissed off at him. Maybe both in equal amounts.

"I had a few nonmalignant cysts on my colon, all removed. I did a couple of radiation treatments just to be sure. I'm here because...well, I won't lie. I came to try to talk you into coming back to medical school, but I realize I was wrong about that, too."

I stared at Dad as he sat quietly, looking straight ahead toward the restaurant. I honestly didn't know what to say. I didn't recognize this stranger next to me who resembled my father.

Finally, he turned to me. "I'd like to make things right, Lance. Is that possible? Life is short and I can't risk you hating me forever."

I was overcome but not with compassion. Not with anything resembling empathy or sympathy for my father and his health. I only felt red-hot flashes of anger. How dare he put this on me? Dropping a bomb like telling me he has cancer, then basically saying he needs my forgiveness, so he doesn't die with regrets. *Fuck him.*

I took a couple of deep breaths to calm myself and force my temper down. I wanted to have a civil conversation, if for no other reason than to avoid alienating Dad, because I didn't want to make being around him difficult for Allen and the girls.

"Dad, listen, I'm a little overwhelmed by the cancer talk. I'm assuming you haven't told Allen yet, which also puts me in a bit of an awkward spot here." I shifted, so I was looking directly at him. If I was going to have my say, I wanted to do it face-to-face and not with me cowing in my seat.

"You do remember that you kicked me out of the house, right? You took away all access to money, including the money I earned myself, and basically forced me to either do what you wanted me to do or be homeless. I nearly was, if not for Allen. And hell, I didn't even have his phone number. I barely had enough money to buy a bus ticket to Crawford City."

Dad gave a single nod in understanding but continued looking straight ahead. I expected to see him clenching his jaw, but instead, he seemed sad.

"I'm never going to be a doctor, Dad. I tried, I really did, but attending medical school made me miserable. I hated it. I don't like the study of medicine and I tried to explain that to you before, but you blew up and threw me out of your life. Having one son follow in your footsteps should be more than enough, and that's Allen, not me."

I could feel the ire rising in me and wanted to get out of the car and storm off before I made a bad situation worse. But I couldn't leave, not when we were finally hashing out a conversation that should've happened long before I'd even enrolled in medical school. So instead, I leaned my head back against the headrest and closed my eyes, like Dad had done just moments before.

"I was wrong. I realize asking you to forgive me is a tall order, but you should know I thought I was doing the right thing at the time. Up until this past week, I still thought you belonged back in New York with me."

I sat quietly for a moment before I asked, "How is making me homeless and penniless with no warning doing the right thing? Do you know how close I came to living on the streets? Hell, I even considered contacting Kassidy, but you cut off her phone in the divorce. If it hadn't been for Allen and his willingness to forgive me for being an ass to him my entire life, I'd probably be dead by now. So, help me understand, how was that doing the right thing?"

"It wasn't. I know that now. I never dreamed you'd actually leave. I never thought you'd stand up to me. I thought you were throwing your life away to *spite* me."

I humphed. "You've never listened to anything I've said. So, by ignoring me, you decided my desire to go into a field that I'd chosen for myself was to spite you. My God, Dad, are you even able to hear yourself?"

He nodded slowly. "I can continue to apologize, Lance, and I will if that's what it takes. What I did was wrong. Worse, it was a betrayal of you and Allen. Catherine told me he gave up his inheritance from my parents so you could afford to go to school."

"He's also let me live rent-free at his house and kept me fed, Dad. He even found me a job with one of his friends, who took pity on me since I basically had no skills. But I've made something of myself here. I have friends now who care about me, and a real family. The kind who only wish for your happiness and stick by you even when things turn to shit. I'm sorry, Dad, I can't do this right now. We can take this up tomorrow."

I made a move to open the car door, but Dad stopped me.

"Son, I can take you home. Please, let me do that much. I talked Catherine into letting me pick you up. We don't have to talk unless you want to, but let me get you back to Allen's safely."

I wanted to get out, tell him to go to hell, and slam the door shut without a backward glance. But I couldn't unless I wanted to call and ask Jake for a ride, which I didn't want to do. He would've been there in a heartbeat, but the last thing we needed was for me to drag him directly into my family drama just because my father was an ass.

So, I nodded, and Dad pulled out of the restaurant parking lot, heading toward Crawford City. We rode in silence for at least a half-hour because it took that long for my initial anger to cool. Given I lived with five other people, including three little girls whose eyes and ears were everywhere, I didn't want to make a spectacle airing dirty laundry in public. I figured it was now or never to hash things out if I hoped for privacy.

"I don't think I will ever be able to forgive you for abandoning me to the streets. I made it clear I was never going back to medical school, but even then, you didn't back down. Not to mention the money thing. I didn't expect you to give me any more of your money, Dad, but I'd planned to use the inheritance money to get my master's in architectural design at NYU. I knew I could afford that. I had over thirty thousand in the bank that I'd been saving since high school. Money that *I earned*, that I scrimped and saved. When you offered to put it in an investment, I thought it was great you could help build it, never dreaming that adding your name to the account would bite me in the ass. Because I trusted you, Dad. I mean, I knew all along you'd cut me off when you found out I wasn't going to be a doctor, but I had no idea you'd lock me out of access to *my own money*. My own fucking money!"

I'd never cussed in anger at my father before. The truth is, I was always a little afraid of him, but as we rode through the dark countryside, I realized there was little he could do to me now. Violence was never my father's way, certainly not hitting me in the nose like Jake's father had done. No, my fear of him came in thinking I'd be a perpetual disappointment to the only family I thought I had. That no matter how hard I tried, even if I'd become a surgeon like him, he'd scrutinize and criticize every aspect of my life until he died.

"I put the money back in your name months ago, but you wouldn't return my texts and I didn't know at the time you were living with Allen. He didn't let that slip until I was on the verge of calling the police to track you down. It's like you vanished."

I turned in my seat to face him. "I blocked your number when you texted me that I was worthless."

"Yeah, another thing I regret. I was drunk when I did that. That's not an excuse, but well, I'd just found out I had the polyps. You know my dad died of colon cancer. Mom had breast cancer and although that hadn't killed her, it was a bad experience."

"So, when you found out you were sick, you lashed out at me. Thought that'd make you feel better? Or was your having cancer somehow my fault too?"

"Lance," Dad said with an exhale. "I'm not a good father. I mean, where you and Allen are concerned, I'm not even a good man. I screwed up royally. All I can do now is try to explain my reasoning in how I raised you, even if it was seriously flawed."

"So, what? Now you're fine with me going to school for architecture?"

"More than fine, I'm proud of you."

"What changed?" I asked, not letting his remorse filter into my thoughts yet.

Dad sighed. "Two things. First, Catherine reminded me how my father had treated me when I resisted going into the Air Force." He chuckled. "You know, you and Allen were the only two people named in his will. He'd intentionally disinherited me because he never forgave me."

"And the second reason?" I asked, determined not to let him off the hook.

"I didn't know you had a boyfriend. Jake seems like a likable guy. I'll admit, I wasn't too happy that you're um..."

"That I'm gay?" I asked, causing Dad to nod.

"Yeah, I've never understood that about you or your brother. But after seeing what Jake's dad did to you, then learning what Jake and his brother had gone through, I realized I was being just like him. Like him and *my* father." Dad glanced over at me before looking back out the front window. "I swore I'd never become my father and put the burden of my own expectations on my kids like he did to me, but damned if that's not exactly what happened."

I took a deep breath and when I let it out, I allowed myself to accept my father's reasons, even though I was still far from forgiving him.

"Just so we're clear, I have my money back? Where is it and how do I access it?" I asked, ready to type the details into my phone.

"It's been moved into a low-risk investment account with the same company and you can access it anytime you want. You just need to contact Raul, who set your account up to begin with."

"That includes my inheritance from Grandma and Grandpa?" He nodded. "Good, so I can at least pay Allen back for what he's spent."

"I've already done that," Dad said.

My head snapped around then. "You paid him back for me?"

"You would've never used his money if it hadn't been for me."

Well, I'd certainly never expected that from my father—him accepting responsibility for how he'd screwed me over, and footing the bill. I waited for a moment before I decided to let him off the hook a little more.

"If it hadn't been for all this, Dad, I would've never come to stay with Allen. I know now that you actively worked to keep him and me apart. I know what you told me all those years about how he and Catherine hated me was a lie. That's something else you'll need to atone for."

I waited for my dad to react, but even in the darkness of the car, he appeared as stoic as ever. Flabbergasted by that, I continued. "Allen is now one of my best friends. I'm also more than a little partial, to say it like they do down here, to Catherine too. You never should've kept me from them or let me continue believing they hated me. Through the years, I could've used my brother and I'll never get that time back."

For the first time in my life, I saw a tear slip out of my father's eye and roll silently down his face.

We then rode in silence until we came to the town center. Dad pulled off at the park, right where the sidewalk ascended the stairs to Allen and Gib's place.

"I've made a lot of mistakes in my life, Lance. Next to being a terrible father, the biggest one was losing Catherine. She was...she *is* the love of my life."

"So, what? You blame me for breaking you and her up?"

"No," Dad looked at me, genuinely shocked. "The only person responsible for Catherine and me breaking up was me. I was jealous of Catherine's career and her commitment to her family. I let my own selfish attitude destroy our marriage. And that happened even before I started wooing your mom. No, you aren't responsible for my fuck ups."

"Why did you try to keep me away from Allen?"

"Because Allen represented all my failures as a dad, as a husband. I didn't want you to hate me."

"You thought he'd tell me what you'd done? That's why you kept us apart? Seriously, Dad, I already knew. Hell, it was you yourself who told me Catherine hated me because I was born."

Dad put his head on the steering wheel between his hands. "I wouldn't blame you, Lance, if you never want to talk to me again. I don't blame you or Allen for pushing me out of your lives forever. I deserve it. But I pray you won't do that." He turned to me then. "I've spent nearly a year entirely alone. When your stepmother Kassidy found out what'd happened with you, she signed the divorce papers and all but threw them in my face. I guess I now know what my future looks like. What is it that Gib says? The chickens have come home to roost."

I nodded. "It sounds like you've had it coming. Dad, this whole conversation is making my head hurt. I probably need to ice my nose again, too, if I don't want it to be the size of a balloon tomorrow. I need time to think." I opened the door of the car, ready to climb out. "If it helps, I still love you. I always will, but I have a lot to process. When are you going back to New York?"

"I'm not, or at least I don't have to."

I looked at my father, puzzled. "Why? What about work?"

"I resigned. Right after the cancer scare, I decided I'd worked there long enough. I still have a board position, but I can attend those meetings virtually."

Of all the things my father had told me tonight, that surprised me the most. Everything in my father's life revolved around that job. I'm not even sure who he'd be without work. I wondered if he didn't know either.

"Okay, that's officially too much for me to process tonight. I'm going to go now. If you're sticking around for a while, I'll let you know when I'm ready to talk again."

I got out, grabbed my bag from the back without saying goodbye, and shut the door behind me. I'm sure I'd have run to the house if my nose wasn't beginning to hurt again. Gib had told me not to exercise for at least another week and with all that'd happened, I didn't want to aggravate it. So, I deliberately walked up the stairs and into the house without looking back.

I had my savings back again, and the first thing I planned to do was buy a reliable vehicle. I'd grown close to Allen and Catherine since I'd come here, but I'd be damned if I ever ended up in another situation like tonight, where Dad showed up as my ride. The prospect of not having to deal with my dad or rehash all the shit from my childhood while my nose throbbed like a son of a bitch made shelling out several thousand bucks for a car totally worth it.

When I crept into the house, the girls were already in their rooms, and I was able to just wave at Gib and Allen instead of having any more conversations tonight. I went into the kitchen, took some pain medication, and then dashed up the stairs to call it a night.

I tugged on my pajamas and propped myself against my pillows, trying to get comfortable despite my painful nose, then texted Jake to ask what his plans were for the weekend.

Jake: *Just my usual, why?*

Me: *I just had a weird-ass conversation with my dad. I need some time away. You up for company?*

It only took seconds to get a text back.

Jake: *Yes! When can you come?*

I thought about it for a moment, and while I'd usually never ask to come over on a weekday, Jake only lived a few blocks from the school. If I could stay with him for the next couple of days, too, that would take care of me having to face my family until next week.

Me: *What about tomorrow night?*

The three dots came and went as I waited for his response.

Jake: *That works. I have dinner plans with my family on Friday night, but you can come with or hang out here.*

A few moments later, I got another text.

Jake: *I could also cancel.*

I chuckled. He would do that for me, too. I knew he would.

Me: *No, I'd like to have dinner with your family. Mine not so much.*

A few seconds later, my phone rang, and I shook my head. I should've known he'd call after that comment.

"Hey."

"Hey, what's going on?"

"Too much to get into tonight, but let's just say my father and I had the heart-to-heart I've been dreading."

"Was it awful?"

"Yeah. You could say that."

"Is he going home?"

I laughed. "No, staying indefinitely. Believe it or not, he's asked me to forgive him."

I knew the silence on the other end meant Jake was pondering what to say. "I'm guessing you're not ready for that?"

I sighed. "Jake, I'm not sure what I'm ready for. No, that's not true. I'm ready to put this bag of ice on my face and try to get some sleep. Then, if you're open to it, I'm ready to spend a few days with my boyfriend and his family."

"Your boyfriend would like that very much." I could hear the smile in Jake's voice and that made me smile, too, for the first time all evening.

"Thanks, boyfriend," I said, and the little thrill that always shot through me when I thought of being Jake Hudson's boyfriend did so again.

"You're welcome, sweetheart," he replied. "Now get some good rest. Want me to come pick you up tomorrow after school?"

"Can I text you?" I asked.

"Yeah, or if I can get away early, I'll text you. Does that work?"

Of course it did, and once we agreed on that plan, I hung up. I put the ice pack over my throbbing nose and willed the Ibuprofen to do its magic.

I fell asleep with the ice numbing the pain and thoughts of how much my father had done over the years to make my life miserable. I thought about what he'd said about Catherine. Luckily, the usual guilt I felt when I thought of her didn't hit me quite as hard as it used to.

I guess, in a way, Catherine had begun to feel like a mom to me too. She had been a solid force in my life since I'd known her, and she'd been nothing but kind and gracious since I'd come to live with Allen. She even ran interference at times, as a mom would, bridging difficult gaps between my brother and me.

Yeah, I could understand why my father had loved her and, apparently, still did. I just had to wonder what kind of nonsense would cause him to throw his relationship with her away instead of embracing it for all it was. I still struggled to reconcile my feelings about my father self-sabotaging what could've been a happy life with Catherine and Allen as a family, and knowing that if he hadn't done so, I wouldn't exist. But I didn't have the energy to let my mind venture into that weird emotional space tonight.

I lay in bed thinking of how I'd never do that with Jake. I'd never cheat on him or let our love for each other just wither away. I already knew he was my life's love, and I'd do whatever I could to make sure to nurture and build that relationship. I'd make it my life's mission to ensure he always knew what he meant to me and never doubted my commitment to him.

Before drifting off, I considered ways to convey to Jake how much I cared for and appreciated him. Other than being devoted to his family and friends, and having an admirable work ethic, the man didn't seem to care about anything other than the mercantile project in downtown Crawford City. That gave me an idea. I'd need to call

Tom tomorrow and see if he could give me a basic sketch of the building's exterior.

If all went to plan, this could be the perfect way to show Jake how much I loved him.

Thirty-Six

Jake

THE EMERGENCY FAMILY COURT hearing on Wednesday had been as routine as such things could be, or so Mrs. Lidia informed us. I hadn't been able to get out of an important client meeting to go, and Claire and Anita stayed home with Derek because he wasn't feeling up to school that day. But Mrs. Lidia assured us we weren't needed and, if anything, having us attend would've made things more difficult–on us.

She said once the evidence was presented, the judge swiftly determined that Dad had created a dangerous situation and posed a serious threat to Derek. Furthermore, any visitations or potentially returning to the parental home was not in my brother's best interest and wouldn't be for the foreseeable future.

Work was chaotic all day Thursday, so I ended up sending my assistant Charlie to pick up Lance from school. I'd given her my spare key to give him and un-beknownst to him, I didn't plan on taking it back. Of course, the moment she picked him up, he called and fussed at me about not letting him just take a cab.

"I didn't want you in a cab, and Charlie said she was happy to do it. You know, I think she's got a little bit of a crush on you."

I heard Charlie in the background confirm that she did and something about him being the hottest single guy in Nashville.

"He's *not* single!" I shouted into my phone, loud enough for both to hear.

Lance snorted, then whined that doing so had hurt his nose.

"If you think this bloated snout is hot, then there's a lot wrong with both of you."

"Aah, honey, I'd think you're hot even if your entire head was swollen."

"Yeah, yeah, I'm getting off the phone now. Do you want me to fix dinner?" he asked.

"Nah, just make yourself at home. I have a friend who just opened a new seafood restaurant, and I told him I'd try it out. I'll have him put together his favorite dishes, then I'll bring that home tonight."

I knew he was shaking his head. He thought it was amusing that I knew so many people around town.

"Okay, babe," he said, and I smiled at the endearment. "I'll see you when you get home. I've got a ton of home-work I need to finish, so I'll just focus on that."

"Perfect, see you around five then," I said, and we both hung up.

It felt so right to have Lance headed to my condo. I got a little happy jolt as I thought about him being there when I got home.

I also thought about how much things had changed since I'd met Lance. Just a year ago, I'd dated this super-hot model who'd shown up at my condo unannounced, fixed a beautiful gourmet meal, and met me at the door wearing only a thong. I couldn't break up with the guy fast enough. Cuddling up with my boyfriend on the sofa while we ate takeout and talked about our day was much more my speed. Although, come to think of it, imagining Lance standing in my entryway in a thong just waiting for me...wow, that vision would take a moment to overcome. Good thing I was alone in my office.

I quickly opened the marketing plan Charlie had sent me just before she left. I concentrated on the boring, wordy document to get my suddenly raging libido back under control. Maybe I could revisit the thought of my sexy man wearing barely there underwear when I didn't have a multimillion-dollar contract meeting in the next half hour.

THIRTY-SEVEN

LANCE

I NEEDED THAT. A weekend free from family and free from disruptions. I adored my nieces, but the fifteen times a day they came by my door made concentrating difficult, to say the least.

I'd also needed time with my boyfriend, although that hadn't panned out quite as expected. Except for Sunday, Jake had been intensely busy with work, some of it being unplanned client crises. We'd had dinner with his family on Friday night, but besides that, I'd mostly had his condo to myself to get my schoolwork done.

On Sunday, we took a nice walk around his neighborhood. One of his many friends that owned restaurants made us a picnic with all the trimmings, including a basket and plastic wine glasses. We lounged on the grass in a nearby park, eating our lunch and just enjoying each other's company, and I couldn't have asked for a more relaxed and romantic afternoon.

"I love you," I blurted, when Jake leaned over to kiss me. A wide smile lit up his handsome face, and he admitted the same. After that, we lay on the blanket, looking up at the sky and sharing slow, soft kisses as clouds passed lazily over us.

Jake ended up having to work late Sunday afternoon on a project he had to have ready for Monday, so by the time we were cuddled together that night, I was all caught up with schoolwork. In fact, I was able to jump ahead using my syllabus and get the next week's assignment done as well.

I'd loved the walk and the picnic, but I enjoyed our quiet together time the most, including working side by side. More than once, I'd been stretched out on the sofa, reading a textbook, and he'd lift my legs up and slip under them, resting my legs on his lap while he looked over some document he was working on. I could envision us doing that for years, me sketching out building designs on a notepad and Jake securing a client's next big contract, from the comfort of his sofa. Well, maybe *our* sofa someday, but that was getting ahead of myself.

By the end of the weekend, I couldn't help feeling a little down in the dumps that our time was coming to an end. I knew I was being silly, and I loved my brother's family, but I was hungry for this kind of companionship. Between all of our responsibilities–school, work, our families–I felt like I'd hardly spent any time with my boyfriend, and I craved more. Jake was in every way someone, *the* one, I wanted to spend time with; I wondered about the possibility of seeing him more often once I had my own vehicle.

After I called the bank and verified that the money was in my name, then had it transferred into a solo account without my father's name on it, I started looking up used car dealerships between Crawford City and Nashville. I also called over to the winery to speak to Matt about drawing a basic sketch of Jake's future building, so he'd have something to show people who inquired about the construction project.

Not that I couldn't create a passable sketch myself, but it'd be nothing as high a quality as what an artist like Matt could produce. He didn't even hesitate to say yes after I'd explained it'd be a gift for Jake, a friend of his and one of his best customers. In discussing it further, we agreed the commission would be a painting on canvas rather than a sketch because that was Matt's specialty and his rendition of my vision for Jake's project needed to be a showstopper. The price seemed incredibly reasonable, too, considering Matt was a highly sought-after artist and could've easily charged more.

I was so excited about commissioning the painting, I almost said something to Jake but caught myself. This gift would be much better as a surprise than something he expected.

Tuesdays and Thursdays were light class loads for me, and since I had all my homework caught up for the week, I didn't have the same pressure to spend those days camped out in the campus library. So, I texted my father and asked if he could meet me after classes on Thursday at the Greek restaurant he'd wanted to take me to last week.

He instantly responded yes, and I felt good that I was being mature enough to put the family reconciliation ball in motion.

I spoke to Jake right after and told him I'd be having dinner out with Dad. He asked if I'd like to spend the night again at his condo, just so I didn't have to spend time with family after what might be another tense conversation.

"Are you sure it won't be an imposition?" I asked. "I mean, I did just spend the entire weekend with you."

"Best weekend of my life," Jake said, and I could hear the smile in his voice.

"Okay, but only if you're sure."

"Lance, baby, if it wouldn't scare you to death, I'd want you here all the time."

I chuckled. "Scare me to death, huh?"

"Yep, running for the hills scared."

"You think you're funny?" I asked, and Jake laughed. He really was funny. "Okay, so I'm getting off the phone now, but Friday morning breakfast is on me, provided you don't want to go to one of your hoity-toity restaurants that cost a thousand dollars per plate."

Jake's laughter echoed through the phone. "The way you talk, you're becoming a full-fledged Southerner," he said, causing me to smile.

"You're crazy, and I need to go. See you Thursday night."

"Yeah, but I'll talk to you tomorrow."

"Ok, tomorrow. Have a good night. I love you, sweetheart," he said and ended the call.

It was so simple, just a few words people often mutter without thought, but coming from Jake meant the world. He rocked my world in the best way possible. After we hung up, I went downstairs to spend time with the nieces. When they saw me, they all began talking at once, and I had to hold my hand up so they'd speak one at a time.

This had become our routine, and I secretly loved it. That the girls wanted to hang out with their uncle and keep me updated on whatever drama had happened in their lives that day made me feel like the luckiest man who'd ever lived. Less than a year ago, my life was going down the drain fast. Now, I had an amazing family, three nieces I couldn't imagine not being in my life, and the world's most handsome, supportive, and amazing boyfriend.

How could I wish for anything more?

Well, maybe one thing. A real relationship with Dad. I spent my entire childhood hoping my dad would become someone who loved and wanted me. That maybe if I'd done enough things right, if I made him proud enough, he'd come around to see I wasn't the disappointment he always made me feel like. I used to have visions of him spending time with me like other parents did...like Catherine did with Allen.

The two of them were the image I always kept in my head when I thought of the perfect parent/child relationship.

Now that Dad apparently wanted that too, I had to push down my vindictive desire to punish him, which I realized would make me just like him. Then there was Jake and Derek's dad. The hateful, horrible son of a bitch who did this to my face.

My dad was not a great person, even he'd admitted that, but he hadn't ever been physically abusive. Emotionally abusive. Yeah, he was an expert at that. And no, his apology would never be enough for that to have ever been okay. Part of me may never forgive him for all that he'd done, but watching him these past few days with my nieces, and even how he was treating Allen and me lately...it was making a difference in how I saw him. A big enough difference that I wanted to clear the air and give him the opportunity to be a real father, the kind I'd always needed. If there was even a chance we could have that type of relationship, now was the time to try.

Thursday came in a flash, and as I sat across from my father at the restaurant table, I studied him for a moment, realizing he was nervous. The change in him was strange and overwhelming, probably for both of us. Not that it wasn't a welcome change. I was tired of being browbeaten by anyone and that included my father.

"How's your week been?" I asked after we'd ordered.

"It's been good. I toured Nashville and was surprised to find it's a nice little town."

I chuckled. "I'm sure none of the people from here would think it's so small."

"They've not been to New York."

"No," I said, shaking my head. "I suppose that's true."

The waiter came then, pouring each of us a glass of wine and putting a loaf of their signature bread on the table before leaving again.

I took a sip of the wine and nodded. It was nice. Several steps above what I'd gotten used to drinking since I'd moved here. The only exception being the red made at Matt and Logan Winery, which was spectacular.

"So, Dad, I asked you here to continue our conversation from last week."

He stopped raising his own wineglass halfway to his lips and set it back down. "I supposed that was the reason," he said, but didn't make eye contact.

"I've not forgiven you. I think that'll take a lot more time. We don't need to rehash everything, but you should've never tried to keep Allen and me from being a family. That's the part I'm struggling with the most. It's also not okay that you forced me into a situation where you basically stole my money. I will never trust you again, not with anything like my finances."

I took another drink of the wine, expecting at any moment for him to lash out at me for daring to be so impudent.

When he didn't respond, just continued staring at his hands on the table, I swallowed and continued. "I love you, though. You are my only parent. Mom has never wanted anything to do with me. I know now you were hurting after losing Catherine and being stuck raising me on your own, and although that doesn't excuse some of the things you did, it does explain it."

I reached over and took Dad's hand, causing him to jolt. "I want you in my life, and perhaps, over time, we can work through the other stuff, but for now, that's what I can offer you. A place in my life, my new one here in Crawford City."

"Thanks," he said, and without warning, my strong-willed, emotionally stilted father broke down right in front of me. I slowly moved to his side and allowed him to lean into me as he quietly sobbed.

Luckily, there were only a few patrons in the restaurant this time of day. The wait staff seemed to understand we were having a moment, and no one disturbed us.

It only took a moment for Dad to get his emotions back under control and he turned to me and drew me into a hug. "Thank you, Lance. I thought you were going to tell me to get lost."

I chuckled. "I thought about it. Lots actually. But, like I said, I want you in my life. You're my dad even if you suck at it...a lot sometimes."

That made him chuckle too. "Okay, okay," he said as he got his wits about him.

I moved back to my side of the table as he wiped his eyes and, as if the wait staff had been waiting for the moment to pass, our food arrived.

The rest of the meal was pleasant. Mostly we talked about anything but what we were both still processing. I did learn that Dad had put his home up for sale because the terms of the divorce were that his ex-wife Kassidy got half the proceeds. But he said his main motivation to sell was that it didn't feel like home anymore. I'd wanted to press him, to ask if it hadn't felt like home because I wasn't there, but I wouldn't have handled it well if his answer had been no.

"Where are you going to live?" I asked.

He blushed, another first. "Well, I've been talking with Allen, and there's an adjunct professor position open at his hospital. I thought I'd do a little moonlighting as a hospitalist and try my hand at teaching. Who knows, it could end up being something I really enjoy."

"Well, you aren't that old. You could totally start a new career."

He chuckled. "I'm fifty-five, so not that young either. But you're right. It feels like the perfect time to try something new."

"And Allen isn't having a heart attack or anything?"

Dad looked at me, startled. I'd never spoken to him like this. Usually, where either Allen or I were concerned, our father would do what he wanted and didn't care what we thought.

He smiled, though, and said, "We had to have several talks, but Allen said as long as we weren't working for each other, it should be fine."

"Lucky that you aren't a pediatrician then, huh?"

He nodded. "Never felt that calling. But I've not been a hospitalist before either. Although through the years that I ran the hospital in Queens, I thought that would be a job I'd really enjoy. You get to have your hands in several pots but don't really have to focus on any one patient for very long. It's like the perfect job for me."

"Either way, Dad, I'm sure you'll find your place," I said. "You're like a cat in that way, always landing on your feet."

Dad cocked an eyebrow. "You sure you haven't been down here too long? You're beginning to use colloquialisms like you were born here."

"It does rub off fast, trust me. If you're here long enough, it'll get to you, too."

"Seriously doubtful, son. Your grandmother was the daughter of a very strict English teacher and even though we traveled all over, she controlled my language like the officers control the recruits at basic training."

"You say that now. Just wait, it seeps in when you least expect it."

The rest of the conversation was easy and by the time Dad left, I was feeling hopeful. Like we'd turned over a huge new leaf. No, nothing about this was perfect, but it felt like we were on the road to healing.

"Hey, Jake," I said when he answered his phone. "Whatcha doing?"

"Just finishing up with Charlie. You ready?"

"More than. Hey, I need a favor?"

I waited while Jake answered some question Charlie asked in the background. When he came back, he asked, "Yeah, what's that?"

"I need a car. Do you have any interest in going car shopping with me?"

"Sure, like tonight?" he asked.

"Yeah, like tonight. I talked to a classmate earlier today. He said he got his car not far from here and he thought the dealer was pretty reputable. I checked, they're open late."

"I'll tell you what, if you're serious, I've got a friend who owns a car dealership, and he owes me a favor big-time. I'd be happy to call in that favor for you."

I laughed. "I'm not looking to buy a Mercedes or anything. I just need a used but reliable vehicle to get me back and forth from Crawford City without breaking down somewhere in between."

"Still perfect. He auctions off the trade-ins and I'm sure he'd be willing to make you a deal on one of them."

"Now, that sounds promising. Okay, call in your favor and I'll do you a favor as well."

"What's that?" he asked.

"Chocolate Factory is on me!"

"Yes!" Jake said, like this was some big deal. I knew he had an account with them and gave chocolate gifts from the local chocolatier on a weekly basis, but hey, it was a place we both loved, so I knew he'd play along.

"Want to meet me there in like an hour?"

"Charlie!" Jake yelled across the room. "Will we be done in time for me to meet Lance in an hour?"

I heard her speaking in the background, but couldn't quite make out what she said.

"No, you can't come too." When he laughed, I knew she was teasing him about me. Something I thought was both embarrassing and funny at the same time.

"Charlie said I can be there in an hour and a half if I work *really* hard."

I chuckled. "Then work really hard and I'll see you then."

"Do you need me to send a car?"

"No, I'd rather walk. I'm doing better. My nose hardly hurts any longer, and I miss exercise."

"Okay. Love you," he said and hung up. Even before the phone disconnected, I could hear him getting back to the work Charlie had mentioned. He was so freaking lucky to have an assistant like her. I hardly knew Charlie, but she seemed smart as a tack and seemed to love what she was doing as well. In fact, everyone who worked for Jake appeared to be happy in their jobs.

After having to fight for the right to live my life, I valued that. More than I even knew I could.

Thirty-Eight

Jake

I WENT TO THE interview with Derek, when he was scheduled to speak to the social workers and his court-appointed attorney about what our father had done. The interview was being held at Anita and Claire's home, so no one questioned why I was there.

Derek was distraught, of course, but my brother's personality was stronger than mine had been at his age.

When he was asked questions, he stilled himself and answered honestly, and although he was clearly emotional, he handled it well.

After we were done, Derek went to his room while the adults discussed the results. Mrs. Lidia looked at me and sighed. "Your father will have to spend the next few weeks in jail. He's also being prosecuted for assault, attempted kidnapping, and public intoxication on top of it."

I nodded. "That's good. At least it means he won't be trying to harm my brother again anytime soon."

They left shortly after the interview concluded, and I made sure Derek was okay before I left as well.

I ended up calling the sheriff in Crawford City, and when she referred me to the prosecuting attorney for my father's case, I contacted him.

"Your father is being charged, so I can't really speak to you directly."

"I assure you, Mr. Jenkins, I'm on your side of this."

The man made a sound that showed how little he believed me. However, he did tell me the date of the arraignment hearing.

"Sir, I'd like for you to ask for the maximum bail. He tried to kidnap my brother, and he beat up my boyfriend. I prefer he not be set free anytime soon."

This time, the noise he made sounded more promising. "Are you willing to tell that to the court in front of your father?" he asked.

I thought for a moment before responding, knowing this was a pivotal decision in all of our lives. "Yes, I believe my father is a threat to all of us at the moment."

I hung up, feeling knots in my stomach. I didn't believe Dad cared about me any longer. Maybe he never had, but it still felt something like betrayal to actually testify against the man. I assumed this was how Derek had felt during his interview.

The arraignment happened the next day, and fortunately, it didn't require either Derek or Lance to be there. I sat in the back of the courtroom and was surprised when Dad came in and looked right at me. When he turned away, I realized he didn't recognize me. His first-born, and he didn't even know who I was.

After my father was read the charges against him, the prosecutor said he was asking for the maximum bail due to his being a danger to Derek and other members of the community. Of course, the defense attorney argued that wasn't the case and that he had just been drunk at the time.

I could tell the judge was being persuaded by the argument, so I was pleased when Jenkins said, "Your Honor, I have a witness who knows Mr. Hudson personally, who is willing to testify not only to the violence Mr. Hudson poses to the community, but he was also at the event and can testify to what happened that day."

My father turned around then and scanned the crowd. When he landed on me, this time he hesitated, and I watched as recognition dawned on his face. He quickly leaned over and whispered something to his attorney, who then turned to face me as well.

"Your Honor, we object to this witness. The prosecution has brought Mr. Hudson's estranged gay son here to disparage him."

"I object, Your Honor," Jenkins said, and there was a whole bunch of arguing between both attorneys until the judge finally called everything back to order.

"Mr. Jenkins, is this Mr. Hudson's son you have here to testify?" he asked.

"It is, Your Honor," the attorney replied.

The judge hesitated for a moment. "I don't think that's necessary." He scanned the documents in front of him and, after pulling one piece of paper up and reading it, he addressed my father.

"Mr. Hudson, you are accused of attempting to kidnap your son, a minor no longer in your custody. You are also accused of assaulting a man who tried to stop you from doing so. All the while being legally intoxicated at a public gathering. You will have your chance to defend yourself in a trial set by this court. However, you were already under a court order not to have contact with your son, Derek. An order you blatantly disobeyed. Because this court has a concern that this was a crime against a child, and there is concern for the safety of that child, bail will be set at one million dollars."

The defense attorney jumped up, but the judge was already banging his gavel and had stood to go. "He's a faggot," my father screamed to the courtroom, stopping everyone in their tracks.

"That man right there is a faggot!" he yelled, so angrily that he was literally spitting, and pointed at me. "If allowed to go without punishment, he will turn my youngest son into a faggot as well. You will all burn in hell if you allow him to get away with converting an innocent youth into an abomination!"

Dad's attorney put a hand on my father to prevent him from saying anything further.

The judge was red faced as he faced my father's attorney. "That's enough. Get this man out of my courtroom before I charge him with contempt."

The bailiff quickly came forward, cuffed my father, and led him out the side door to what I assumed was the jail. Before he was gone, he turned toward me, and I saw for the first time nothing but pure hatred. He was different from when he kicked me out of the house all those years ago. Back then, he still had a soul.

I shuddered as he was pushed through the door. Not even a glimmer of my dad remained in that man. I'd just stood to go when the prosecutor stopped in front of me. "I'm sorry you..."

I shook my head. "No, it was good for me to see it. I now know what he is. It's been a long time since I've laid eyes on my father. I didn't know what he'd become."

I continued shaking my head, then looked up. "Thanks for what you've done. I'm sure now he would've come after my brother again, and next time it would've been much worse."

"Well, we aren't out of the woods yet. He could still post bond, but more importantly, we need to prove his guilt in court."

"Will Derek have to testify?"

He nodded. "Yes, but I can probably arrange to have that testimony given in the judge's chambers since he's a minor and a ward of the state."

"And Lance, I'm sure he'll have to testify."

The prosecutor nodded. "Yes, along with the other witnesses."

"Okay, then let's do what has to be done. I'd rather my family not be put at risk any more than necessary."

I was depressed as I drove back to Nashville. I hadn't been prepared to see how my father had changed. I also regretted Lance and Derek had to endure all they were going to go through because of him.

From the courthouse in Mayville, I ended up going to Crawford City instead of driving home because, frankly, that felt like a place where good people still lived. It was so much like the town I'd grown up in, but instead of leaning toward hate, they leaned toward acceptance and even friendship. I totally needed that tonight.

If not for Todd and Ash having three toddlers to deal with, I'd have been tempted to call and crash at their place. Except there was someone else in this town I needed to see and talk to right now, even more than my oldest friends. I pulled my car over and called Lance.

"Hey, are you back home yet?" I asked.

"Yeah, just got to the house. Why, are you in town?" he asked.

"I will be in a moment. Do you have time for a walk? I'm just getting back from my dad's arraignment."

"Oh, yeah of course. Want to walk around here?"

I thought for a moment. "Yeah, I think I'd like to walk around town and have dinner at the café."

"Come on then. I'll see you when you get here."

After we hung up, I thought about the little Subaru Lance had purchased when we'd gone looking. It was a sweet little car and because it was all-wheel drive, I was confident it would be able to get him to and from Crawford City even on bad weather days.

It also allowed him to come home when he got out of class rather than having to hang around campus waiting for Allen, which is why Lance was home this early on a Wednesday afternoon.

Just seeing Lance lifted my spirits. He was sitting out on the big front porch swing of his brother's house, reading something on his iPad. I assumed it was homework.

I parked the car in the last parking spot that sat just below the hill leading up to his house. He looked up as I climbed the steps and sat next to him on the swing. "You okay?" he asked.

"I will be. I'm definitely better now that I'm here with you."

He leaned into me. "Wanna talk about it?"

I shook my head. "Not right now. I still need some time to process who my father has become. But I'd rather not be alone while I'm doing it."

Lance reached over and kissed my cheek. "You aren't alone."

I used the arm I'd put across the back of the swing when he'd leaned into me to side hug him. "This is exactly what I needed."

We walked around the town, occasionally stopping to talk to one of the folks we passed. "This is such a great place. I can't wait until the building is done and I can move here," I said.

"Yeah, I can't wait until you're here more, too. Hey, so I hear the groundbreaking date is set."

I smiled. "Yeah, with my dad's crap, it hasn't been as big a deal as it would've been. But we break ground in two weeks, and then Todd and Amos plan to dig in."

Lance leaned into me as we walked, holding hands. "Oh, Linc told me you didn't have any problems with the town council. That's good news."

"Yeah, a couple council members are friends of the former mayor who'd burned the mercantile, so we always thought they'd object to the rebuild, but even they seemed to have come full circle now. Of course, it's going to bring some nice new shops and a hotel to town. Something that really is needed. "

I realized we'd been talking only about me, so I quickly checked in with him. "How's your nose feeling?"

"Gib said I should be fully healed in a week or so. He doesn't think it'll have to be reset. He thinks it's healing straight."

"Well, at least you have something straight on you."

Lance playfully backhanded me before chuckling. "I don't wanna be straight if that means I can't have you."

"Oh, that wasn't a complaint, just an observation."

We teased each other a little more as we walked toward the café, in an unspoken agreement that we were both ready to eat.

As I sat across from my boyfriend, who was talking about his classes and how much he enjoyed them, I couldn't help but once again come to the realization of how much I wanted to have a life with him. How just spending time with him could ease my anxiety even after looking into the face of hatred. Hatred from a man who should've loved me unconditionally.

I resolved then that it was time to buy the engagement ring. I would do that tomorrow. Usually, I'd have asked Todd or Jen to go with me, but they were both leading insanely busy lives. So, I decided I'd send a text to Derek before I headed home to see if maybe he'd like to go with me to pick it out.

Then I smiled at the thought. I had three people I thought of as best friends. Todd and Jen would always be that for me. They'd had my back for a very long time. But somehow, my little brother had begun to become that too. The family I never thought I'd have again.

And if my brother's wish came true, soon Anita and Claire would legally be family too. I guessed I should probably plan on taking them all out to dinner tomorrow and announce that I planned to ask Lance to marry me. Maybe Derek and I could go ring shopping this weekend.

I looked up and saw that Lance had stopped talking. "Oh, um, sorry, my mind drifted for a moment."

Lance reached over and took my hand. "It doesn't surprise me after what you've been through. I'm sure you're reeling after all that."

I chuckled. "No, baby, I wasn't thinking about that. I was thinking about how lucky I am to have you in my family. I've been alone for a long time, but now, even in the face of seeing a man who has lost all concept of familial connection, I see the things I *do* have. I can't tell you how much I appreciate that, Lance."

He blushed, then took a breath. "You know I love you, right?" he asked.

I nodded. "I love you too. More than I ever thought I could."

We were looking into each other's eyes and holding hands across the table when I heard someone approach us. When I looked up, Todd and Ash were standing there awkwardly, looking a bit embarrassed.

"Hey guys, what's up?" I asked.

"We didn't mean to interrupt," Ash said. "But we thought you might enjoy joining us. We have the big table in the back since we have Donna, Louisa, and the kids with us. Our dads are joining us soon, too."

I looked over at Lance, who was smiling, and he nodded. "Okay, yes," I said.

We went to the back, where the kids were already in their highchairs and making a mess with the food their aunts had gotten them.

Lance and I spent the rest of the evening playing with Todd and Ash's toddlers and laughing with our little group of friends.

I drove home that night convinced I'd somehow won life's lottery. The people I'd just spent the evening with were by far the best friends a man could hope for. Nothing my birth father said or did would ever dim the light that had begun to shine in this little town. All we had to do was ensure that everyone I loved stayed safe.

When I got back home, I quickly looked up a private investigator I'd used a couple times in the past to get ahead of bad press. Someone who could dig up enough dirty laundry to fill a washing machine, even on my most upstanding clients. *Know the devil before he attacked* had long been my philosophy when dealing with famous people. Know it, then you could be prepared to deal with it.

I shot her a quick email asking that she do some digging on my father to assist in a criminal investigation against him. I knew country prosecutors like Jenkins often had tiny budgets, and I wasn't going to let that keep my father from being held accountable for his actions.

I took out the business card the prosecutor had given me and gave him a call. I was sure he wouldn't be too happy about my hiring a PI, but hell if I cared. In the end, he had a job to do, but so did I. Hopefully, my efforts would prove useful in the end and the people I loved would be safe.

THIRTY-NINE

LANCE

MY HEART WENT OUT to Jake in the weeks following Labor Day. His father had really done a number on him and Derek. Not to mention my nose.

After his father's arraignment, Jake hired a private investigator who began unearthing some pretty scary stuff about his dad, including his involvement in paramilitary groups. One group even had multiple members arrested at a rally where they were planning a physical attack on capitol buildings in Nashville and Washington, DC.

Jake's father had been arrested at the time but later released since it was the first rally he'd attended and there was no evidence he was involved in the efforts to attack either capitol.

The first hearing happened in early December and since I had been subpoenaed to attend, I'd taken time off school. I would've anyway, though, just to support Jake and Derek.

I was sitting on the far side of the courtroom, mostly to stay out of the way. But also because the attorney mentioned that since Jake and I were dating, it was best if we didn't sit together, so as to not stir the pot, although the defense attorney would probably figure it out anyway.

When the prosecution called their first witness, Jake jumped like he'd been shocked. "Will Lena Manning please take the stand."

"Objection," the defense argued. "This witness was put on the list last-minute, Your Honor. We haven't had time to prepare a defense."

"Who is this witness, Mr. Jenkins?" the judge asked.

"Your Honor, this is the defendant's daughter. We added her name to the list as soon as we got it. Also, Your Honor, the defendant knew we were putting his children on the stand. The defense shouldn't need any more time to review this individual as they did for Mr. Hudson's sons."

The judge thought for a moment. "I'll allow it but, Mr. Jenkins, I'm putting you on notice. From now on, you need to give adequate notice of any new witnesses, understood?"

"Yes, Your Honor," he said.

Lena came forward and was sworn in, then she took her seat.

"Mrs. Manning, would you please state your full name for the court?"

Lena answered all the questions about who she was and when she'd contacted the prosecuting attorney.

"Why did you approach my office, Mrs. Manning?" Jenkins asked.

She took a deep breath and looked over at Jake. "I'm afraid for my brothers' lives," she said.

"Objection," the defense yelled, and once he explained what sounded like a bunch of crap to me. The judge seemed to agree with my assessment.

"Overruled. Please continue, Mr. Jenkins."

"Would you please explain why you thought your brothers' lives were in danger?"

She nodded before wiping at a tear that'd rolled down her face. "I was visiting with my parents the week we'd found out Derek had requested to be adopted by a lesbian couple. Dad had blown a gasket and Mom had asked me and Richard to come over to help calm him down."

"And Richard is?"

"Richard is my husband," she said.

"When we got there, Dad was in the back room talking to three men I didn't know. I couldn't hear everything they were saying until Dad got agitated and told them he wanted that 'faggot' killed," she said, using air quotes when saying the hateful word.

"Did you know who he was referring to?" Jenkins asked her then.

She nodded. "Yeah, he told them. His first-born was an abomination and had to be gotten rid of."

"What else did he say?"

Lena's tears were streaming down her face now. "That they were supposed to take Derek away, too, and put him through conversion therapy."

She looked at her father then and her face hardened. "Then Dad told them if Derek couldn't be saved, they should get rid of him, too."

"Objection."

"Overruled."

"What did your mother say about this?" the prosecutor asked.

"She told me we had to stop him. That we couldn't let these men kill our Derek."

"Did your mom say anything about your older brother?"

Lena nodded. "She said even though she thinks it's a sin, being gay, she believes in the Ten Commandments more."

Lena turned again to her father. "Thou shalt not kill."

Their father jumped up and shook his fist at his daughter. "Honor thy mother and thy father!" he yelled. "A man who lies with a man is an abomination and should surely be put to death."

The judge was banging his gavel, but Jake's father wouldn't stop yelling. Finally, the judge ordered the bailiff to remove Mr. Hudson from the court and even then, he yelled all the way out of the courtroom.

"Mr. Graves, you need to control your client. For now, we'll recess until tomorrow."

The bailiff returned and escorted the jury from the room.

Lena left the stand and looked in Jake's direction with a sad expression before she left the courthouse. I waited to follow Jake out of the courtroom until most of the crowd had dispersed. When I got to my car, I saw Jake talking to Lena a short distance away.

I smiled as they hugged. This really was a big deal for Jake, and I hoped the hug was an indication that things were going to be reconciled there as well.

I decided not to approach Jake just yet, keeping my distance. As I drove home, I thought about the reconciliation with my own father.

Since our talk, things had vastly improved between us. No surprise, his house sold almost immediately. He'd moved to a really nice apartment in Franklin, not far from Catherine, and it looked like they were working on their own form of reconciliation. Although, one night when we were all having a picnic at her house, I heard Catherine telling Chrissy that she wasn't going to marry her grandpa again, but they were trying to be friends.

When I got back home, I went to my room and opened the link my professor had sent me. I could watch a recording of class so I wouldn't get behind during the trial. It sucked that we were in court right before finals. I was confident I would be okay, but this wasn't the time to fall behind.

I was watching the end of the lecture when Allen knocked on my door asking how the trial went.

"It was intense. Jake's sister was the first on the stand and she basically told the court her father was planning to kill Jake and possibly Derek."

"Wow, really? Is Jake okay?"

I shrugged. "Not sure yet. I think he'll come by, but when I left the courthouse, he and his sister were in the parking lot. I assume they decided to meet somewhere to talk."

"That's good, at least. So, does it look like the jury was hearing what she said?"

I shrugged again. "To be honest, I wasn't watching the jury. I was too overwhelmed by what she was saying. The fact they had to drag the old man out of the courtroom yelling scripture about killing gay people probably didn't help his case any."

"Dear God," Allen said. "Do you think Jake is still at risk?"

"There's a good chance. Lena, his sister, testified there were three men she didn't know in the room with him when he was planning to kidnap Derek and possibly murder Jake."

"Well, I'm guessing you should be careful, too. Why don't you let me drive you to school until this is over?"

I laughed. "Now you're sounding like Jake. I don't think I'm on anyone's radar quite yet. Maybe if I end up testifying, then we should be a bit more cautious. For now, I'm pretty sure I'm okay."

Allen looked at me as if he wanted to argue, but decided to let it go.

"I took off early today so I could be here when you got home and fix dinner. So, if Jake gets in contact, let him know he's invited."

I nodded. "I'll do that."

Allen left my room and I put my energy into the assignment for the class I'd just finished watching. Rather than a final exam, this course ended with a term paper, which I had mostly completed. I quickly signed into the program where I was taking notes for the paper and added a couple things I'd gotten from the lecture, then closed out of schoolwork altogether. I laid back on the bed and closed my eyes.

I thought about Jake and how we'd both had difficult childhoods in different ways because of our fathers, and how those men were on opposing life paths now. Mine was finally coming to terms with the horrible human being he'd been as I was growing up and actively working to reestablish our relationship. Jake's had taken a blowtorch to any decent feelings he'd had for the man and was becoming more hostile and even violent toward his children.

I must've dozed off because when my phone began ringing, I saw that I'd missed a couple texts before answering Jake's call.

"Hey, you okay?" I asked.

"Yeah, um. I have a strange request."

"Okay," I said, waiting to hear it.

"My sister, Lena, the one who testified today, would like to meet you."

"Um, do you think that's a good idea, all things considered?" I asked.

"I do, but only if you feel comfortable meeting her."

"Well, I mean, maybe. Allen is cooking dinner for us, but if you'd feel more comfortable, we could meet at the café."

Jake paused a moment. "Why don't we meet for coffee there? It's still early enough that I doubt anyone is using the back area. Besides, the new woman they hired makes the best cinnamon rolls I've ever eaten. Then, after I've spoiled my dinner, we can go eat Allen's cooking."

I chuckled. "He's getting better, although marginally."

Allen was not the best cook around. Usually, Gib or I cooked dinner, although I wasn't much better than Allen, if I'm honest. Catherine had begun teaching me how to cook from the very first day I arrived. So, I was a little better than my brother. What Allen could cook, though, was his homemade chocolate chip cookies, the rest...well, we were all a work in progress.

Lena was a shy version of her outgoing brother. The two were remarkably similar in features, and now that I saw her close up, they really did look like siblings.

She was gracious when I met her, but I could tell she was leery of me. Of course, after what I'd heard today, I had to assume she'd heard some pretty awful things about gay people. It was probably a miracle she was comfortable enough to sit this close to two gay men, even if one of them was her long-lost brother.

We spent over an hour at the café. After the initial greeting, I mostly just listened to the two siblings reunite. The conversation was strained when I'd first showed up, but before long, they began teasing each other over things they'd done when they were growing up.

Lena was just over a year younger than Jake, and it sounded like they'd been pretty close before he'd been kicked out. Lena told Jake about her family. She had three little boys who she said were hellions. Her husband was a youth pastor who'd come to work at the church they'd grown up in. He'd grown up in Pennsylvania. She'd just finished community college when he'd come along, and they'd fallen in love and been married within a few months.

I could tell she really was in love with him. She showed us pictures of her boys and laughed when she said the oldest was so much like Jake it was scary. He got into trouble at home and at school. Not because he was mean, but because he was inquisitive and wanted to try everything out.

Jake laughed and laughed as she told us about his antics. "You should get the boy insurance 'cause you know that's not going to change, right?"

Lena shook her head. "He's going to be the death of me."

It was fun watching the siblings reconnect. Lena looked at her watch. "I really should be getting back. I've got an hour and a half drive to get back home."

Her face sobered before she sighed. "It's been great reconnecting Jake. I fought for you when they kicked you out. Dad told us if we didn't shut up, he'd kick us out next. I was too young to do anything other than shut up. I tried to find you several times after..." She shook her head. "Dad even found out once. He made it clear I wasn't to go looking for you again, only not with words."

"He hit you?" Jake asked, alarmed.

Lena looked at him for a long moment. "You don't know him, Jake. He's changed over the years. He got darker and darker, even to the point where he left the church and joined some really creepy place that even Mom refused to go to. I'm afraid for you, Jake, and for Derek. You should watch your back. I think those men he talked to that day were from his church. I don't know much about them, and I'm not sure if they agreed to help or not, but you need to be careful."

"I'll be okay," Jake assured her. "I've got security at my condo and also at my workplace. If it helps, I'll let them know they should keep a closer eye on things until this trial is over."

"It couldn't hurt, brother," Lena reached over, putting her hand over his. "I don't want to lose you again. I know you probably hate all of us, but we love you and miss you. Always have."

I think Jake was about to make some retort, but tears were flowing from Lena's face, and it was clear she was being genuine.

"Thanks, Lena," he said instead. "It means a lot to hear you say that."

She smiled at him before saying it'd been nice to meet me.

We watched her leave, then Jake turned to me. "I never would've dreamed the day would come when I'd talk to my sister again, much less have her come to my and Derek's defense. Especially not in court."

"People surprise us when we least expect it," I said, thinking of my own father and his turnaround. "So, we should probably get back and pretend like whatever Allen cooked is palatable."

"Ugh, can't we pretend like we got caught up with Lena and just ate here?" he asked.

"Sure, but everyone here will tell Gib they saw us eating tonight. Do you want to explain that to my brother?"

"No," he said with a sigh. "I guess not."

"Buck up, you ate two of those huge cinnamon rolls, so even if Allen makes his horrible eggplant stuff again, you'll be full."

"On purpose, Lance, I did that on purpose."

We walked out of the restaurant laughing. It'd been a hell of a day, but at least it had ended on a good note.

FORTY

JAKE

THE PROSECUTION RESTED ON Friday. Dad was too violent to have in the courtroom, so he was left in the jail cell and attended court through closed-circuit TV.

Lance took the stand for less than half an hour and he was one of the last to be questioned. Mostly, the prosecution just asked him about seeing Dad pull Derek toward the parking area and why he'd stopped him. Hearing Lance's play-by-play account of how he'd run to help my brother automatically, without even thinking, only deepened my pride in him and gratitude for his swift actions in a way I couldn't even express in words.

The defense didn't ask about him and me being in a relationship, but I assumed that was because I hadn't been called to testify.

As my private investigator uncovered, much to the satisfaction of the prosecution, Dad's participation in nefarious activities went a lot deeper than even Lena knew. Most of the trial showcased how Dad had gotten involved with several paramilitary groups and even though most of them weren't considered a major threat by the FBI, it appeared that he was trending toward more violent groups such as the one who'd been raided by the FBI last summer.

The threats he'd made that Lena testified to were reiterated by other people the prosecutor had found through my PI. It wasn't until the trial started that I knew the information had been found. Of course, I'd instructed the PI to do whatever the prosecutor needed to help with the case. So, when Jenkins had told her not to share the information with me, she had complied.

Saturday afternoon, Jenkins called me to tell us Dad's attorney had approached him with a plea bargain.

"If he agrees to this, your dad would get ten years without the chance of parole to avoid the more severe charges of conspiracy to commit murder, kidnapping, and assault. If he ended up being convicted of those, he could end up serving a life sentence, especially since he'd been heard conspiring to kill his underage son, who was in the custody of the state at the time."

"Do you think that's the best way to go?" I asked, thinking that seemed a bit light for a man conspiring to have his sons murdered.

Jenkins sighed. "Listen, juries can go either way when it comes to families. They might push for the maximum or they could let him off with a slap on the wrist. Personally, I think it's better for all parties to go for the sure thing, which would ensure Derek has enough time to grow up before having to face your father again."

I couldn't argue that point. Although, as I learned later, I think the main reason Jenkins wanted to accept the plea deal was because, in exchange, Dad had agreed to give up details on people he'd associated with in the paramilitary groups. The men he'd been conspiring with were bad characters and the FBI wanted information on them.

Whatever the reason, if it meant my brother was safe and that my dad would end up being ostracized by those bad people, I was all for it.

That night, I went to eat dinner with Derek and our moms and explained what Jenkins had told me. Derek's reaction was shock, then sadness. I comforted him as best I could, but I could see the conflicted emotions on his face and knew this was stuff he had to work through on his own.

Before I left, Derek said, "Come get me tomorrow morning and lets go out for breakfast. I'm not sure if I'll be up for talking about all of this, but I'd like to hang with you, okay?"

I nodded. "Of course. Hey, I talked to Lena again, and she wants us to come visit her and the boys. You up for that?"

Derek frowned, then shrugged. "Maybe eventually, but it feels like they all threw me away, Jake. I'm not ready to forgive them just yet."

I nodded. "I get it, Derek. I'm still dealing with those same feelings."

The next morning, I picked him up and took him to the local Waffle House. Claire hated the food there and said it was like eating in a closet, so anytime it was just Derek and me, we tended to eat there. We both liked the greasy food and comfy surroundings.

When the waitress had taken our order and left, Derek immediately launched into why he'd wanted to come out.

"So, Dad was up to some major stuff, like dangerous and probably illegal stuff. I mean, I think we all knew it was happening, but it was just easier to pretend it wasn't."

I nodded and let him talk. I'd wondered how much he'd known. Dad seemed to have kept everything away from the family until Lena had stumbled upon him and his cronies plotting to kill us.

"What was he like when you were growing up?" I asked, curious if I could pinpoint when Dad had begun to noticeably change for the worse.

"Moody. I mean, sometimes he'd be carefree and fun, and he'd play ball with us, or he'd tease us and Eric, Chelle and I'd end up in a pile on the floor laughing."

I hadn't thought of Eric and Chelle in a long time. They were both still in diapers when I'd left. For that reason, I still pictured them as babies.

"And other times?" I asked.

"He'd get so angry. And none of us knew why."

"Did he ever hit you?" I asked, feeling concerned.

"He'd spank us, but never when he was angry like that. Those days, he'd rant about something none of us really understood, screaming about politics, then he'd disappear, sometimes for a day or two."

I didn't know how to respond, so I decided to talk about the dad I once knew.

"He was always in a good mood when I was little. He'd antagonize me or Lena and we'd end up jumping on him and he'd tickle us and sometimes throw us in the air, then catch us. He loved church and was even a deacon when I was little. I remember his favorite times were Sunday mornings before church, and he'd dance around the kitchen with Mom, telling her he loved her, and he'd grab us all up in a group hug. I mean, he had dark days even then, but he'd never done anything hurtful, not until the day he kicked me out. That's why it'd all come as such a shock at the time. That day, he was dark and mean. Although, to be honest, Derek, even then I could tell he knew what he was doing was wrong."

I let the tears fall from my eyes and didn't even try to wipe them away. I didn't want to hide my emotions from Derek because I didn't want him packing down his feelings either, even if it meant crying over waffles in a crowded restaurant full of strangers.

"I'd never known what betrayal was until that day. But Derek, he was not the same man I saw in court. That man is angry and violent. All the good I remember seems to have disappeared and he..."

"He became a monster," Derek finished for me.

I nodded and wiped the final tear as the waitress put the food we'd ordered in front of us. "Thank you," I managed to say and the older woman gave me a polite smile, clearly having noticed I'd just been crying.

Derek and I ate in silence as I pondered the past few weeks, and I assumed he was doing the same. Halfway through our meal, he changed the subject, asking, "So, when are you going to pop the question to Lance?"

I about choked on my bite of waffle and started coughing. Derek just grinned at me, knowing the one-eighty in our conversation had caught me completely off guard. "Wow, way to warn a guy about changing the subject here," I croaked out, then took a long drink of water.

"Well, I mean, Dad is an awful man who'll be in prison for a while, which hopefully will knock some sense into him, so why aren't we talking about something positive?"

I laughed. "You're right, although you're too young to be this smart."

"Pfft," Derek scoffed. "Dude, just 'cause I'm sixteen doesn't mean I don't have a little common sense. So, stop changing the subject. When do you plan to propose?"

I smiled. "Well, if you must know, I was waiting until all this court crap was done. So, now that it is..."

"You should do it at Christmas. Give it to him as a present. He won't be expecting it."

I laughed. "You've been thinking about this, then?"

"Well, yeah, I went ring shopping with you how long ago now? I bet that thing has been burning a hole in your pocket every day since. And Lance is sweet and good-looking. You're not likely to convince someone like him to fall for you again, so make him my brother-in-law before you screw up or something."

"Dude!" I said and threw some of my biscuit at him.

"You did not just pick a food fight with me," Derek said, breaking off a chunk of his waffle to lob back at me.

"No, he didn't," the waitress said as she came up to our table. "And if you start throwing food, I'm gonna paddle you both."

We laughed as the woman refilled my coffee, gave us both the eye again, and turned around before she could smile.

We were both rolling with laughter as we finished our meals, and I left a huge tip for the woman who'd helped us find some humor when we both really needed it.

FORTY-ONE

LANCE

"H ERE'S TO YOUR FIRST Christmas in the wilds of Tennessee," Jake said as we cuddled up in the little cabin he'd rented for us by the lake above Fall Creek Falls State Park.

We clinked our eggnog glasses together, then after drinking, cuddled back under the blanket on the sofa, and listened to the logs softly crackle in the fireplace.

"This was a great idea, Jake," I said. "Since everyone's coming to Allen and Gib's house tomorrow, it's nice just to have Christmas Eve to ourselves."

Jake kissed the top of my head. "I'm glad you approve."

I was feeling drowsy as the alcohol in the eggnog and the warmth from the fire began to take its hold on me.

"Wanna open one of your presents?" Jake asked.

"Um, I didn't bring yours. Why don't we wait until tomorrow and you can open mine at the same time?"

Jake chuckled. "'Cause this one is more private."

I leaned up, looking at my boyfriend. "What did you do?" I asked, causing him to laugh out loud.

"Nothing like that," he assured me.

"Okay, I'll play. Where's this gift I can't unwrap in front of my family?"

Jake got up from under me, went into the bedroom, and brought back a huge box wrapped with a giant yellow ribbon.

"How did you get that in here without my seeing it?" I asked.

"Elves helped me," Jake said, tongue in cheek.

"Elves, huh?" I said, chuckling. "Okay, hand it over, Santa."

Jake knelt on the floor next to the big present and smiled like the Cheshire Cat as I unwrapped it.

When I pulled the top off the box, I was perplexed. The box was empty except for a much smaller present in the bottom. I pulled it out, and Jake knocked the big box out of the way. It didn't register to me what was really happening until I'd unwrapped the small box and Jake took the ring box from my hand, opening it.

"Lance," he said, as I gaped at him in shock. "I've known for the longest time that I'm head over heels in love with you. Your compassion, kindness, and warmth undo me. I already consider you part of my family, but if you'll have me, we can make it official. Would you consider being my husband?"

I was already crying like an idiot the moment he took the box from my hands. I'd thought about proposing myself, but since I was still in school, I'd decided to hold off until I had something to offer him.

"You want me even though I'm just a student?" I asked, feeling a little silly for being hung up on that, but then, I was already a blubbering mess.

Jake laughed. "I want you no matter what you are, Lance. You're still *you*, the man I love. So, what do you say? Be my husband?"

I launched off the sofa and into his arms, knocking him onto his back. I kissed his face until I found his mouth. I poured everything I wanted to say but couldn't find the words for into devouring his lips.

When we finally pulled apart, I gasped, "Yes! Of course, yes, yes, yes!"

Jake face was full of merriment as he pulled us both to our feet. "I love you, Lance McCartney, for always. Merry Christmas, fiancé."

Forty-Two

Jake

I HADN'T KNOWN HOW to propose. I knew I didn't want to do it in front of Lance's family because I never liked how people did things like that in public. What if he wanted to say no? It's not like he'd have been able to without feeling worse by embarrassing me in front of a crowd.

I thought about taking him back to the chapel at the vineyard, our special place. But another big renovation project was underway to add a larger storage area next to the barn where they processed the wine, and they were also adding an extension to the old mill since they'd long ago run out of room for large events.

I also thought about proposing in front of the mercantile project site, where I hoped our new home would soon begin looking like an actual building. The symbolism would've been sweet, but at the moment, the active construction site looked more like a pile of rubble and not remotely romantic.

It'd been Todd who eventually suggested I do it in the state park in McMinnville. Doc and Amos had gotten married there a few years back, and the wedding had been beautiful. I'd stayed in one of the cabins with Jen and her boyfriend at the time and had loved how quaint it was. I knew as soon as he mentioned it that the quaint cabin would be a perfect spot.

I was a nervous wreck, but determined not to let Lance pick up on it. I'd rented the cabin a day early, brought the present down, and stored it in a back closet. Then I did everything possible to keep him from looking in the closet.

I'd waffled on when and how to best propose, possibly over breakfast or maybe by setting the gift on top of the car, so he'd see it when we ventured outside for a brisk nature walk. But when Lance cuddled up to me on the sofa, all warm and cozy and just about to fall asleep, I knew the time was right. So, I grabbed the box, which I'd disguised as a Christmas gift like Derek had suggested, and brought it out for my boyfriend to open.

His stunned and emotional reaction was everything I'd hoped it would be. He caught me a little off guard when he mentioned being a student, as if that were some sort of deterrent to my wanting to share my life with him. He had no idea all he brought to the table, which had nothing to do with his profession. I loved Lance McCartney with all my heart for the person he was inside, for his strength and caring, and the way he looked at the world. This man was everything to me, and I couldn't imagine my future without him.

The next day, we arrived for the family Christmas party just as Anita, Claire, and Derek pulled into the parking spot below the front of the house.

We pulled in next to them and helped carry armloads of gifts up the stairs and into the beautifully decorated sitting room, where our giant Christmas tree stood. The girls were running around like crazy. Gib's foster mom, Mrs. Margaret, was there along with her wife. Allen and Lance's father was there, as was Allen's mom Catherine. They all embraced my family as we walked in and we'd just unloaded our gifts and taken our coats off when Derek noticed the ring on Lance's finger.

"You did it!" he exclaimed, and everyone stopped talking to look at us.

"Did what?" Allen asked.

Derek looked shocked, then embarrassed, and I couldn't help but laugh. "You might as well show them," I said to Lance.

Lance was smiling from ear to ear as he walked over to Derek. "He did, and I said yes. So, I guess that makes you my little brother."

Derek grabbed Lance into a hug as the family swarmed around us, giving hugs of congratulations and angling to see the ring.

LANCE

WE HAD PLANNED TO tell everyone over dinner, but Derek had seen the ring first thing and announced it before we'd even sat down. Of course, that just made it that much more amazing and special. When Derek grabbed me into a hug, I could tell he was crying, which caused me to shed a few happy tears myself.

Dad stood back as everyone rushed in for hugs and to see the ring. Even Catherine oohed and aahed over it. I couldn't read Dad's expression, but I could guess he was overwhelmed. Both of his sons had come out as gay, and even though he'd come to terms with it, as well as he could at least, I don't think it hit him until right then that I was about to marry a man.

I tried not to think about it as I allowed the love from everyone else to sweep over us. This small group of people were my family, my people, my tribe. When I'd shown up here broke and desolate, these people took me in and loved me. They helped me find my way when I was utterly lost, and helped me rediscover myself in the process.

Once the excited group dispersed and only Jake and I remained standing near the coat closet, I tugged him into a kiss. "I love you," I whispered between us.

When I drew back, just far enough to meet his eyes, Jake winked at me and mouthed, "I love you too."

When I looked back toward the sitting room, I noticed Dad staring at me with a determined look on his face.

"I want to pay for the wedding," he quickly said. "I should've done more for Allen and Gib's wedding, but I was stupid. I regret that and I don't want to regret not showing you boys how proud I am of you ever again."

Dad wasn't talking loudly, but the intensity in his voice must've caught everyone's attention because another hush fell over the room.

He looked around, embarrassed, then he sighed. "I've made so many mistakes with my family, with all of you. I am so proud of my boys. I mean, look at this family you've created. Three beautiful granddaughters, friends, a beautiful home in a wonderful little town. I couldn't have designed better lives for you if I'd tried."

Dad never exposed his feelings, especially in a crowd, so his declaration felt a bit awkward. No one knew quite what to say, including me, but before it could get worse, Catherine picked up her wine glass and yelled out, "Here's to family!"

"Here's to family!" the group, including the three girls, shouted at once and just like that, everything was back to laughter and fun.

I looked over at my dad and smiled, willing myself not to cry, again. "I'd like that. And Dad?" I said quietly, stepping closer to him. "I'm so happy you're back in my life. Christmas or not, that's the best gift I could've wished for. Thank you for just wanting to be my dad."

Forty-Four

Jake

AFTER AN INCREDIBLE DINNER courtesy of Catherine and Gib, we sat around opening presents, which took some time since there were a lot of us, and a lot of gifts being given.

I had bought Lance a pair of hiking boots, since he didn't own a pair, and I was determined to get him out into some of the backcountry over the following spring and summer. He'd worked all last summer, and we hadn't been able to get out much, so I was determined to change that in the coming year.

After all of the gifts under the tree had been un-wrapped, or so I thought, Lance brought me one last present, wrapped in regular brown paper sealed with masking tape. I could tell it was a picture of some sort, but I didn't have a clue what it might be.

I slowly unwrapped it, since I could tell it was on canvas, as everyone watched with curious expressions.

When the paper fell away and revealed a painting of the building we were constructing in downtown Crawford City, my breath hitched. Even more astonishing, the artist signature read Matt Brinks.

"H-how did you get him to paint this? This is exactly how you described the building to me. It's like your sketch in full color."

Lance laughed. "I told him what it was for, and who it was for, and he jumped on it. Matt ran with my idea and put it on canvas, so now you can show everyone the amazing building you're bringing to this town."

I smiled, but didn't trust myself to say anything without choking up. Matt had such a way of expressing himself through his art. What should've been a boring old brick building was expressed so beautifully, so regally.

"We're gonna live there, Lance. You and me," I said to my fiancé, who was beaming. "Someday, this'll be our home."

"It'll also be a place of business," Catherine said and smiled when I looked her way.

"You concentrate on that," I told her. "And I'll concentrate on making this the best home I can for the man I'm crazy in love with."

Catherine winked at me, and I could feel my face blush, although I wasn't sure if it was because of how Lance made me feel or our public display of affection.

I placed the painting on the fireplace mantel in front of the big mirror Gib and Allen had hanging there. It was the safest place for it, since it looked like a wrapping paper explosion had hit the entire sitting room.

We cleaned everything up and everyone except Lance and I went to the dining room for dessert. Once they had gone, I kissed Lance and said, "I can't believe you arranged for Matt to create this. It's the most amazing present ever."

"I'm so glad he agreed to it. You should thank him yourself, though."

"I will, but right now, I wanna thank the man that inspired it and inspires me. *You*." Emotion washed over me as I wrapped Lance in my arms.

He sagged into me and sounded teary when he said, "I just love you so much, Jake. It's hard to put it all into words."

"Shh," I said and held him a little tighter. "You don't have to find the words, sweetheart, 'cause I'm feeling the same way. I'm yours and you're mine, for always."

FORTY-FIVE

EPILOGUE - LANCE

"U NCLE LANCE, ARE YOU okay?" Ruby asked. I chuckled as I bent down and pulled my niece into a hug.

"I'm okay, sweetie. I'm just emotional about today."

"Are you happy, Uncle Lance?" Chrissy asked, sounding concerned.

"I've never been happier in all my life, Chrissy," I told her.

Catherine came in to check on me and the girls, and smiled when she saw the four of us bundled together in a bear hug.

"Okay, girls, we need to let Lance get ready. Lance, are you okay, or do you need help?" she asked.

I quickly wiped my eyes and smiled at my friend. "I'm okay, Catherine. But girls, thank you for keeping me company."

Catherine hurried them away to finish getting ready, and I couldn't help but feel grateful about how much those three young ladies added to my life.

I finished tying my bow tie, then sat down on the chair that occupied the corner of the room.

The basement of the chapel was made for events like today. Both Matt and Lia had come in to check on me earlier and make sure the venue was working out okay. I was so appreciative of the space.

Jake and I had decided to get married in the spring, here in our special place, just as things were blooming and coming alive. Daffodils lined the walkway up to the chapel, as well as being naturalized throughout the woodland, just like Lia had told me it would be during the wedding. One of the few memories I had of my mom was picking her daffodils as a young kid. Even though she wasn't here and would probably never be a part of my life, the fragrant sweet yellow flowers always made me think of mothers in general.

Knowing the daffodils would be in bloom had certainly helped us decide on getting married this time of the year, but the symbolism also played a part. My life had been desolate and bleak before I'd come to Crawford City. Now, having reconnected with my family and met the love of my life, my life was like its own spring renewal.

I went to the mirror and used a damp cloth I'd grabbed earlier to wipe my eyes once again, hoping to rid my face of the blotchy redness and knowing I wasn't going to have any luck.

I heard the door open and turned to see my dad standing there. "Hey," he said almost shyly.

"Hi, Dad. Is it time?"

He nodded. "Almost, but I wanted to spend a moment with you before you go."

Dad and I had talked several more times since last September. Mostly about the stuff we discussed *in* September. He'd changed so much since then. I actually liked the guy he'd become, and I can certainly say I didn't like the man he was before.

"Um, so I wanted you to know how much I like Jake, and how proud I am of you today."

I'd just wiped my face and put the cloth away, accepting the fact that I wasn't going to be stopping the tears anytime soon. When I turned back around, Dad pulled me into a hug.

It took several moments to register what was happening. My father never hugged me. He barely ever even touched me, so the sudden affection came as a surprise. My arms seemed to know what to do, though, and I embraced my father for a moment.

"Okay," he said as he pulled back. I shouldn't have been surprised to see his own tears threatening to spill over. "Let's get you out there and get you married."

I laughed. "Sounds like a great plan," I agreed.

Jake had the biggest family, so he agreed to stand out front by the altar. Todd, Jen, and Derek stood with him.

Allen and Dad stood with me at the back of the chapel, as did Linc, who'd immediately agreed when I'd asked him.

Dad escorted me down the aisle where the rest of the wedding party was already waiting. Chrissy and the twins followed behind, sprinkling rose petals, which they insisted was necessary for a wedding. I'd learned when my nieces decided something, it was best just to roll with the punches.

"Who gives these men to be married on this day?" the minister asked.

"We do," Dad, along with Anita and Claire, who'd stood up when we began to walk down the aisle, said at the same time.

It was a little old-fashioned, but Jake wanted to include his newly adopted moms in the ceremony.

When they sat down, the minister followed the traditional script. "Dearly Beloved..."

As I suspected, I had no control over the tears that slid down my face as the ceremony went on. Luckily, I was able to read my vows first, knowing I'd be bawling after Jake read his.

I cleared my throat, then began. "Jake, my life was dark and empty when I came here. The moment I met you, it was as if a light had been turned on. Since then, that light has only grown brighter and the warmth of it has filled me." I looked at what I'd written and realized, with Jake, the minister, and our entire families staring at me, that it felt stilted. Jake deserved to hear my words from the heart, so I decided to wing the rest.

"Baby, you are my light, but also my missing pieces." Tears increased in volume as I searched for the right words. "I have never felt this complete. I've never felt so loved in all my life. Thank you for loving me."

Jake put his hand on my cheek, and I leaned my face into it. Somehow, even though my words weren't quite adequate for the occasion, at least he could feel it through our touch.

"My beautiful Lance," Jake said just as the emotions took him too, his voice thick. "You are my inspiration, my own private sunshine. On my darkest and most depressing days, just having you near, or seeing your smile, or your leaning into me fills me with happiness and chases the shadows away. I didn't know it was possible to love someone as much as I love you... To feel this happy just because you exist in my world. It is my promise, sweetheart, to cherish you with all that's in me."

The minister had us exchange rings and then announced, "Ladies and Gentlemen, I now give you, Misters Jake and Lance McCartney. Husbands."

Jake cupped my face and leaned down, and we exchanged a mind-blowing kiss. He then pulled me into a hug and rocked me gently, which probably better signified just how much love and compassion we shared than the kiss. When we pulled apart, I couldn't help but seek out his lips again.

"Okay, okay, boys, do that on your own time," Catherine said loudly from the front row, causing us both to laugh.

I pulled back and stuck my tongue out at her before we walked down the aisle and out of the beautiful chapel that was even more our special place now than it had been before the ceremony.

Matt and Logan had built a brand new reception hall just off the old mill for events just like this one. Luckily, the chapel was close enough to the hall that most people walked, including my new husband and me.

"You know I'm madly in love with you, right?" I asked, suddenly realizing I hadn't actually said the words in my vows.

He leaned into me. "You know you make my heart soar, right?"

"God, I hope so." I leaned into him, too, as we walked, and he put his arm around me before kissing my temple.

"Wanna run away and start the honeymoon?" I whispered.

"Hell no, I'm ready for some of that cake!" Jake teased. He'd been threatening to steal a slice since it'd been delivered. Of course, the fact that it'd been made by the Chocolate Factory meant it'd be over-the-top delicious.

I was ready for the honeymoon, but like him, I was equally excited about celebrating this day with our family and friends. And eating that cake.

The reception, which resembled one giant party, was one for the history books. Just like meeting and loving Jake had changed my life, so had all the people who were there. Todd, Ash, Amos, Doc, Linc, Jake's friends from Nashville, including Lexie and her contingent. Townsfolk who hadn't fit in the little chapel had shown up for the reception, so many that it looked like the whole town was here.

Logan had taken on all the food prep for us, and he and Matt served barbecue from a small pit that'd just opened up between town and their winery. They had opened a commercial kitchen and served everything appropriate for a Southern wedding, or so Jake told me. Baked beans, which both Jake and I avoided since it was our honeymoon, coleslaw, potato salad, and everything under the sun in the way of sides.

We sat at the table and listened to my brother and father make their speeches. I laughed hysterically as Derek pegged his brother perfectly in what could only be described as a roast, but ended in obvious love and compassion.

Jake's sister Lena and her family had shown up for the event, too, although none of the rest of his siblings did. I could tell her being there had touched him deeply.

Finally, the evening drew to a close and my new husband and I drove back to Nashville to spend the night in his condo before we flew out to Greece for our honeymoon. A trip my father had said was our family's tradition and that he'd paid for.

Allen rolled his eyes when Dad had suggested it, but after Dad was out of earshot, he said, "Dad and his Greek trips. But trust me, that cruise is one hundred percent different when it's just you and your man."

I blushed at what he was insinuating, but I agreed to the plan to take the yacht we'd rented every year since I was a kid, to bump around the Greek islands. Especially when I saw how Jake's face lit up at the idea.

It's funny how strange life could be and how it changed just because you had someone new in your life. I'd hated those family vacations in Greece, but Allen had been correct that it would be transformed just because Jake would be a part of it. I guessed that was an à propos example of my life now. A life I savored every aspect of. Even simple things like studying while he sat across from me doing his work was like the best entertainment money could buy.

I smiled up at the sun after catching its reflection in my ring, and I counted my blessings I'd found the man who was now officially mine. Jake filled my life with happiness and a completeness that was difficult to explain, not that I needed to since he felt the same way. That's what it meant to be in love.

JAKE

C HAOS. IN MY WORK, in my personal life, and on the building project, I hated chaos. The dedication for the new commercial property and our condo was this weekend. I had three new clients who needed to be assigned. Charlie was going on vacation, and both Derek and Lance were graduating in the next two months.

It's like everything was happening at once, and I was having a hard time keeping all the balls in the air.

"Honey," Lance said when he came over and took my arm, pulling me toward the living room. "Why don't you have a glass of wine and join me on the sofa."

My gut reaction was to say no, that I had too much to do, but I'd been neglecting my husband since our one-year anniversary. So, instead, I took the wine and sat down next to him.

"Listen, everything is going to be fine. You're stressing yourself out over nothing."

I chuckled. Lance was quick to pick up on my moods, even though I hadn't told him I was stressing. Of course, the pacing in front of the long bank of windows in the condo while reading emails on my phone might have given him a clue.

Lance took the phone out of my hand and said, "Those will be there in the morning, and Charlie already has everything set up for you next week. She's called me at least a dozen times this week to make sure I know the people who are in charge of keeping you from falling apart." He laughed. "You know she's as afraid of taking a vacation as you are of her going."

"Charlie keeps everything running," I said, and Lance cut me off.

"You and Charlie keep everything running together, and there's always going to be a hundred excuses for her not to take time off. If she doesn't, she's going to burn out. Trust me, you're going to be fine."

"But your graduation..."

"Is already planned and doesn't require anything from you, and certainly not her. You just have to show up," he said and kissed me on the cheek.

"The dedication, though," I said, shaking my head.

"Honey, that building is built. We're talking about a little dedication party, and Catherine has all that planned already. So, please stop fretting. I promise it's going to work out."

I leaned back on the sofa and, for the millionth time, wondered what magical skill my husband had for calming my nerves.

I drank the white wine he'd poured and was expecting sweetness to hit my mouth, which, to be honest, I didn't care much for. Instead, a pleasant flavor filled my palette and I looked at the bottle.

"Of course, this would be one of Logan's wines," I said, smiling.

"Yeah, it's their new white blend. He wants to make it the signature drink for the hotel."

"I'm a total yes. It's great."

Lance kissed my temple, stood up, and came around the back of the sofa. "Relax and I'll give you a little massage. You're radiating tension."

I moaned as his magic hands began to rub my stressed muscles. Lance just seemed to know where my muscle pain was and went directly to the worst spots, willing the knots away with his fingers and soothing the pressure points.

By the time he'd finished, I was finally feeling sleepy.

Charlie had agreed to be at the dedication on Sunday because neither of us was able to give up that much control. Although Lance was right, Catherine had planned it beautifully. Of course, she had been throwing dedication parties in hotels much fancier than this one most of her life.

The event was spectacular, bringing in most of the residents of Crawford City and several of my clients who had heard me drone on about the place enough that they felt like they needed to see it for themselves.

Lance and I were taking the top condo. Jen had agreed to purchase the second, and the third would be placed on the market as soon as the dedication concluded. Of course, both Jen and I had the final say on who would live there, so I'd yet to hire a realtor, hoping that the perfect person would just fall into our laps.

As for the hotel, Catherine had designed the entire spectacular interior, and it sparkled and screamed elegance. Even though the hotel was small, it was something to be extremely proud of, and I couldn't even begin to say how excited I felt that Catherine had been on our team.

She'd also filled all the commercial spaces with local vendors. Matt and Logan's winery had taken a small space in the actual hotel entrance. Catherine had said we needed to designate at least a small section of the first floor for the hotel, so the café down the street had created a breakfast area that served coffee and baked goods like Danish and croissants. Mrs. Cole, the Crawford City Café's owner, had said the micro-bakery offered her the perfect opportunity to expand her business without having to do a complete renovation of the café building itself.

Hotel guests were given a stipend to spend at the bakery every morning that was included with their room fee, which helped to boost sales at the bakery but also meant we didn't have to have a restaurant within the hotel.

Other meals, of course, were encouraged to be had at the café.

Boutique shops filled the rest of the commercial space. Even though we hadn't officially opened, there was already a significant buzz and lots of interest. I'd been really interested to see how successful our first week open would be.

Lance and I walked through the different shops, meeting townsfolk as well as people who'd driven in from Nashville for the event. Thousands of people came and went throughout the day and even though it was a cloudy and chilly spring day, all the stores reported that they'd sold out of most of their merchandise and were scrambling to restock the shelves for the first week.

That was a problem I don't think anyone was upset about.

I'd intended for Lance and me to move into the condo the first week after the dedication, but Lance had all but refused, saying he needed to concentrate on his finals. Then, after graduation, we could begin the move.

I'd already decided to turn our Nashville condo into a place for clients to stay when they were in town, especially since a lot of my newest were from Hollywood, Atlanta, and New York.

Word had gotten out that our PR firm was good for launching new celebrities, not to mention Jen had been interviewed by *Vogue* and mentioned the firm by name. So, our client roster now included several supermodels too.

Although growing my firm had been a goal, having a loving husband at home and additional business affairs to manage, I was no longer as keen on jumping on a plane every time someone wanted PR work. So, I'd restricted my new clients to only those willing to come to Nashville, and I assigned everyone else to other managers. Even with those restrictions, though, I had at least one new client every week. Not that I'd ever complain about that.

I loved my job, and with the new clients had come new employees who loved the profession as much as I did. As the firm grew, it felt more and more like we were simply forming a bigger family. I knew not many companies could boast that.

After the dedication and hell week, Charlie went off on vacation and it was time to focus all my attention on my husband and brother's graduations. I knew Lance thought of his graduation ceremony as just something to attend and be done with, but I'd be damned if I wouldn't make a big deal out of something he'd fought for so hard. First with his father, then for himself.

He'd taken a part-time job with an architectural firm in Nashville after his mentor in Crawford City, Tom, had sent them a glowing recommendation. Tom was convinced Lance needed experience with a large firm to gain real-world experience in all manner and scale of building design, even if Lance had aspirations to one day hang his shingle in a small town like Tom had done.

"You'll need partners in this business," Tom told him. "And I trust these guys."

Of course, he trusted them because the two owners of the firm had been his interns many years ago.

With so many of my Nashville clients establishing homes on the outskirts of the city, and some even planning to move to Crawford City itself, I'd been sending more and more referrals to Tom for design and Todd for construction.

Lance had expressed his interest in taking over Tom's business someday, probably in the near future, and Tom had made it clear he'd be happy to hand it over. I knew Lance would be happy wherever he chose to set up shop, since he'd be living out his career dreams regardless, but I secretly loved the idea that our lives were becoming more ensconced into the little town I'd come to think of as home.

Anita and Claire had a family randomly stop by and offer them a ridiculous amount of money to buy their home, which they accepted. After Derek's graduation, and with nothing else keeping them in Nashville, they planned to move here as well. Luckily, my moms had met Todd and Ash's lesbian friends, Donna and Louisa, and the two couples had hit it off, although Donna and Louisa were quite a bit younger. So, Anita and Claire had already purchased a home across the street from theirs.

My sister Lena and her husband were considering moving out to this area too. Lena's husband had been interviewed by a large church in Mayville that'd lost its minister due to some crazy harassment the man had done to Matt and Logan, of all people. The church had lost a lot of its membership over that debacle and they were looking for someone who had connections with diverse family members.

That made me laugh since just a year ago, Lena had been alienated from me because I was gay. Oh well, the world moves and changes and we have to let it. That's how things improve.

If he took the job, Lena would be living close to me and Derek. I wondered if that would bring us closer or drive us further apart. Our relationship was still strained, but hopefully, it would continue to improve over time.

I climbed the stairs to our new condo's roof, where we'd built a rooftop garden and yard. We could see out over the entire town from here, but no one could see us, including hotel guests in the enclosed pool area on top of the hotel's main building.

As I surveyed my new home, I thought how quickly life could change and how amazing that change could be. Lance had told me time and time again, I was why his life changed, but I thought that was only partially true. Lance was a powerhouse of a man who was just coming into his own when he came seeking his brother's help.

I knew for a fact that both our lives had improved tremendously because we'd found each other, and through our relationships, we'd become more. We loved life more and held onto those we loved a little tighter. *Our* family.

I peered down at the street below where it all began, where I'd rounded a corner one chilly day only to be plowed over by a sexy man who would change my life forever. I'd always thought of Crawford City as a special little town, where love and acceptance were given without a second thought, and having met the love of my life here only solidified that. After years of searching for a place that felt right, and with Lance by my side, I'd finally found home.

Continue the Coming Home Series with ***Bound for Home***

Available at your favorite bookseller!

Join Blake's email list to get advance notice of new books and receive his occasional newsletter:

www.blakeallwood.com

MM Romance
By Blake Allwood

Transitions Series
Aiden Inspired
Suzie Empowered (MF Romance)
Bobby Transformed

Chance Series
Love By Chance
Another Chance With Love
Taking A Chance For Love

Romantic Series
Romantic Renovations (1)
Romantic Rescue (2)
Romantic Recon (3)

Melody Series
Melody of the Heart
Melody of the Snow

Road to Rocktoberfest Anthology
Changing His Tune - 2022

Coming Home Series (2023)
A Long Way Home
Family Home
Discovering Home
Finding Home
Bound For Home
…and many more

Novellas
Tenacious
Moon's Place

Romantic Fantasy
By Adam J. Ridley

Big Bend Series
Love's Legacy (1)
Love's Heirloom (2)
Love's Bequest (3)

The Witch Brothers Series
Emerald Earth (1)
Diamond Air (2)
Ruby Fire (3)
Sapphire Water (4)

Science Fiction
By Adam J. Ridley

Superhero Series
Emergence

Blake Allwood was born in west Tennessee, then moved to Kansas City MO after earning a degree in Early Childhood Education from Graceland College in Lamoni, Iowa. He met his husband Shaun in 1995 and they officially married in 2015, once gay marriage was legalized; although they still consider Valentines Day 1995 as their true "anniversary date". Twenty-two years later (2017), after fostering 12 children together, he and his husband sold their home, purchased an RV and began traveling the country with their two dogs.

Typically, Blake can be found relaxing in the RV or by the fire with his laptop and their Jack Russell Terrier, Buddy, curled up between his legs demanding attention. Denver, their Siberian Husky mix is often asleep at his feet or playing tug of war with Blake's husband.

Most of Blake's stories are inspired by the places they have visited in their ongoing travels. His first book, *Aiden Inspired*, was released in 2019 and he has now written over 20 books. In 2023 he is releasing the *Coming Home* series which is comprised of ten-plus sweet contemporary romance novels that are based on a fictional town in his home state of Tennessee.

Blake also writes under the pen name of Adam J. Ridley for his urban fantasy fans looking for stories revolving around gay characters. His first series is The Witch Brothers Saga, starting with ***Emerald Earth***.